Shug'ah

By
Imani Writes

Shug'ah by Imani Writes
Copyright © 2014 by Artistic Words Publishing, LLC

All rights reserved. No part of this publication may be reproduced or transmitted in any form or by any means – electronic, mechanical, photocopying, recording, or any information storage or retrieval system – without prior written permission from the publisher except in the case of a brief quotations embodied in critical articles and reviews.

This is a work of fiction. The characters, incidents, dialogues are product of the author's imagination and are not to be construed as real. Any resemblance to actual events or persons, living or dead, is entirely coincidental.

ISBN-10: 0990326500
ISBN-13: 978-0-9903265-0-2

Cover design by Tammy Capri, Nu Class Publications
Edited by Carla M. Dean, U Can Mark My Word

Printed in the United States of America

Discount pricing for bulk orders of ten (10) copies or more.
Email: orders@artisticwordspublishing.com

For information regarding the other releases under Artistic Words Publishing, please visit us at www.artisticwordspublishing.com or connect with us on the following social media websites:

Facebook - Artistic Words Publishing
Twitter - @Artistic_Words
Instagram - ArtisticWordsPublishing

For my children, LaSherice, Kevin, KJ, and April. You give my life purpose.

And for the young women who have been silenced by fear, may you all find your voices.

Shug'ah

Artistic Words Publishing, LLC
"A Gallery of Literary Masterpieces"
www.artisticwordspublishing.com

Introduction

Summer 2004 ~ Long Beach Boulevard

    The summer sun is blazing relentlessly, and I'm brushing the sweat from my brow as if it will provide some relief. I wish I could jump in my Escalade and take a spin down the California coast with the windows down. But, that isn't going to happen anytime soon, if ever. I'm not about to risk my life by going outside just to escape this hellish heat. My crew and me are hiding out, so our only taste of the outdoors is looking through the dingy glass window of this cheap motel room. I can't help but wonder when the police will kick down the door and lynch us for killing a cop. He was a dirty son-of-a-bitch, but he was still one of them.
    Upon first glance at our crew, the first thing people probably notice is how small in number we are, but regardless of that fact, we still made a name for ourselves. I'm the lone woman of a crew that functions in a man's world. No, I'm not talking power suits and corporate boardroom drama. I'm talking street life. Once this life grabbed my soul, my body willingly followed into the depths of the never-ending LA war zone.
    Look at them sleeping peacefully as if we don't have the

entire Los Angeles police department on the hunt for our asses. I've always admired their 'I don't give a fuck' attitudes. I think that's why we've lasted so long. Up until last month, I didn't give a fuck about anything or anyone, either.

My birth name is Samantha Ruiz, but they call me Shug'ah. Don't let the sweet name fool you. I have plenty of blood on my hands. The t-shirt I'm wearing is adorned with blood splatters from two days ago. Most people would have changed into fresh clothes, but I'm wearing that dirty muthafucka's blood like it's a fuckin' gold medal.

I envy my crew for being able to sleep and wonder what each of them is dreaming about. I haven't slept in days, but it feels more like years. Every time I attempt to sleep, my dreams are haunted by a memory that will be with me until I die. It's funny to me when people say they've found heaven on earth, because almost every door I've opened has given me a glimpse of eternal damnation.

Great! My shrink is blowing up my cell. Today isn't one of those days where I feel like being in touch with my feelings, so I ignore his call. Truth is, I wish I could erase everything in my life, or better yet, erase my entire existence like that movie *The Butterfly Effect*.

How did I end up here in such a fucked-up world? Since day one I've experienced nothing but drama on a never-ending rollercoaster. Are you sure you want to enter my reality?

Chapter 1

July 1994 ~ Riverside, CA

"Guess what, Samantha?"

"What, Mom?"

"I'm getting married."

My nine-year-old little sister Melanie was happy, but I was a little taken aback.

"Married to who?" I asked slowly.

"To Jackson, silly."

"Mom, you've only been seeing him for a few months. Are you sure you're ready?"

"Yes, I'm ready. And you know it's been longer than a few months. I've been dating Jackson for about two years. I haven't been serious about anyone since your father passed. It's been years, and I'm ready to be married again."

My mother always became sad when talking about my father, who died while she was still pregnant with Melanie. I remember the day like it was yesterday. It was my birthday about nine years ago, and he was teaching me how to ride my new bike. As I struggled to keep my balance while riding down the sidewalk, I heard shots. I fell off my bike and turned to see my father lying on the concrete struggling to breathe. Unfortunately, he died before I could get to him. That was the first time I saw death, and I wished it would be my last. I never rode a bike again.

"Are you happy?" I asked, while washing the dinner dishes.

"Very. You know Jackson has that good-paying construction job, so I can finally quit working at the diner and spend more time with you and your sister."

Working as a part-time nurse at MFI Recovery Center during the day and a waitress at The Chicken Shack at night kept her absent around the house. So, I liked the idea of her being at home more. I had just turned fifteen, and having to cook almost every day, maintain a B average in school, and take care of Melanie was a little overwhelming at times. If Mom stopped working so much, maybe I could have a life outside of home and school.

The late August wedding was beautiful, but the honeymoon didn't last long. Mid-September, Jackson got fired because a trace of marijuana was found in his system after a random urine test. So, in order to make ends meet, Mom had to return to her other job. I complained to her about Jackson not getting off his ass to find another job. I should have known she would go back and tell him what I said. One day, he cornered me and told me to stay out of his business. That was fine with me. I didn't like him anyway, and I had much better things to think about than him.

"So will you go with me?"

It was the beginning of October, and Kareem Valentine, the cutest junior at Arlington High, had asked me to the school's Halloween dance.

"I'll have to ask my mom, but it should be okay."

Shug'ah

"Ask her now. Is she home?" he asked, peeking through the window.

"No, she's at work," I replied, gesturing with my hand for him to sit on the porch swing with me.

"Oh, so the house is empty," he said, leaning in for a kiss.

Suddenly, the front door swung open and Jackson stood there drunk. "No, it ain't empty," he said, as if someone had been talking to him.

"Call me later," Kareem said and stood to leave.

"She won't be calling you at all. Now go home. Samantha, come in the house."

I was on fire from embarrassment. I didn't even get to say goodbye to Kareem before he ran him off.

"How dare you?" I yelled after he closed the door. "You're not my father!"

"Yes, I am, and I say you can't see him."

I ran down the hall to my room and slammed the door as hard as I could. While I started undressing to change out of my school clothes, my door swung open. I quickly grabbed my shirt from off the bed and placed it against my chest to keep him from seeing my bare breasts.

"You don't slam doors in my house!" Jackson said.

I should have let it go, but he had already pushed me too far already. "Your house? What fucking bill have you paid?"

He slapped my face so hard I tasted blood. I tried to get the phone to call my mom, but he snatched me by my hair and shoved me against the wall. The smell of cheap rum reeking from his mouth nauseated me, and I became scared.

"This is my house!" he yelled. "And you won't have these little boys sniffing around here. It would break your momma's heart if you became pregnant. You don't want that to happen, do you?"

"It won't happen."

"Why?" he said, then experienced a short coughing fit. "You sayin' you a virgin?"

"Let me go!" I shouted.

"Shut up before I smack you again. Let's see how much of a virgin you are."

Jackson had a tight grip on my hair, and with his other hand, he began pulling my pants down.

"Please don't," I cried.

Even though I stood at 5'8", I was no match for Jackson, who was over six feet tall and weighed close to three hundred pounds.

"If you don't be quiet, I might have to hurt you…or Melanie."

I immediately stopped screaming and resisting. I loved my little sister and would do anything to protect her. At times, I felt like her mother, and the asshole used my love for her to get what he wanted. He threw me down on my bed and forced himself inside of me. As the torturous flames of him ripping me open engulfed my body, I was stripped of my innocence. Tears streamed down my face as I endured the pain. I often dreamed of Kareem being my first, but Jackson turned that fantasy into a nightmare.

"Well, what do you know?" he said, pulling up his pants. "You *were* a virgin. That was some good, tight pussy." He walked to the door, and when he turned back around, his pleasured smile turned into a mean expression. "Remember what I said. You tell anyone about what just happened and I'll have to hurt Melanie."

Once he left my room, I lay there with my head throbbing in pain and my eyes dry from being cried out. Everything hurt. I heard Melanie come home, so I got up as fast as I could, pulling on my sweats and a shirt. When I entered the living room, she was in Jackson's arms.

"Melanie!" I snapped. "Come here!"

"Hi, Samantha. You okay? You look funny."

I took a deep breath. "I'm fine. Go to your room and start your homework."

I watched as she skipped down the hall to her room. Then I went into the bathroom and tried to scrub his filth off of me.

Shug'ah

I showered for almost an hour.

Home was no longer my safe haven. I even tried staying after school until Melanie's school let out. That way, I could bring her home with me, and since there's power in numbers, Jackson wouldn't dare force himself on me in front of her. However, that didn't work. Jackson would send her next door to play with her friend, and I'd find myself being victimized again. Whenever I tried to resist him, he reminded me of the hurt he would bring on Melanie. I hated the power he had over me. The weeks turned into months, and I eventually created a place in my mind that I would escape to while he violated me. That place became my safe haven. In reality, I wanted to kill Jackson.

When summer rolled around, I surrounded myself with people and made sure I was too busy for him to rape me. I offered to keep the neighbor's children during the workweek, and on Saturdays, Melanie and I would take the bus to Memorial Park. We'd spend the whole day playing and swimming or we'd go to Keisha's house. Mom was always home on Sundays, so I was protected seven days a week.

"Happy Sweet Sixteen!" my family and friends yelled when I walked into the house with my best friend one hot afternoon.

A smile formed on my lips, something that hadn't been happening too often. "Now I know why you kept me out in the hot-ass sun, Keisha."

She laughed. "I am soooooooo bad. You know I love you, girl."

"I love you, too," I responded, giving her a hug.

I approached Mom in the kitchen. "Where is he?"

"He who?" she asked while placing candles on the big,

13

pink cake.

"Your husband."

"I sent him out. I told him this was a female thang."

That was the best gift she could have given me. Even if for only a few hours, knowing he wasn't around allowed me to let my guard down so I could enjoy my party. I didn't think of his threats or abusive ways that he had used to control my life. For the first time in the past year, I felt free. I took a deep breath and embraced being sixteen. I really enjoyed myself that evening up until everyone left.

"I'm glad you're here, Mom," I told her as we cleaned up.

"Now where else would I be?" she said, smoothing down my hair. "You and your sister are the most important people in my life. Too old for a hug?"

I shook my head and hugged her tight. I knew she would string Jackson by his nuts if she knew what he was doing to me.

"Mom, there's something I have to tell you."

Jackson suddenly walked in. "Well, well, well, is the party finally over?"

"Hey, baby," Mom greeted as she left my arms and went into his.

"So, what's on your mind, Samantha?" he asked me.

"What?"

"I heard you say you have something to tell your mother." He grinned devilishly and taunted me by scooping Melanie into his filthy arms. "So, we're waiting to hear what it is."

My mind was screaming to tell her that he was abusing me, but my mouth wouldn't open.

"What is it, love?" Mom asked sweetly.

I looked at Jackson and became nauseous as he kissed Melanie on her cheek. "I just wanted to tell you how much fun I had today."

"You're welcome, baby. Now go watch TV. Birthday girls don't do dishes."

"C'mon, Melanie."

"Can we listen to your new CDs?"
"Sure."
"Good! I wanna listen to Immature first."
"Someone is crushin' on Immature."

We both laughed. Jackson standing in our path cut my laughter short, though. I pulled Melanie behind my back as Jackson put his arm around my shoulder.

"I'm sorry I didn't get you anything. Tell you what, I'll give you your gift real soon."

I tried to pull away, but he held on tight.

"You don't need to give me anything."

"Samantha," Mom said sternly, "if Jackson wants to give you something, let him."

Only God, Jackson, and I knew what gift he wanted to give me.

I watched Jackson and my mom for a few moments. They appeared to be so in love, giggling and tickling each other. He always acted so perfect when she was home. I thought back to last Thanksgiving when he sat at the table and said grace before we had dinner. I wanted to laugh out loud. The nerve of him to act so godly while in the presence of others, but doing ungodly things to me behind the closed door of my bedroom. As he carved the turkey, I stared at the knife, remembering what Ms. Celie did in *The Color Purple*. I wouldn't stick the knife in the table, though. I would use it to castrate the motherfucker.

Chapter 2

Kareem became a very important part of my life. Although he wouldn't come to the house anymore since Jackson chased him off that day, he always met up with me at the pool. We would swim all afternoon or sit on the edge and talk while watching Melanie play with her friends. A few times, I saw Jackson drive by the pool to an out-of-the-way liquor store. Kareem knew I hated Jackson, but he never asked why, and I was thankful for that.

"I want you to be my girl," Kareem confessed one Saturday afternoon at the park.

"Ooooooooooh!" Melanie sang. "Samantha's got a boyfriend."

I shushed Melanie and looked at Kareem. He was too fine. With his 6'2" stature and athletic build, he towered above a lot of the guys at school and on our basketball team. He was the color of roasted almonds and had a smile that made butterflies flutter in my stomach. His dark brown eyes seemed to sparkle in the late afternoon sun, and they were becoming impatient waiting for my answer. I thought of nothing at that moment except wanting him to hold me and never let me go.

Imani Writes

"I want to be your girl," I replied softly, ignoring Melanie's giggling.

"*My* girl," he whispered, then kissed me.

I was pretty much on clouds nine, ten, and eleven when Melanie and I walked into the house. I was so lost in thought that I forgot to tell Melanie not to say anything. Usually, I would have warned her.

"Samantha belongs to Kareem now!" she announced loudly.

Her words instantly brought me down from my high and sent me crashing to the ground.

"What are you talking about, Mel?" Jackson interrogated, his eyes piercing my soul.

"Kareem asked Samantha to be his girl."

"And?" Jackson pressed.

"She said yes and then they kissed," she said. The animated one, she started making kissing noises.

"I thought we talked about this, Samantha. You don't belong to nobody."

Nobody except you, right, Jackson? I thought to myself.

"Awwwwww, I think it's sweet," Mom chimed in. "It's about time you have a boyfriend."

"Baby, I don't think—"

"Oh, come on, Jackson." Mom silenced him with a hug. "It's just young love. Now leave it alone."

"All right, all right," he said, surrendering reluctantly.

I knew it was far from over, though.

Later that evening while I was washing the dishes, he came up behind me and hissed in my ear like a wounded snake.

"You belong only to me!"

Tears formed in my eyes, but I refused to give him the satisfaction of seeing them fall. I picked up the long, sharp knife from the soapy water with thoughts of plunging it into my tormentor.

Shug'ah

"Sam, you know what I was thinking," Mom said, slicing through my thoughts.

I placed the knife back in the warm water. "What were you thinking?"

"Next weekend is the last weekend you have before you go back to school. You and Kareem should go out that Saturday night."

"I can't. I have to watch Melanie."

"I'll call Carol and tell her I can't come in on Saturday. I'm sure they can spare me. I'll find out tomorrow when I go to work."

I loved her idea, but her reminding me that there was only a week left of summer break was where my thoughts dwelled. When that week was up, my hell would start all over again. I thought of what I could do and who I could tell. I had to confide in somebody. I knew I couldn't survive another year of Jackson raping me. I decided Kareem would be the first person I would confide in.

"You look funny," Melanie said, laughing at the curls Mom was doing for my Saturday night date.

"Melanie, that's not nice. Apologize to your sister right now."

Melanie looked at Mom and quietly said her apologies.

"It's cool, because when you get older and go on your first date, I'll be there to do your hair."

"You can," Melanie said, slipping off the bed. "Just one thing…" She paused at the door. "I don't want those funny-looking curls, silly!" She laughed and ran down the hallway.

"Pay her no mind, love. You look beautiful. Don't you think so, Jackson?"

19

I stiffened when she asked him.

"She looks too grown. Take some of that make-up off her face."

"She's fine," Mom insisted.

The doorbell rang at the perfect time. I rushed to open it, and Kareem stood there looking so good. From his facial expression, I looked good to him, too.

"Wow!" was all he could say, and that was enough.

"Samantha, be home at eleven. Okay?"

"Okay, Mom."

"Have fun, you two."

Before we could get in Kareem's car, Jackson started arguing with Mom about me looking too grown, which I found to be ironic since he was the one who forced me into womanhood.

Kareem took me to see *Virtuosity*. It seemed like everyone was out that weekend. As we walked out of the movie theater, he held my hand tight.

"Did you like the movie?"

"I liked it just fine. Speaking of fine, Denzel Washington is fine as frog hair."

"Fine as frog hair?" Kareem laughed. "Uh, frogs don't have hair."

I tried to keep a straight face. "Yes, they do. It's just so fine you can't see it."

"You are too funny, Ms. Thang. I want to see it again tomorrow night. Care to join me?"

"My mom might not let me because I have school the following day."

Kareem looked into the night sky as if asking the man upstairs for help. "Why don't we go to the three o'clock movie?" he suggested.

"Yeah, why don't we? Besides, I missed a bit of the movie."

"Why?" he asked as we got in his car.

"I couldn't concentrate."

"And why couldn't you concentrate? Too busy watching the sexiest man alive, huh? At least that's what *People Weekly Magazine* considers him to be. But, I think I got that brotha beat."

I smiled when I heard a tinge of jealousy in his voice. Then I thought of the possibility of losing him since we hadn't been intimate yet. I took a deep breath and let it out slowly.

"Well, actually, all I could think of was this." I leaned over and kissed him. His lips parted and his tongue danced on mine. When his hands started to explore my body, that's when I became tense.

"Please stop," I voiced softly.

Being the gentleman he was, he did what I asked.

"I'm sorry," I muttered.

"Don't be. It's cool," Kareem said assuredly. "I don't want to push you to do something you don't want to do."

"I want to," I whispered. "It's just that my body won't let me."

"What?"

Of course, he didn't know what Jackson had been doing to me, but I felt it was the perfect moment to tell him. I wanted him to understand that I wanted him to touch me and make love to me the way a man should. I wanted someone else to help me carry the secret that was becoming too heavy for me to carry by myself.

"I..." I paused and remembered the threat against my ten-year-old sister. "I'm really sorry, Kareem."

"Baby, any time I get to spend with you is golden, and I don't want to mess it up. Now is you hungry?" he asked, smiling.

"Yes, I is," I joked back.

He drove us to the local hot spot, which happened to be where my mom worked.

"Uh, Kareem, not here."

"Why not?"

"My mom works here, and I'm tired of eating this food."

"But they have the best chicken wings," he countered.

"Trust me, I know. Look." I flapped my arms and clucked. "If I eat anymore, I will fly away."

He laughed, but I wished I could really fly away.

"Samantha, have a cheeseburger or something. I want some wings."

I gave in, and we had to share a booth with some people from school and Keisha. The place was packed with moviegoers reciting lines from the movie they had just came from seeing.

"Y'all ready for school?" one of the girls asked.

We all looked at each other, then balled up our napkins and opened fire on her.

I took a big bite of my cheeseburger and glanced at Kareem, who was happily knee deep in chicken wings and fries.

"Hey, baby!"

My mother's voice almost made me choke on the food in my mouth. "What are you doing here?"

"As you can see, I was called in. This place is crazy tonight."

"Did you take Melanie to Jessica's house?" I asked after forcing the food down my throat.

"It was such a last-minute's notice, I left her home with Jackson."

"Please tell me you didn't!"

"Baby, what's wrong with you?" Kareem asked, confused.

"I don't feel too good. I'll be right back."

I acted like I was going to the bathroom, but instead, I went to the room where the employees keep their personal belongings. It was a good thing I knew the place like the back of my hand. I found my mom's car keys and walked quickly out the back door without anyone spotting me. After maneuvering her car out of the crowded parking lot, I raced home.

It's going to be okay. He wouldn't hurt her, I kept repeating in my head to myself.

Chapter 3

The only sound in the house was the TV, which played to an unoccupied couch. I tripped over an empty bottle of Jackson's cheap vodka and noticed a half-smoked joint in the ashtray. I felt the burnt end; it was cold. I walked into the kitchen and there was a half-eaten peanut butter and jelly sandwich on the counter. Without even thinking, I took the knife I had often thought about using and clutched it while walking down the hallway. It seemed to take me forever to reach Melanie's room. Her door was locked, so I kicked it several times.

"I'm coming, Mel!" I shouted.

Finally, I got the door open, and that's when my heart felt like it had stopped. Jackson was on her bed asleep, but Melanie wasn't there. I glanced at the open window, praying she got away from him. As I walked slowly towards the bed, I brushed away the tears that were preventing me from seeing my worst fear. Melanie was in the bed, her little arm barely showing from underneath his huge body.

"No!" I screamed, then sprang into action as I tried to roll his heavy body off of her.

He wouldn't budge, so I plunged the knife deep into his back. He moaned in pain and rolled onto his side. That's when I was able to push him off her and onto the floor.

I lifted the pillow from over Melanie's face. Her big, beautiful, lifeless brown eyes stared back at me with fear. Her mouth was open as if still fighting for a breath that could save her. I trembled with pain, frustration, and disappointment. I was supposed to protect her and keep her safe, but I failed to be there when she needed me. I closed her eyes and mouth and kissed her cheek.

"I love you, Melanie," I cried. "I'm so sorry I allowed this to happen."

As I stared at her lifeless body, his laughter filled the room. I grabbed the knife and stood over him.

"What the fuck are you laughing at?" I yelled through my tears.

"You got someone new, so I had to get someone new, too."

"Shut up!" I yelled as loud as I could.

Instead of taking me seriously, he continued laughing. So, I had to silence him. My anger went into motion, and I watched as the knife went in and out of his body repeatedly.

"I never told," I screamed. "I never told anyone!"

When I finally stopped stabbing him due to my arms growing tired, silence filled the room. My heavy breathing echoed in my ears as I watched the pale, pink carpet absorb Jackson's blood. I put the knife down on the nightstand, took off my blood-soaked shirt, and sat on the bed next to Melanie.

I pulled her to me and held her close. I wailed into the silent night. My beautiful sister's life was cut short at the age of ten. He had put the pillow over her face so she couldn't scream, but in his drunken and high state, he passed out while on top of her and she suffocated. It was only right for me to die, as well, since it was my fault. I picked up the knife with every intention of plunging it into my broken heart.

"Police! Drop the knife! Let her go!" an officer demanded.

"No!" I yelled. "You're not taking her from me!"

"No one wants to take her from you," a female officer said calmly.

"This is my sister. She's mine."

"What happened here?" she asked, using the same gentle tone.

"Jackson…he killed her…and I killed him."

"You need to let her go so the paramedics can take a look at you."

"I'm fine. Can they help Melanie?"

"What's your name?" she asked, avoiding the question.

"Samantha."

"Samantha, my name is Sergeant Young. Now, the paramedic is going to give you something to help you relax."

Before I could protest, a needle was stuck in my arm. Seconds later, I felt them take my beloved sister from my arms and carry her out of the room just as my mother arrived.

"My baby! Oh my God, my sweet baby!"

"Mom," I called out to her weakly.

When she entered the house and saw Jackson being placed in a body bag, she began screaming again.

"Mom," I said again, while carefully standing and walking over to her. I was hoping for a hug, but got a slap in the face instead.

"You did this? You killed my man?"

"He…*your man* killed Melanie!" I screamed in her face.

"No, he didn't. It was an accident!"

I couldn't believe what I heard. What happened to her two daughters being the most important people in her life? Feeling stronger, I wrenched free from Sergeant Young's grip on my shoulders.

"Was it an accident that he tried to rape her the way he's been raping me for almost a whole year?"

She slapped me across the face again.

"You're lying!"

27

"Mom, he would rape me almost every day when I came home from school. I never told because he said he would hurt Melanie."

"Young man, you don't belong here," Sergeant Young said.

I looked in the direction of the doorway and saw Kareem standing there with a horrified look on his face. Less than an hour ago, he had been having dinner with me. Now I stood before him a bloody mess as a victim of rape and a murderer.

What my mother said next broke my stare. "You are no child of mine," she spat through clenched teeth, then walked out alongside the gurney carrying her dead husband.

Those words pierced my heart and went deep enough to kill me. I felt my knees weaken.

"Samantha!" Sergeant Young's voice sounded so far away. "Give her air. She's coming to."

"What's going on?" I asked weakly. "Where's my mother?"

"You fainted. Are you okay?"

I looked around while accepting the shirt she handed to me. I knew I would never be okay.

"Just relax and come with us," Sergeant Young instructed. "We have to take you in."

"In? What do you mean?" I asked, putting on my t-shirt.

"You're under arrest for the murder of Jackson Price. You have the right to remain silent…"

Soft-spoken Sergeant Young read my rights to me and placed me in handcuffs. When she led me to the police car, it seemed as if the whole world was outside. Keisha, who was standing next to Kareem, burst into tears when I walked by her. Kareem approached the patrol car, kissed his middle and index fingers, and placed them against the window. Then he stepped back as the police car pulled away.

Shug'ah

At the precinct, I was sitting at a table when Sergeant Young came in with two cups. She handed me the cup of water and kept the coffee for herself. She gave me a little smile as she removed the cuffs from my wrists. Then she sat down opposite of me and sighed heavily.

"How old are you, Samantha?"

I took a sip of the cool water before answering. "I'm sixteen."

"You're so young," she said almost in a whisper.

"What's going to happen to me?"

"You'll be held here until Monday morning. That's when your court-appointed attorney will come and talk with you. Do you have any other family?"

"I think my grandma is alive in Puerto Rico."

"Your father's mother?"

"Yes. After he died, she never called or wrote us again."

"And on your mom's side?"

"I never met anyone from her side. I remember her saying they disowned her because she married my father too young. She was being a rebel, I guess."

"So you have no one?"

I thought about it and she was right; Because of Jackson, I now only had myself.

"I didn't do anything wrong. He had to pay for what he did."

"It seems as if your actions were premeditated because—"

"Of course, it was premeditated. I wanted to kill him for months."

Sergeant Young held up her hand. "I'm advising you not to say another word until you speak to your attorney. Now, let's get you cleaned up."

29

I followed her to the locker room and took a much-needed shower. She handed me police sweats and suggested I get some sleep, but sleep never showed up.

"Morning," Sergeant Young greeted me the next morning. "Get any sleep?"

I shook my head as she unlocked the cell.

"Here you go."

"What's this?"

"Breakfast and some magazines. It's going to be a long Sunday," she told me.

I ate the pancakes, but couldn't taste a thing. My family and I would have been in church at that moment had it not been for Jackson. I closed my eyes and imagined we were sitting in the pew listening to Reverend Samuel preaching. Then I opened my eyes. *Reality is a bitch.*

"You have a few minutes," I heard one of the officers say.

"Hey, girl!" Keisha said, trying to sound upbeat. "We missed you at church today."

"Well, take a look around. I don't think church is on the list of places I can go."

Keisha blinked quickly, fighting the urge to cry. "What happened?"

"That's the question of the day," I replied.

I took a deep breath before filling her in about my life for the last year. Reliving it drained me.

Keisha was speechless. After she left, I closed my eyes and began praying for sleep. This time, it finally showed up. However, what seemed to be a short while later, I was awakened by Sergeant Young and another officer talking near my cell. I sat up when I realized they were talking about me.

"She stabbed him thirty-two times," I heard the officer tell Sergeant Young.

"Thirty-two times?" I echoed out loud.

Sergeant Young quickly turned toward my cell. "I'm glad you got some sleep."

It didn't feel like sleep, but more like passing out from sheer exhaustion.

"Did I really stab him thirty-two times?"

"I'll tell you what; let's play cards while we wait for the pizza."

Sergeant Young was good at two things: avoiding questions and remaining calm.

"Melanie liked playing cards." Her name exiting my lips made my eyes water. "Melanie," I whispered.

I said her name over and over, hoping if I said it a million times she would appear. Sergeant Young sat down next to me, and while she held me in her arms, I cried a sea of tears until I drifted off to sleep again.

Chapter 4

"Samantha. Samantha. Wake up, silly."
"Melanie?"
"Samantha, come play with me."
I followed her laughter through a thick forest, but I couldn't see her.
"Where are you, Mel?"
"Right here next to you."
I looked to my right and then to my left, but she wasn't there.
"Melanie, come on. Stop playing games."
"Why, Samantha? Don't you wanna play with me?"
"Of course, I do. I can't see you, though."
"Do you see me now?"
I was now out of the forest and floating on a cloud in the bluest sky. I saw her big smile and her long hair dancing around her face. She was so beautiful.
"Melanie, I can see you!"
She laughed. "I see you, too."
Our clouds were side by side. I reached out to her extended hand, wanting to pull her to my cloud. Right when our fingers touched, she began to fall and everything turned dark.

Imani Writes

"Samantha!" she screamed as she fell.

My cloud kept rising, so I couldn't get to her. As she screamed continuously, I jumped off my cloud and landed hard on the ground.

"Melanie!" I called out into the darkness, ignoring the pain in my chest. "Melanie, answer me!"

She screamed again. We were back in the forest. I tripped and fell, and when I looked up, I noticed the trees had turned into hundreds of laughing Jacksons.

"Melanie!" I screamed.

"Sam, help me...please." Her voice was so weak.

"She's my new thing." Jackson's voice burned my ear.

I turned to see Melanie in his arms. Suddenly, a knife appeared in my hand.

"Let her go!"

"I can't. She belongs to me now."

Melanie seemed to be gasping for air.

I held up the knife, ready to strike Jackson. "She will never be yours!"

I closed my eyes as I felt the knife meet flesh. Jackson's laughter was all around me.

"What have you done?" Melanie asked, taking shallow breaths.

I opened my eyes only to discover Melanie lying there with the knife in her chest. I couldn't move. I couldn't speak. Melanie held up her arm and pointed at me. Her eyes were wide with fear.

"It's your fault! It's all your fault!"

I screamed as Melanie took her last breath. Upon hearing Jackson's laugh, I kept screaming.

"Wake up! Wake up!" the officer yelled, shaking me awake.

When I opened my eyes, I realized I was screaming.

"What the hell is wrong with you?" he questioned.

She blames me. Melanie blames me. I looked at the officer

Shug'ah

and rolled over. That night, I fought off sleep. I didn't want to ever fall asleep again.

"Rough night?" Sergeant Young asked early the next morning.

I looked up at her and nodded.

"I was told you were screaming in your sleep. Care to talk about it?"

I shook my head.

"Okay. Well, the lawyer will be in after nine. I think you should shower and eat something."

During my shower and while eating breakfast, the nightmare replayed in my head. I didn't care to live. I didn't care if they locked me up and threw away the key.

While in a daze, my concentration was broken by my cell being opened.

"Good morning. I'm Leon Sampson. I'll be representing you in court. Explain to me what happened the night of the alleged incident."

Leon looked like he just graduated from law school. *I should be in school right now*, I thought as my mind drifted back to the life I once had before Jackson stole it from me.

"Samantha?"

I stared at the young man. His well-kept locs danced on his shoulders as he looked in his briefcase for a notepad.

"What do you want to know? Would you like to know how a man that was supposed to be my father figure raped me almost every day? Do you want to hear how he was trying to rape my ten-year-old sister and ended up killing her? Maybe you'll get a kick out of the fact that I stabbed the asshole thirty-two times, or the fact that my sweet mother would rather cry over her dead husband than be here for me."

My last statement made me realize that in the two days I had been locked up, my mom hadn't visited. I wasn't surprised, just saddened.

"Get some rest. We have to appear before the judge tomorrow morning. I'll see you then."

Before leaving, he turned and gave me a reassuring smile that let me know he cared.

I sat for an hour listening to Keisha give me the rundown on the first day of school. She told me everyone in school was talking about me, which didn't shock me.

"You know Kareem's moving away, right?"

"What?"

"Yes. His momma is all about the drama, gurl," Keisha said between popping Bubblicious bubbles. "They're moving to NYC. His mother thinks he's traumatized, so they're leaving the environment."

"How do you know all this?"

"I was in the office this morning and heard those two busybody, nosey-as-hell ladies talking."

"Ms. Fabio and old-ass Charlotte?"

"Uh-huh."

More grape-scented bubbles popped inches from my face.

"Are you gonna give me some or what?"

"You can have gum?"

"Keisha, you can be so dense. I'm in jail, not on Weight Watchers."

She laughed, and hearing it made me feel good. I didn't want anyone feeling sorry for me.

"Hurry up and open the door!" Leon's deep voice roared,

interrupting us. He came over to the bars and stood next to Keisha. "I have good news."

"Who dis?" Keisha asked.

"Gurl, hush. This is my lawyer." I directed my attention back to Leon. "Good news about what?"

"I have two words for you: justifiable homicide."

"Translation, please?"

"I can prove you had just cause to kill Mr. Price. He was raping you for almost a year, he was trying to rape your little sister, and in the process, he killed her. I simply have to get the court to agree that he had to be stopped."

"He did have to be stopped. That's why I did what I did."

"I know. I'm going to the DA's office to see if I can get them to agree to justifiable homicide." He smiled and patted my hands that were gripping the steel bars.

"This is good news," Keisha said happily. Her jaws finally gave the bubblegum a break.

"It is, but don't go all Fabio and Charlotte on me and start telling my business."

"Why not?"

"I don't want to jinx it."

"I understand. Well, I'm about to go home. I'll see you later."

"One more thing, Keisha. I need you to do me a big favor."

"Name it."

"Find Kareem and tell him I want to see him."

She grinned and mouthed the words *I love you* before leaving. She cared, too.

About seven o'clock, Sergeant Young showed up with dinner. I ate and told her what my attorney said about using justifiable homicide as my defense. I couldn't help but notice she wasn't too surprised about the news. I got the feeling she had already talked to Leon. Suddenly, this world didn't seem so bad.

By eight-thirty, I was flipping through my last magazine when I got a surprise visit.

"Hey."

I looked up and saw the most beautiful sight. "Hey, Kareem!"

"Keisha left a thousand messages on my pager. I would've come sooner, but there's been a lot of things going on lately."

"I know. You and your mom are moving to New York."

"Yeah." Kareem stared down at his shoes as if they had sprouted heads, and then he looked up with tears in his eyes. "Why didn't you tell me? I could've helped you." His voice wasn't accusing or mean, just filled with pain.

"He told me not to."

"I would've killed him if I knew."

"I wanted to tell you. I swear I did."

Kareem stepped closer to the bars. I reached out and wiped away the tears that escaped his eyes and rolled down his cheeks.

"Still my girl?" he asked with a smile.

My heart began to beat faster and the stomach butterflies fluttered.

"Always."

I needed to connect with someone, and as if reading my mind, he held my chin. The bars had enough space between them for our lips to touch. As he kissed me gently, the bars seemed to melt away. The officer cleared his throat as a warning, breaking our union. We both backed away from the bars.

"Kareem, I might be free this time tomorrow."

"This time tomorrow I'll be on my way to New York."

"So soon?" I asked, trying to hide the disappointment.

"Yes. My mother doesn't want me to miss too much school."

"I'm sorry you have to leave because of me."

Shug'ah

"We were going to move away next summer, but with all that has happened, she thought it was best we leave now."

"You never told me that you were moving away."

"I was hoping she would change her mind or I could stay here and live with my dad. You know I'll be back."

"Yeah, that's what everyone says."

"I promise I'll be back."

"I'm going to hold you to that promise."

"Well, I better go. My mother would freak if she knew I came here to see you."

I smiled to cover up the pain I felt from his statement.

"Good luck tomorrow. I know it will all work out for you."

"From your sweet lips to God's ears. Please write me," I told him, forcing a smile.

"I will."

"Promise?"

When he didn't say anything in response, a part of me felt I would never see him again.

I heard the main cell slide open and then slam shut. My eyes felt heavy and the butterflies died down. I was left alone with my thoughts. Kareem was gone and it hurt to see him go. I temporarily forgot the promise I made to myself to stay awake in order to avoid that nightmare. Fortunately, sleep came easily and no dreams surfaced.

Chapter 5

"All rise!" the bailiff belted out, grabbing the attention of everyone in the courtroom. "This court is now in session. The Honorable Brenda Wilde presiding."

"You may be seated," Judge Wilde instructed. "When this case was given to me, I was appalled. This should have never happened, and because of it, two people are dead." She looked my way with an empathetic expression. "Because the defendant is a minor, this hearing will be closed to the public. I will now hear both sides."

The prosecution lawyer stood, smoothed down her blonde hair, and started speaking in a no-nonsense voice. "A young girl is claiming she was raped, but did she have the right to kill Jackson Price? She stabbed him thirty-two times for a crime of rape, which has not been proven. I have but one witness that can hopefully shed light on this case."

She walked back to her seat and leafed through a small stack of papers. I stared at her witness—my mother.

"Your Honor," my lawyer began as he rose to his feet, "my client was in an unthinkable situation for a fifteen-year-old girl. Did she have the right to kill Jackson Price? It is not my job to give my opinion. The facts that led up to the death of Mr. Price are not in black and white. Records that my client was raped over the course of a year by her stepfather are not in any police station's file because she feared what Jackson Price would do to her mother or little sister. So, to protect them, her abuse was not told to another soul.

"However, I believe Samantha. I see the hurt and emptiness in her eyes. The loss of her sister was more than she could bear. Speaking of her little sister Melanie, she was as much a victim in this tragedy as Samantha, but she is not here to speak about it. Why? Because Jackson Price killed ten-year-old Melanie while forcing himself on her. All of these circumstances led up to the killing of Jackson Price." Leon paused and looked my way before continuing. "So, I ask the question again. Did Samantha Ruiz have the right to kill Jackson Price? She certainly did, and I will prove her actions were justified. I have but one witness myself."

When the judge looked at me, I diverted my gaze down to my wrinkled purple skirt. As Leon took a seat next to me, he patted my clenched hand.

"Ms. Bishop, please call your first witness."

"I call Yolanda Price to the stand."

I watched my mother walk to the stand and be sworn in. She sat there glaring at me. I couldn't understand the hatred she had for me. All the love she once claimed to have for me was quickly replaced by hate.

Ms. Bishop began her questioning. "When did you meet Mr. Price?"

She cleared her throat and rubbed her nose. "I met Jackson about...well, a little over three years ago at MFI Recovery Center. That's the hospital where I work."

"What is your job there?"

"I'm a nurse."

"Was Mr. Price a patient?" Ms. Bishop asked.

"Oh, no. He was there checking up on his heroin-addicted father."

"So, at what point did the two of you decide to get

married?"

She smiled at a distant memory. "I would say after almost two years of us exclusively dating."

"Was your daughter supportive?"

I felt uneasy that Ms. Bishop didn't pluralize the word daughter as if Melanie never existed.

"She was at first."

"Can you be more specific?" Ms. Bishop pressed.

"She stopped hanging with me and started always hanging around him."

Leon jumped to his feet. "Objection, Your Honor. Hearsay and speculation."

"Sustained. Please keep your answers to the facts," Judge Wilde requested.

"So you say your daughter stopped doing things with you and spent most of her time with Jackson?"

"Yes."

"She's lying," I leaned over and whispered to Leon. I couldn't believe what she was saying.

"Let's talk about the night your husband was murdered."

She shifted in her seat. "I was supposed to be off from my second job that night, but I got called in to work."

"And your second job is?"

"*Was*. I quit after that night. I worked at a diner in our neighborhood. Everyone calls it the Chicken Shack. I was a waitress there."

"Go on."

"Well, I was happy that night because Samantha was going out on her first date, and even happier when I saw her come in with her date to get something to eat. She didn't seem happy to see me, though. After a few minutes, she ran to the bathroom and never came back. About thirty minutes later, I got a call from my neighbor telling me that I should get home as soon as possible."

"Then what happened?"

"Well, when I went outside my car was gone. So, I ran back inside and asked her date to give me a ride home." She paused and wiped the corner of her eyes. "Then when I got to the house…" Her voice changed from a somber tone to anger. "…he was dead. They didn't even let me see him. And she was standing there covered in blood. She killed my husband!"

Tears formed and I let them fall. Not once did she mention her; not one recognition of my beloved sister.

"No further questions."

Judge Wilde sighed and looked my way. "Mr. Sampson."

"Mrs. Price, you seem to be forgetting something."

"I'm not forgetting anything," she replied with hostility.

"Let me rephrase that. You are forgetting *someone*."

She was silent.

"Melanie Ruiz. Can you tell me who Melanie Ruiz is?"

There were no tears and no change in tone. "My daughter."

"How old was Melanie on the night of Mr. Jackson's murder?"

"She was ten."

"Why is she not here?"

Ms. Bishop yelled an objection, and the judge ordered him to redirect his line of questioning.

"One question, Mrs. Price. Do you think what your husband did to your two daughters is forgivable?"

"He didn't do anything!" she shouted.

Leon shook his head. "Nothing further, Your Honor."

"You may step down," Judge Wilde told her. "Mr. Sampson, your witness."

I looked away as she walked to her seat. I didn't want to look at her. I waited until she was seated before I got up and walked to the stand.

"How are you?" Leon asked me once I was seated and sworn in.

"I don't know."

"Just take your time and answer my questions."
I nodded.
"How old are you?"
"Sixteen."
"How old were you when your mother married Jackson Price?"
"When I found out she was getting married to him, I had just turned fifteen. They married about a month after that right before school started."
"How did you and Melanie adjust to the new father figure?"
"We were fine. Mom was happy and home more often, so Melanie and I were very happy."
"Did it last?"
"Not really. About a month after the wedding, Jackson got fired from his job, and Mom had to get her other job back. She wasn't home much anymore after that."
"When was the first time he raped you?"
"Objection," Ms. Bishop said. "Rape has not been proven."
"Overruled. Mr. Sampson, please rephrase your question," the judge requested.
Leon ran his hand through his locs before continuing. "Samantha, how old were you the first time Jackson touched you inappropriately?"
"Objection!"
The judge grabbed her gavel and slammed it. "Sit down, Ms. Bishop!" Then she turned back to me and said, "Please answer the question."
I scratched my head and cleared my throat. "It was in October."
"I know it's difficult, but please tell us what happened that day."
"I came home with a friend. He and I were sitting on the porch talking, and he invited me to the Halloween dance at

school…"

"What's the name of your friend?" Leon asked, interrupting me.

"Kareem."

"Okay. Please continue."

"A few seconds later, Jackson opened the door and chased him away. He was drunk. I was mad at him and probably shouldn't have yelled, but he made me mad."

When I took a long pause, Leon motioned with his hand for me to continue. Tears filled my eyes. It was hard going back to the time when he first raped me.

"I went to my room and slammed my door. While I was undressing, he walked in and told me if I was having sex and became pregnant, my mom would hate me. I told him that I wasn't sexually active and it really wasn't his business. That's when he pushed me against the wall and told me that he wanted to see how much of a virgin I was."

"You're a liar!" my mother yelled.

The gavel came into play again. "Control your witness, Ms. Bishop. Continue, Samantha."

"He pulled my pants and panties down and forced himself inside of me."

I began to cry. I would have done anything not to relive the pain of that day. Yet, I had no other choice.

Sensing my agony, Leon moved on, but the questions didn't get any easier to answer. "How often did incidences like what you just described happen?"

"Once or twice."

"A month?"

I sighed deeply. "No, a week."

My mom attempted to say something, but the prosecutor silenced her.

"Samantha, let's talk about what your mother said about you not spending time with her and spending more time with Jackson."

Shug'ah

I looked at my mother as I began explaining. "Mom started working two jobs again after Jackson got fired, so she was never home. I never went anywhere with him, and I tried to avoid him as much as possible. I hated him for forcing me to have sex with him. I hated him because he lied to me."

"What do you mean?"

"He told me if I kept quiet, he wouldn't hurt her."

"Please be specific for the judge, Samantha. Who is her?"

"Melanie. He said if I told, he would hurt her. So, I never told. I never told anyone."

"Thank you, Samantha. I have nothing further, Your Honor."

The judge informed Ms. Bishop that she could begin her cross-examination.

"Did you like Mr. Price?" she asked while pacing in front of the stand.

"No," I mumbled.

"Never? Not at any time? Not even in the beginning of your mother's relationship with him?"

"Yeah...at first, I did."

"Did you dress seductively around him?"

My lawyer objected numerous times during Ms. Bishop's questioning. By the time Judge Wilde put a stop to it, I felt as though it may have been my fault that he raped me. Could it have been the clothes I wore, the things I said, or the fact that I sat too close to him on the couch while we watched TV.

"Your Honor, I'm withdrawing from the agreement of justifiable homicide. I'd like to request that the defendant get the maximum in a juvenile detention center," Ms. Bishop announced to the court.

After taking a break for lunch, we returned to the courtroom for the judge's decision.

"All rise!"

Judge Wilde motioned for us to sit. "We have a case here that sickens me," she began. "I understand Mr. Sampson's claim for justifiable homicide. This should be an open and shut case. Samantha, right now you should be going home with your mother."

"That slut needs to be locked up!"

At that point, Judge Wilde had enough. "Remove Mrs. Price from my courtroom now!"

As the bailiff began escorting my mom out of the courtroom, she continued hurling insults at me like bricks.

"You little bitch! You should be the one dead, and Melanie should be here! You nasty slut!"

As the doors of the courtroom closed, my mom could no longer be heard. Still, her words continued to resonate in my head. I sat in shock at the woman who birthed me referring to me using such vulgarity. Me! Her own child—her firstborn.

"The behavior of your mother is why I…" Judge Wilde stopped and looked at me. She drew in a deep breath and let it out slowly before continuing. "Your mother is not going to take you in, and you have no relatives who are willing to step forward to care for you. Therefore, I have no choice."

Leon rose to his feet. "Oh, no! Your Honor, no!"

"Mr. Sampson, I can understand how you feel, so I'm going to overlook you interrupting me during sentencing. Be seated, Mr. Sampson. Samantha Ruiz, you are reprimanded to the juvenile center in Stockton to serve the maximum time for manslaughter. You will be free on your twenty-first birthday."

Her gavel slammed on the desk as the exclamation point to her decision.

"We'll appeal," Leon told me, trying to offer some comfort.

The guards cuffed me and escorted me out of the courtroom onto a bus. I never felt so scared and so alone. The other girls on the bus talked to each other as if they were going to summer camp. Overwhelmed with sickness, I moved closer to the window.

Chapter 6

January, 1996

It was five months into my sentence and nothing had changed. I followed instructions, did my schoolwork, and kept to myself. No one knew what I was in there for. A few asked, but they never got an answer. I dreaded going to sleep because my nightmares continued, and when I did sleep, it was only because my body grew tired and I lost the battle to stay awake.

I looked forward to Saturdays when the mail was given out. Teachers and a few friends would write me occasionally, but I always got a weekly letter from Keisha. Kareem sent his letters in purple envelopes. I got about two letters a month from him. I would go to my room and read his words over and over again. They were filled with love and hope for a future together. He told me about the fun he was having in New York, but expressed that he missed me more. I knew as long as I got his letters I could survive being in that place.

My biggest problem was Special K, a seventeen-year-old who taunted me from day one. She never lightened up.

"Well, if it isn't Ms. Snobby," Special K said, sitting next to me at my table. "You always sitting over here by yourself. You think you too good for the rest of us?"

I put a spoonful of mashed potatoes in my mouth.

"Mmm, that's okay, sweet Shug'ah."

Shug'ah was what she started calling me a few days after I arrived there.

"You ain't gotta say nothing. You may not be good for them, but you're damn good for me."

I shook my head trying to ignore her.

She ran her hand through my hair. "It's so soft. Would you mind if I pull it while you lick my pussy?"

I had been silent long enough. "Are you fucking crazy?"

"Of course, I am. I'm in here, ain't I? I can't wait to taste you, Shug'ah."

"Well, you gonna be waiting a long-ass time." I looked around and noticed a few eyes were on us. "No dyke's gonna tongue–fuck me." I raised my voice to expand the listening audience. "I don't swing that way, and if I did, I would fuck a prettier girl than your ass, bitch! You ugly motherfu—"

Before I could finish ranting, Special K grabbed my hair and slammed my face into the table. "Next time I won't be so nice, Shug'ah."

Her so-called crew surrounded her, but then they moved on as one of the guards walked up.

"You alright?" the guard asked.

Tears stung my eyes, my nose throbbed, and my mouth ached.

"Tilt your head back," a soft voice said.

"Juanita, go back to your dinner," the guard instructed.

"I just wanna help."

"Then help. Don't hinder," the guard told her.

Juanita tilted my head back. "Now swallow."

I swallowed. The taste of blood sent a wave of nausea through my body.

Shug'ah

"Her lip is split, and I think her nose is broken. She needs stitches. Juanita, help me get her to the nurse."

The two of them helped me, and within a few minutes, I was lying on an examination table. I ran my tongue over my lip trying to assess the damage.

"You know you got some serious mental issues to talk to K that way."

I finally got to see Juanita's face. I had seen her before, and ironically, she kept to herself, too.

"Well, she has men-tool ihht-uses if—"

"Girl, shut up. Your busted lip is making you sound retarded."

"Alright, you two. What happened?" the nurse asked us.

The look on Juanita's face was enough to tell me to be quiet. The nurse stitched my lip and informed me that my nose wasn't broken, but it was going to hurt like hell until the swelling went down. After a few weeks, my stitches were removed and I was able to talk normal. Special K still kept after me, but having Juanita around lessened her threats. By then, everyone had started calling me Shug'ah.

"So why have you never asked me?" Juanita said as we watched TV in the recreation room one afternoon.

"Asked you what?"

"Why I'm in here."

"'Cause I don't want you to ask me why I'm here."

Juanita drew in a long breath and volunteered her story. "About a year ago, my boyfriend and I went into a store that he decided to rob. He shot the cashier, but he didn't die. My man had two strikes, so I did what I had to do."

"You took the rap?"

"Yeah, I did."

"That was dumb," I told her.

"No, that was love."

"Ha! No, it wasn't. He used you."

Juanita sighed deeply and looked out the window. I

assumed someone had told her that before.

"I'm going to my room."

"Look, girl, I'm sorry, but the truth hurts."

She shifted on the battered couch and faced me. "What about your truth?"

"See, here we go."

She sat there searching my face for answers until I finally gave in.

"Fine! I killed my stepfather."

"Whoa! Damn, girl! Why?"

"Let's just say my actions were justified."

I didn't want to tell her the story. The last thing I needed was someone else pitying me.

"If they were justified, why you up in here?"

"I wish I knew."

One of the male guards walking by cleared his throat and grinned.

Juanita looked up at him. "Keep moving, Michaels. There's nothing here for you to see."

"You can talk to them like that?" I asked after he walked away.

"Naw, just his ass. He's one foul son-of-a-bitch."

"What do you mean?"

"He's a watcher."

I was confused. "A watcher?"

Juanita smiled. "Well, you got me, so you'll never have to find out. I'll keep that dyke away from you, too."

"Amen!"

Juanita kept her word to me. Whenever Special K so much as looked in my direction, Juanita would flex on her. She taught me a few self-defense moves, as well. She never talked about her life on the streets, though. Right after my birthday, a few new girls came in. One in particular made Juanita tense. They spoke a few times, but I could tell there was no love lost between them.

"So how does it feel?" Juanita asked while we ate breakfast.

"What?"

"Well, you've been seventeen for a month now and you got your GED."

"I don't feel any different."

"You should," she replied. Then quickly, her smile faded.

I turned to see what got her attention. It was that same girl.

"Who is she?"

"Who?"

"Bitch, stop playing."

"That's Coco. I guess you could say we worked together. We were cool until I found her fucking my man."

"The same one you're in here for? That's fucked up."

"What's in the envelope?" she asked, changing the topic.

"I got another letter from Kareem."

"It's purple. I should've known."

We laughed.

"Read it. Wait! Before you do, I got to thinking about what you said about me being up in here for something I didn't do. I contacted my lawyer, and we're going to appeal this shit."

"No shit? That's what I'm talkin' about."

"Now read it! Let me feel the romance," she said in a very bad Italian accent.

My Darling Samantha,

I apologize for taking so long to write. I'm so happy you liked the gift I got you for your birthday. I wish I could've been there to hold you and give you what you really wanted. My heart is still overflowing with love for you. I didn't tell you this, but I took my mother to the prom as my date. Don't get me wrong, I was asked a lot, but you're my girl no matter the distance. Mom had fun. A few of the guys cut in a lot, and

Imani Writes

she thought she was all that.

My love, I'm not sure how to tell you this, but remember I told you Dad moved to Paris for a change of scenery? Well, I'm going to Paris in August to stay with him for a while. He wants me to go to college over there. I'm not sure about that, but it will be the perfect place to pursue my love for designing clothes.

I promise I'll continue to write you. I want to make our future stronger financially because you know we got the love thang down. I'm going to marry you and restore your faith in life. Stay beautiful and remember I will always love you. ~ K

"Awwwwwww, he is so sweet," Juanita commented. "I can't wait to meet him. You're so lucky to have a man who cares so much about you."

"I know."

It felt like everyone that I loved was moving further away from me. First, Keisha moved to North Carolina and then Kareem to Paris.

For the next couple of months, Juanita was escorted to and from court as she appealed her case. I knew it would work out for her. I had to admit I was a little nervous at the thought of being left to fend on my own. Juanita was my rock and my protector, but I knew once she was released, I would no longer have her to hide behind. She and I still did our exercise routine. She had me lift anything to build up my arms, whether it was one side of my dresser or the jumbo-size cans of pork and beans we snuck from the kitchen.

"Why are you smiling?" I asked Juanita as we sat eating the detention center's version of Thanksgiving dinner. All of us who didn't have visitors ate in our rooms.

"I've been waiting for this day to tell you."

"Tell me what?"

"I did it."

It took me a second to figure *it* out. "Really?!"

Shug'ah

"Yeah. I leave next week."

Tears tickled the corners of my eyes. My emotions were mixed; I had happy tears for her being able to leave the dump we were in and sad tears because my only friend would no longer be there with me.

"I'm happy for you," I said, forcing a smile while fighting back the tears.

"I'll be back to see you for Christmas. You will not be up in here eating by yourself."

The day she left was difficult. She told me to be strong and promised me that three and a half years would go by fast. I was just happy when Christmas Eve showed up. Keisha sent me some CDs, and Kareem sent me tons of pictures of him in Paris. He also had a friend here in California send me an orchid. Kareem wrote that the orchid was a symbol of our love—always growing and always beautiful.

While lying in bed enjoying the CDs and looking forward to seeing Juanita the next day, the faint glow from the blinking Christmas lights glaring under my door made me sleepy. As soon as I closed my eyes, Melanie wanted my attention. I opened them quickly, but I wasn't in my room alone. Thinking I might have been still dreaming, I closed my eyes, but they were still in my room when I opened them again.

Chapter 7

I took the headphones off. "Who the fuck's in here?"

When I went to get out of bed, someone turned on the lights, blinding me for a moment.

Special K stood in front of four of her girls. Then Officer Michaels came in.

"Oh, thank God. Get these bitches out of my room, please. I need to get some sleep."

He grinned and closed my door. "Just relax. You might enjoy it."

Before I could grasp that they were setting me up, Special K introduced me to her right fist. I was caught a little off guard, but she didn't sway me much. Despite her being a big bitch, her punch had no power. Clearly, I was outnumbered, but I didn't let them see my fear.

Special K took a step back and let her girls take over.

"See," she said, breathing hard. "I told you one day I would get you."

I wanted to beat the shit out of her, but I was already too busy fighting off my attackers. I threw punch after punch until my hands felt broken. Someone kept hitting me in my face. I got dizzy. Unable to stand my ground any longer, I finally buckled and fell to the floor.

"Hold her ass down on the bed!" Special K instructed.

My arms were held above my head by one of them, and I felt my clothes being ripped from my body. I didn't fight because I couldn't. Special K tugged at my panties so hard that the fabric burned my skin before they finally ripped. I lay there naked and in pain. My legs were yanked open and held for Special K, who touched me and began licking me. I felt nothing, though.

I escaped to the place I would go when Jackson used to put his hands on me. Just like back then, I focused on something in my room and let my soul leave my body. I looked Officer Michaels dead in his eyes and finally knew what Juanita meant about him being a watcher. Allowing my mind to take me to Paris, I mentally flipped through the photos Kareem had sent me. I don't know how long Special K took me, but I came to my senses when I felt a sharp pain in my vagina. Special K was shoving Officer Michaels' club deep inside of me for his viewing pleasure, while he leaned against the wall and masturbated until he came.

Silence fell on the room, and I was alone again. I tried to get up to shower, but my legs wouldn't allow me to stand. I fell to the floor and stayed there until morning when I woke up to indescribable pain. Hoping to be the first one to the showers, I got my robe and towel, but I had no such luck. Gasps and whispers filled the area as I looked for an empty shower stall. I didn't know what they were all whispering about until I looked in the mirror. The scratches and bruises all over my body broadcasted last night's events. My left eye was damn near swollen shut and I looked like shit. Ignoring the pain, I stepped into the shower. My womanhood had once again been violated, but this time, I promised myself it would be the last time.

After showering, I quickly returned to the privacy of my room. However, Ms. Kingston, the center's director, didn't grasp the definition of the word privacy.

Shug'ah

"Samantha...what happened to you?"

I remained silent.

"Who did this to you, sweetheart?" she pressed, her voice caring and her eyes showing concern.

"I don't know," I lied.

"You know I can't help you if you don't tell me."

I nodded.

"I think you need to go to the nurse."

"I'm fine," I replied firmly.

She didn't question me further about it. "You have a visitor."

"Thank you."

Ms. Kingston left without saying another word.

I tried to smile at the thought of having a visit, but the tenderness of my face made it a bit difficult. Once dressed, I made my way to the visiting room. My eyes searched the area for Juanita, but instead, I saw Leon. His expression changed the closer I got to where he was sitting.

"Samantha, what happened?"

"Santa gave me an ass kicking for Christmas. What does it look like?"

"This is not a time to joke. I'm your lawyer."

"Not anymore," I told him.

I wasn't in the mood. He was only going to get me pissed off before Juanita showed up.

"I care about you. I can't sleep thinking about you in here," he expressed, taking on a more personal tone. "I'm still working on your appeal."

I stood up. "Look, Leon, it's not your fault. You did your best the first time. I'm not going through another trial, so drop it. This is my life now. Don't give me a second thought. Go home and get some rest. We're done here."

I walked through the growing crowd of visitors and made it back to my room. I was happy to lie down and get some rest. Hours went by and no one came to tell me that my best

Imani Writes

friend was waiting for me. It was close to eight in the evening when a guard finally came for me, but instead of saying I had another visitor, she told me to go to Ms. Kingston's office. I went there immediately and knocked on her door.

"Come in."

"Is Juanita here?" I asked as soon as I entered.

"Samantha, sit down."

I hated her tone. I slowly sat in the chair in front of Ms. Kingston's desk and looked at her with an expression that let her know I was awaiting an answer to my question.

"There's no easy way to tell you this. I know you and Juanita were very close while she was here."

"We still are. So what if she isn't coming. She'll come another day."

Ms. Kingston sighed. "I hate to put this on you now, especially after last night, which I will get to the bottom of. Samantha…a few days ago, Juanita was shot and killed."

I sat there shaking my head. "You're wrong."

"I wish I was. Her lawyer informed me of the news. Her funeral is the day after tomorrow. You have my permission to attend, if you would like."

"No. I don't want to attend," I said, then stood to leave.

I left her office and took my spot on my bed again. My body was numb with physical and emotional pain. That night, I cried for the last time. I shut myself off from any and everybody in the center. Coco tried stepping to me a few times. She was cool, but I had a new rule: *No more friends*.

I let someone get close to me again and they got killed. There was nothing I could do to save them. Not wanting to feel that pain again. I decided I would rather be alone.

Keisha went off to college and her letters only came on holidays. After March of 1997, there were no more purple envelopes. Ironically, the orchid died, as well. There were also no letters from anyone else. I officially became one of the forgotten.

Life went on. Each day, I got up and went through the motions of living, if you could call it that. Revenge kept me going. I couldn't wait to settle the score between Special K and myself. I got my chance one day in April of 1998, the night before her release.

It was movie night at the center. I usually looked forward to it, but this night, I had my own screening to attend. I got word that Special K was going to pack during the movie. That was perfect!

As we sat in the recreation room, I noticed Special K's fat ass head off in the direction of her room. Needing a reason to be excused, I pretended like I was going to throw up. So, one of the guards practically forced me to go to the restroom. After leaving the recreation room, I dashed to Special K's room. When I got there, she had her back to the open door. I leaned against the doorframe as she placed the headphones on her head. Finally, she noticed me while moving around.

"What the fuck are you doin' here, bitch?"

I didn't answer. Instead, I closed the door so no one would hear us. She was about to say something, but I ran over and slapped the shit out of her.

"It's just the two of us tonight, sweetheart, and I'm about to fuck you up!"

"Whatever, bitch. You don't fuckin' scare me!"

She swung a few times, but missed. I would have loved to continue playing the game of cat and mouse, but I had to get back to the recreation room before the guard came looking for me. I ducked her next swing and then punched her in the ribs with a hard right. As she doubled over in pain, I held onto her shoulders and drove my knee into her face.

"Stop it!" she begged, stumbling around the room. "Please stop."

"Awwwww, you want me to stop the same way I asked you to stop that night you raped me?" I taunted.

I ripped off her shirt and continued delivering hard blows to her ribs with evil intentions. She got fists filled with years of frustration and kicks filled with the power of vengeance. As she lay on the floor bloody and barely conscious, I gave her three hard kicks to her ribs. I then pulled her pants down and pulled at her panties until they ripped. I wanted her to feel as degraded as I felt the night she and her girls attacked me. While standing over her, I pulled her head up by her hair and began punching her in the face until my hand started to hurt. I could have beaten her to death, but I stopped myself.

I went to the restroom, cleaned up, and then ran back to the recreation room.

"Do you feel better?" the guard asked.

I smiled. "I feel so much better now."

"Good. Now sit down and watch the movie."

Right before the movie ended, the lockdown sirens sounded and some of the guards left the room. One of the guards returned to the room and demanded that the girl who assaulted Special K step forward. No one moved or said a word. The guard threatened us with hard work, no food, and no privileges, but still no one talked. The only person that knew it was me was the guard who let me go to the restroom, but he didn't say a word. If he had spoken up, he would have gotten in trouble for not going with me to the restroom. The paramedics came, and an hour later, we got word that Special K had suffered serious internal injuries that required surgery.

In the days following Special K's attack, I found out that most of the girls knew it was me who whooped her ass. I didn't care about anyone knowing except for Ms. Kingston. The last thing I needed was trouble from administration.

July 5, 2000

Two years passed and my release date finally arrived. Ms. Kingston called me to her office to go over what would take place.

"Samantha, it's your big day. I know you've had this day embedded in your brain since the time you first stepped foot in this facility."

"You're right, and I'm ready to get up out of here."

"I understand that, but let me ask you a question. Do you feel you've been rehabilitated?"

"Look, there wasn't anything wrong with me in the first place. It was a justifiable homicide. I should've never been put here."

"The court didn't think so."

"I don't give a damn about the court. That's in the past. I did my time and now I'm ready to go."

Ms. Kingston looked at me long and hard as if she could see through me. "I contacted the judge who handled your case. She's on her way. I'll send for you when she comes."

On the way to my room, I passed Michaels in the hall.

"I'm going to miss you," he taunted. "You were by far the best show I ever had."

That was the wrong fucking day and the wrong fucking moment for him to bring up. I flexed my fingers and brought my hand up with all the force I could muster, connecting the palm of my hand with his nose and breaking it instantly.

"You bitch!" he yelled.

"Tell it to someone who gives a fuck."

A few hours later, I was summoned to Ms. Kingston's office. Judge Wilde was there waiting. She looked different from the last time I had seen her.

"Samantha, how are you?" she asked.

"Ready to get out of here."

Ms. Kingston spoke up. "That's why we're here. I think Samantha needs to be held in a women's prison until she is twenty-five."

"Excuse me?" I asked.

"Are you insane?" Judge Wilde shot back. "This girl had no business being sent here in the first place, but I had no choice because no one would take her in. Placing her here was one of the hardest decisions I had to make as a judge. Now you're telling me that she needs to go to a women's prison for four more years? That's not going to happen. When you called me with your concerns regarding Samantha, I made some calls and pulled a few strings. She is to be released today."

Ms. Kingston stood her ground. "She's not mentally well. She has been through so much."

"And your solution is to send her to another hellhole? No offense."

"I've tried to reach her for years, and she still hasn't come to terms with what she has done."

"Are you a shrink?"

"No, but I—"

"Were you raped by your stepfather?"

Ms. Kingston paused and looked at me. "No, but—"

"Did your mother disown you?"

"No."

"Then don't do my job. Release her now."

With no other choice, Ms. Kingston got up and left to get the paperwork.

"Samantha, I found a place for you to stay and a job at a supermarket not too far from here. There's a taxi waiting for you outside. I already paid the fare. He'll take you home. I also have some money for you." She handed me a wad of cash and the information on my new home and job. "One more thing. In September, you'll be starting psychiatric meetings with a friend of mine named Dr. Luke."

"Do I have to?"

"The one thing I agree with Ms. Kingston on is you need someone to help you deal with what happened. Consider the meetings your probation. You'll go twice a month 'til you turn twenty-five."

"I'll do it," I said, knowing it was better than what Ms. Kingston had in mind.

"Great. Now sign this agreement. It states that you promise to attend the sessions."

I signed it while Judge Wilde and I waited for Ms. Kingston to return with the forms. I was so thankful that Judge Wilde came on my behalf, and I was even more surprised that she had a job for me and a place for me to stay.

Felt like it took forever for me to finally reach twenty-one. Not many girls entered that place and left as women. I had seen many come and go, and when they turned eighteen, they were granted their freedom. On the other hand, most girls who were convicted of manslaughter ended up being tried as adults and sent to a maximum-security facility for twenty-five to life. However, there were a few like me, because of special circumstances, who got sentenced until they were twenty-one in a juvenile facility.

Damn. Melanie would be fifteen years old now, I thought to myself.

Ms. Kingston returned and placed a small stack of papers in front of me. "Here you go. Sign the highlighted areas. I do hope you get your life together."

Looking up from the papers, I told her, "My life has always been together. It's just that people like you come into it and try to fuck it up."

"Samantha," Judge Wilde said softly. "Just sign the release papers."

I signed my name, and out of respect, I shook Ms. Kingston's hand. I'm sure she was more than happy to see me leave.

Judge Wilde followed me to my room and helped me pack what little belongings I had. I pulled out the letters from Kareem that I kept under my mattress. For a brief second, I wanted to throw them away, but instead, I simply tossed them in my bag.

"From someone special?" Judge Wilde asked.

I frowned. "He used to be."

I took one last look around the little room that had been my home for five long years. Then I walked out without looking back. As we walked through the halls towards the exit, no one ran over to give me a hug with tears in their eyes and choking out goodbyes. Not one person said they would miss me. I might as well have been a ghost that used to haunt the halls, but that was fine with me.

When I stepped through the heavy doors, the sun warmed my face. How ironic that the previous day had been Independence Day? I soaked in the feeling of my personal independence day. I couldn't help but feel overwhelmed by the wave of different emotions. I was happy and relieved to be free, yet at the same time, scared and anxious because I was free. When I walked into the detention center, I was only a child, but now, I was stepping out a grown woman on my own with no one in my corner.

"Well, I guess this is it," Judge Wilde said.

My heart started beating hard. "I guess," I replied, then got in the taxi. "Thank you for everything."

She closed the door. "My pleasure."

After telling the driver the address of where to take me, she stood waving as we pulled off. I took in the scenery as we drove away from a place that was already becoming a faded memory.

Chapter 8

The judge set me up in a home that served as a shelter for abused and battered women. Mrs. Tyson, the director of the home, was really nice and very trusting. I enjoyed living there and slowly allowed myself to become friends with all of the women. A few of them had been sexually abused by their husbands. So, like myself, they understood the pain of being betrayed by the ones they loved.

Working at the supermarket was good, but I always felt like my manager, Mr. Howell, was watching me carefully. He constantly looked over my shoulder.

"Well, well, well. If it isn't the prettiest girl from Arlington High."

I searched the stranger's face for some spark of recognition.

"Oh, you're going to break my heart."

"I'm sorry. I don't remember you."

He smiled. "Rome."

"Rome Rawlings?"

"Yes, baby girl. Good to see you."

"What are you doing with yourself these days?" I asked while scanning the few items he was buying.

"I'm just doing my thing, you know. Whatever happened to your boy?"

I knew he was talking about Kareem. The two were good friends in high school and played together on the basketball team.

"Your guess is as good as mine. He went to Paris and that was it." I glanced at his total. "Thirty-four twenty-eight."

He handed me a hundred-dollar bill. "Paris, huh? Damn. Keep the change."

"I'm not your waitress. I can't keep the change. The minute I would go to put my hand in my pocket, I'd get tackled and strip-searched," I said, giving the change back to him.

"I feel you on that one." He laughed and looked at me like he forgot something.

"Do you need anything else?"

"Not really. I was just wondering about something."

"Well, can you wonder off to the side? I have customers behind you who are waiting to check out?"

"If I gave you something, would you use it?"

I glanced at the cashier next to me named Niquee. Like always, she was being nosey. We didn't care for each other at all.

"Give me what?" I asked, ignoring Niquee's signal for me to wrap up my conversation.

"My number."

"Well, give it to me and you'll find out."

Taking the pen from my hand, he scribbled his number on the back of his receipt and gave it to me.

"Anytime, anything you need. Even on my dime. Okay?"

"Okay. Now go! You're going to get me in trouble," I told him, not knowing trouble was already brewing.

That afternoon at the end of our shift, Niquee and I were counting our money. My drawer came up almost three hundred dollars short. I looked at Niquee, who kept staring at me as if she were expecting something to be wrong.

"Is there a problem, Samantha?" she asked sarcastically.

"Mind your business," I snapped.

My reaction got Mr. Howell's attention. "What's the problem, ladies?"

"I think her money is coming up short."

Mr. Howell shot her a look as if to let her know she gave out too much information. "Samantha, is that true?"

"Yes, sir. I seem to be three hundred dollars off."

"Three hundred dollars!" he exclaimed. "Let me count it."

I waited until he finished counting the money.

"Give me the money you stole and maybe I will forget about this."

"I don't have the money. I didn't take it. You have to believe me."

"I'm sorry, but I can't believe that, especially with your past record and all."

"Oh, so it's like that? I knew this shit was going to happen."

"Samantha, I need your register key."

"I know the two of you did this. You waited until I went on my break and took the money out of my register."

"Humph! Just like a criminal," Niquee said. "They can't take responsibility for their own actions. Once a thief, always a thief."

"Look, bitch!" I took a step closer. "I wasn't locked up for stealing. I killed someone. Do you think once a killa', always a killa'?"

Mr. Howell pulled me away from Niquee. "You're fired! Now leave!"

"You don't have to tell me twice."

I walked out of the supermarket mad as hell and not knowing what I was going to do. Going back to the halfway house was not an option for me no matter how loving Ms. Tyson was. She would probably believe their accusations about me being a thief.

I slid my hand deep into the jeans pocket and pulled out the wrinkled piece of paper with Rome's number. I smiled to myself and found a payphone.

"Hello?"

"Who the fuck is dis?" the voice on the other end demanded.

I was caught a little off guard. "Can I speak to Rome?"

"Ain't got no Rome here, bitch."

Thinking he had given me a wrong number, I was about to hang up, but then, I heard a female's voice in the background.

"X, give me the phone...Hello?"

"Yeah, I need to speak to Rome."

"This is his sister. Who are you?"

"Just tell him Shug'ah...I mean, Samantha called."

"Oh, his lil' friend from school? He told me to expect your call."

As she repeated his cell number, I memorized it and called him.

It took a long time for Rome to show up. I would have left hours ago, but I had nowhere else to go. So, I sat on the curb waiting across the street to avoid making contact with any of the workers from the supermarket. A few minutes later, a cream-colored SUV with dark tinted windows slowly rolled by the supermarket. Figuring it was him, I walked across the street in front of the ride. DMX boomed from inside the vehicle.

"Are you going to stand there all damn night?" Rome questioned after rolling down his window a few inches.

I walked around to the passenger side and got in.

"Why you got your face all twisted?"

I rolled my eyes and looked out the window. "I asked you to come for me about four hours ago."

Rome chuckled and turned down the volume on the

stereo. "Oh, no, sweetheart. You didn't ask me to come for you. You demanded I come for you. Nobody, and I mean nobody, tells Rome what to do or when to do shit. Even if…" He paused and looked at me. "Even if they are fine as hell."

"Where are we going?" I asked when I realized we were driving away from the city.

"You'll know when we get there."

About an hour later, he stopped at a fast food joint in Compton.

"You hungry?"

"Yeah, I could eat."

"Well, come on then," he said, then got out of the truck.

I sighed. "I got no money."

Rome leaned in and laughed. "Sweetness, this is no time for you to be shy. I got you."

From the moment we walked in, I could feel all eyes on us and it made me a little uneasy. Rome greeted a few people and glared at a few, too. We finally got our order and returned to his car. As soon as I shut the door, I reached in my bag and pulled out a few fries.

"Sorry, lady. There's no eating in my ride."

I let the fries fall back into the bag. "It seems like you're pretty popular."

"What are you talking about?"

"When we walked in, you could have balled up the tension, thrown it on a grill, slapped some cheese on it, and served it with fries."

Rome laughed, then got serious. "Don't notice too much. It might not be a good idea."

I didn't know if he meant it as a warning, but I took it as one. I had a feeling he was into something big. Little did I know what I was about to get myself into.

Chapter 9

After riding for a few minutes, we pulled up to a nice home on Wilmington Avenue.

"Here we are," he announced as we walked inside.

"It's about damn time, Rome. I'm starving over here."

I looked at the overweight woman and figured she could have waited a while longer.

"What woman you bringing up in my house?" she asked, eyeing me up and down.

Rome sat down at the oversized dining table. "First of all, this is *my* house."

She sucked her teeth and looked me up and down once more.

"Samantha, this is my sister Latasha."

When he mentioned my name, she smiled. "Oh, you so pretty. You sounded so mean on the phone when you called." She stepped towards me and touched my hair. "Your hair needs some serious help, though."

Rome kicked out one of the chairs and motioned for me to sit. "My sis owns a salon, so she's always trying to get new clients." He winked at me. "Hey, Tasha, give my girl a job."

She looked at him with wide eyes and a full mouth. "Excuse me?"

Imani Writes

"Give her a job. Oh, and she's staying with us. Hear me now?"

I could tell from her expression she wasn't too excited having me in her space. She seemed about ready to dispute his decision, but the look on his face shut her up quickly. It was apparent he ran the house.

We sat eating in silence until I was startled by the next sound I heard. Latasha got up and quickly went to the bedroom.

"Yours?" I asked.

Rome chuckled. "Hell no. That's my nephew. I'm not ready for no baby." He smiled at the little bundle in Tasha's arms when she returned. "But I sure love to spoil this lil' man." He took him from his sister, and she went into the kitchen to get a bottle.

"What's his name?"

"Malique," he managed to tell me through all the tickles and kisses he was giving him.

From the looks of it, Malique was about a year old.

When Tasha returned, she held Malique and fed him his bottle. "So where is she gonna sleep?"

"She'll sleep in my bed."

"Oh, no, I'm not," I objected, putting my soda down quickly.

"Look, I'm not here at night, so don't get it twisted. By the time I come in, you'll probably be up."

"You could fix up the next bedroom," she told him.

"Nope, that's my office. Considering your options, I doubt you'll complain too much, Samantha."

"Right, but one thing, though. Don't call me Samantha. Call me Shug'ah."

He smiled, showing off his dimples. "Sweet...no pun intended. Shug'ah it is. Anyway, I'm out. See you around, Shug'ah."

He walked around the table to high-five his little nephew.

Then there we sat, three strangers not sure what to say. Malique broke the ice by throwing up on his Baby Phat shirt.

"Q! Now you have to take another bath."

"Well, I'll clean up this mess and you clean him up."

She smiled. "Professor's room is the last door on the right, and the bathroom is across the hall from his room."

"Professor?" I asked, confused.

"Yeah, that's his street name." She shifted the conversation as if she had done it a thousand times before. "You don't have any clothes. Let me see if I can find something for you. I know I'm not exactly your size, but I was before Malique was born. I saved a lot of my clothes hoping to fit back into them."

I looked around the house after I cleaned up. The place was well kept with leather couches, a big-screen TV, a huge stereo system, and every video game system out.

"My brother, the big spender," she said from behind, startling me.

Malique was clean and wobbling around the living room on semi-trained walking legs.

"Well, here you go."

Tasha handed me an armful of clothes, some of which were still covered in plastic from the dry cleaners. There were also panties and T-shirts in their original unopened packaging.

"Thank you."

"No problem. Well, I need to get this one back to sleep," she said, scooping up her son. "Have a good night."

I took a deep breath. "You, too."

After I heard her bedroom door close, I walked down the hallway. Rome's room was a typical bachelor's room, with leopard-print sheets on the unmade king-size bed and unopened condoms scattered on his dresser and nightstand. I put the clothes on the recliner in the corner and made up the bed. I figured it would be cleaner to sleep on top of the sheets. As I looked through the clothes, I noticed there were no pajamas. So, I figured a t-shirt and panties would have to do.

After showering, I laid on the bed. Sleep came quick, and so did Melanie. I fought to wake up, but it was as if I was being held down and forced to watch the dream replay in slow motion. I finally managed to wake up right before I stabbed my sister. I sat up and wiped the sweat from my forehead. It took me a few minutes to adjust my eyes to the darkness, and after remembering where I was, I lay back down and allowed the night sounds from the open window to caress my ears.

Looking out the window, I saw Rome's car in the driveway with two others. I pulled on my jeans and opened the bedroom door. I could hear low male voices coming from his office. When I went to the kitchen to get something to drink, a rather large man was already in there making a sandwich.

"Hi," I greeted softly.

He smiled. "Who are you?"

"A friend of Rome's."

"Who?" he asked before shoving the sandwich in his mouth.

"Professor," I mumbled. "I'm Shug'ah."

He lifted the sandwich to his lips once more, but lowered it for a second to tell me his name was Tiny. *Well, isn't the world full of irony,* I thought to myself. I got my drink of water and left Tiny in his happy place. On my way through the living room, I bumped into Rome.

"What are you doing up?"

"I had a hard time sleeping."

"Well, it's almost five in the morning, so I guess you got a little bit in."

Just then, another man walked into the house. "Hey, Professor, X is on my phone. He says he's been trying to reach you."

"Yeah, my battery died," he said, then stepped outside for privacy.

"Are you the flavor of the week?" the guy asked with a smirk.

"You talking to me?"

"Uh-huh. You Professor's trick?"

"I'm nobody's trick, asshole."

"Damn, it's a bit early for a dirty mouth."

Rome walked in and pushed him aside. "Well, maybe if you didn't have a twenty-four/seven big mouth, then people would be civil to you. Get Tiny out of my kitchen before that motherfucker eats Q's baby food." He looked at me. "Sorry about that. Shabazz is a good seed, but he lacks tact. Why don't you try to get a little more sleep?"

"No, I'm good. Besides, I have to work."

"Tasha doesn't open the doors until ten."

"I'll just watch TV."

"Suit yourself." He turned towards the door, but stopped and turned back to me. "By the way, here."

"What's this for?" I asked as he handed me a wad of bills.

"It's for whatever."

When he left, I counted the money. It was a little over five hundred dollars. I stuffed the bills in my pocket and turned on the TV. About an hour later, Tasha shuffled into the kitchen to get a bottle for Malique. She mumbled a half-dead good morning when she saw me. She was clearly not a morning person. Malique's early-morning lung exercise was in full effect by the time she shuffled back down the hall with his bottle. I turned my attention back to the TV.

At seven, Rome pulled in. He yawned as he closed the door and then took a seat next to me on the couch. I was going to say something about him being out all night, but decided it would be better if I kept my mouth shut.

77

Chapter 10

"Talk to me, Shug'ah."

"About what?"

Rome yawned again. "About your situation."

"I don't really have one."

"Yes, you do. Where were you staying before you called me?"

"Some halfway house for abused women," I replied.

"And it's cool for you not to go back? I don't need anyone beating down my door looking for you."

"It's cool. I was only staying there until I got a place of my own. All I have to do is call the judge and tell her that I'm staying with friends and got another job."

"Is that it?"

"Well, I do have to begin my probation bullshit next week."

"Probation?"

"Yeah. They said I wasn't rehabilitated and felt I should spend four years in a women's prison."

"That's fucked up."

"I know, but this judge told them I should see a shrink twice a month for the four years to work through my anger issues."

"Are you angry?"

"They seem to think so."

"I'm not asking you what they think. I'm askin' you."

"I guess I am."

"You guess? I would be mad as fuck. Your stepfather was raping you and killed your little sister. Then your mother disowned you, leaving you alone to spend four years in juvie."

"Five," I said, wanting credit for every year served in that hellhole.

"And then they wanted you to do four more years? I know you're angry."

"Hell yeah!"

"Good to hear it, but you still better go to your probation officer. You don't want to get caught up with probation drama."

"Can I ask you a question?"

"It depends," Rome replied.

"How do you know so much about me? Better yet, why do you know so much?"

"I'm sleepy. I'll see you later."

He didn't realize he left me with plenty of unanswered questions. Or maybe he did and just didn't care.

I waited until a little after nine o'clock to call Judge Wilde. I was a little nervous, but since she was on her way to court, she quickly approved my address and change of work. Soon after, Tasha put her key into the salon's front door. It was called Nex Phase, an interesting name for a salon in the heart of Compton.

"Just because you're a friend of my brother's doesn't mean you're gonna get special treatment."

"That's cool."

She eyed me up and down while smiling at the clothes that used to be hers. On my lunch break, I planned to go purchase my own clothes.

Shug'ah

"I'm early this morning for a reason," Latasha said as she locked the door behind us. "I can't have you in my shop with your head looking like an extra fuzzy peach. Follow me."

I ran my hand over my "fuzz" and followed her to the rear of the shop, where she washed and conditioned my hair. Since it was time to open, she pulled my wet hair back into a tight ponytail while informing me of my duties in the salon. It was pretty basic grunt work, which included sweeping the floor after every haircut or trim and doing whatever the girls needed me to do, whether it be something as simple as getting a bottle of shampoo or their lunch. There were four other ladies who worked in the salon. All of them seemed nice, but honestly, they were ghetto as hell.

The following Thursday, Rome dropped me off at UCLA to meet with the psychiatrist.

"Here, take this." He handed me a cell phone. "Don't give this number to anyone. It's only to be used for me to contact you and the other way around."

"Cool. I don't know anybody anyway."

He peered over the rim of his sunglasses. "Call me when you're done."

"I guess I'll be waiting long."

"Naw. I have a few things to do in this area, so I'll be around. You know, you sound like a wife."

"Oh, please. I'll never be one of those. I'll call you."

After getting out of his ride, I watched him drive off. I had no clue how to get to Dr. Luke's office and was a little nervous about meeting him.

"Hi. Do you need help?"

I looked at the perky, dark-skinned female standing in

front of me. "Yes. I'm looking for Dr. Raymond Luke's class."

"His *lecture* room is on my way. I'll show you."

Uptight people who thought they knew everything irked me. Her subtle way of telling me it was a lecture room and not a classroom warranted my fist in her mouth, but I reminded myself that I was there to work through my anger. I made sure to memorize the way so I wouldn't have to ask anyone for help my next visit.

"Here it is," she sang as if doing her one good deed for the day.

I knocked on the door.

"Come on in," a voice invited.

I opened the door and took a deep breath. "Hi. My name is—"

"Hold on one second." He stopped me as he shuffled through a stack of papers.

I pressed my lips together and sucked on my bottom lip while looking around.

"Are you nervous?"

"Not really."

"Good," he said, walking towards me and extending his hand. "I'm Dr. Luke."

I shook it and summed him up. He had a "don't-give-me-any-of-your-shit" look plastered on his face, and he sported an afro that had more grey hairs than black. His ears were pierced. I'm not sure if he was trying to recapture his youth or if he pierced them decades ago. His eyes were pleasant, even though I was sure he had seen a lot throughout his years. He looked like an Oakland-Telegraph Avenue kind of brother. If I had dangled a dashiki in front of him, he probably would have put it on in seconds and yelled, *Black Power*! I smiled at the thought.

"Are you finished?" he asked.

"Excuse me?"

"I assume you were silently analyzing me."

"You would be right."

"Well, that's my job. So, leave the analyzing to me." He flashed me a friendly smile. "Follow me to my office. This is where you'll be coming at three sharp. My last class finishes at about two forty-five. At times I may run late, so just wait for me."

He unlocked the door and I entered behind him. His office was a decent size, and he made good use of his given space. He had a lot of books and plants that made it resemble a home. By the smile on his face, I figured he thought I was analyzing him again. I took a seat in a very soft chair positioned in front of his desk.

"Okay, let's see."

He opened a file and read through a few papers. I watched as his eyebrows met his hairline quite often. There was my life summarized and packed into a folder.

"My friend Brenda wanted me to be your psychiatrist instead of someone the court appointed."

"Your friend?"

"Brenda…Judge Wilde."

"Oh yeah. I forgot her first name."

"You've been through a lot, Samantha. Much more than any young woman should. According to your file, you were attacked in the detention center where you did your time."

I nodded.

"I'm surprised you're sitting here in front of me as you are. Let's talk about Melanie."

"No!" I said quickly. "Anything but her, my so-called mother, or Jackson."

"But I'm here to help you."

I looked past him to the beige wall behind him. "I'm not ready for that. Not now."

He pulled out a deck of cards. "Deal. We'll play whatever game you want."

83

"Why are we playing cards?"

"I have to fill the hour up some way."

Although his voice was filled with patience and understanding, I shuffled the cards and wondered how long he would be patient and understanding once he found out I would probably never talk about them. I flipped the first card to him.

"What are we playing?"

I looked him in his eyes and replied, "War."

We played cards and talked about useless things until the hourglass ran empty. We then said our goodbyes. I was about to call Rome, when the cell he gave me rang.

"Hello?"

"I'm out front. Are you finished?"

"Yeah. I'll be out in a few."

A few minutes later, I was getting in his truck.

"Like the shrink?" he asked as we headed back to Compton.

I sighed and closed my eyes. "Too soon to tell."

Not in the mood to talk, I allowed myself to fall asleep.

Chapter 11

The next three months went by quickly, and there was never a dull day at the salon. All the ladies bossed me around, but I didn't mind being needed because it made the days go by faster. I was often the topic of conversation, and my sexual orientation was questioned often. Since they never saw me with a guy, they assumed I was a lesbian. I didn't offer any explanation to them as to why I was without a man. I just laughed it off and told them I was waiting for Mr. Right.

    I actually looked forward to my bi-weekly visits with Dr. Luke, whom I began calling "Doc". He was frustrated because I didn't open up about what bothered me nor did I talk about the people that used to be my family. Truth was I hated reliving that night. I knew what my problem was, and he couldn't help me. I knew I had deep anger and it took a lot to suppress it. I was angry with my father for getting killed and leaving me, and angry with my mom for not believing in me enough to stand by me. It was hard to face the anger I felt for Melanie, but I was angry with her for leaving, too. My anger level for that son-of-a-bitch Jackson wasn't even worth thinking about. I didn't want to go back to the way I was in juvie. I was mad at the world and didn't give a shit about myself or anyone else. At the same time, I knew I couldn't move on until I knew why Melanie blamed me for what happened. Talking about it made it feel too real. During our sessions, Doc would engage me in conversation about other stuff, we'd play cards, or he would push my mind with impossible crossword puzzles.

Rome started getting tired of driving me to UCLA, so I crammed for my driving test and got my license. He rewarded me with keys to a second-hand Honda. Having my own car gave me a sense of freedom that I hadn't felt in a very long time. My life was coming together. However, my curiosity would change that and pull me into a world of serious regret.

One night, I heard angry voices coming from Rome's office. Tossing and turning in my bed, I closed my eyes, but the voices kept me from sleeping. In the past months, I put some pieces together, and with the help of Tasha filling in some of the blanks, Rome's life became clearer to me.

There were seven people in Rome's crew. His right-hand man was X, a twenty-two year old without a care in the world. His real name was Xavier. Then there was Wall Street, a light-skinned man who loved to dress and whose real name was Lee. He was about twenty and the father of Malique. Whenever he came to the house, Tasha would get fidgety. I think she still had feelings for the brother.

The third guy was NIC, pronounced nice. I was a little curious as to why they called him that since he was mean and never let his lips form a smile. Tiny told me it wasn't because he was pleasant, but rather the letters N-I-C stood for Nigga In Compton. I couldn't help but smile. I liked the originality of it. Speaking of Tiny, he was alright to be around. He was Rome's security. His real name was Timothy, and although he was only twenty-one, I was sure he suffered from high cholesterol.

Number five of the crew was a nineteen-year-old named Sebastian Gomez, who went by the street name Shabazz. He was a fast talker and had mad skills throwing out rhymes. The sixth member was Nine. He was twenty-four, soft-spoken, and tall. I never got his real name, but he had a huge fixation with guns. Last and latest to the crew was Joe. He was the youngest at the age of eighteen and started coming around only a few weeks ago. The rest of the crew called him J. He always talked about taking pictures and his desire to go to film school. I admired that goal.

Because of Rome's warning about noticing too much, I kept my distance from them whenever they came to the house. Still, I was intrigued about his life. I didn't know exactly what he did, but Rome being a drug dealer was the first and only thing that came to mind.

As the voices escalated, I got up to listen at the door. That's when I realized he was arguing with Tiny. Rome was really letting him have it. After a few more minutes of arguing, there was dead silence. I looked into the hallway and saw Tiny dragging a laundry bag down the hall. Suddenly, the door I was peeking from behind swung open and there stood Rome with a frown.

"Come to my office."

Damn! I saw too much.

Rome sat down behind a desk and motioned for me to sit. "What did I tell you?"

"What did you tell me about what?"

He scratched the back of his head. "About noticing too much."

I slumped deeper in the chair. "Oh, that."

"Yes, that. I need to know I can trust the people in my house."

"You can. I didn't see anything."

He chuckled. "I heard that one before. What do you think I do?"

"I don't think about it."

"Bullshit! It's my job to read people. You are so fucking curious right now you're twitching."

He was right.

"Go ahead and open it," he said, referring to the tall wooden cabinet. "You keep looking at it. I know you want to see what's inside. Here's the key."

I shook my head. "Nah, it's cool."

"You sure?" He dangled the key in front of my face.

Curiosity getting the best of me, I took it and unlocked the cabinet. I opened the doors and took a step back, stepping on Rome's foot. I didn't know he had gotten up and was standing behind me.

"Sorry."

His hands rested on my shoulders. "What do you think?"

"Wow," I whispered.

Chapter 12

"So I'll ask you again. What do you think I do?"
"Drug dealer?"
"That's a common misconception, but there's too much drama in selling drugs."
I looked at all the weapons in the cabinet. "Sell guns?"
"Well, let's just say I give away bullets."
"You kill people?" I was shocked. That was the last thing I expected to hear.
"Surprised?"
I searched his face for any kind of expression or hint that he may have been joking, but he just stared back at me.
"Yeah, a little."
"I'm a hired gun."
"All of you?"
"Yeah."
"Why?" I asked.
"The money is good and the power is priceless. Have you ever fired a gun?"
"No."
"Oh, that's right. You killed your stepfather with a knife and almost killed that bitch in juvie with your bare hands. You and Wall Street will get along fine."

"Okay, now I really need to know why you know so much about me."

"I've been watching you. Do you think it's a coincidence I came into that supermarket? I live too far away to frequent that location. Look, the night I handed you the money was a test. I wanted to see if you were going to question me. Honestly, I've been testing you a lot. Tonight was your biggest test, and you proved me right. You're curious about my life."

"I still don't know what you want from me."

He stepped towards me, caressed my face, and brushed his lips against mine. My body tensed. I didn't expect that nor did I want it. I pushed him away.

"I'm sorry," I muttered, wiping my lips on the back of my hand.

Rome frowned and walked out of the room. I followed him to his room where he was sitting on the bed holding his head in his hands. I sat next to him, and he looked at me.

"I'm sorry, Shug'ah. I should've never touched you, especially with knowing what you've been through. I guess I wanted to do what I've always wanted since we were in school."

"What are you talking about? We barely spoke in school."

"Because you were my boy Kareem's girl and I couldn't step to you. I've always liked you." He smiled and sighed. "I thought maybe you could be my girl now."

"Another time and place, who knows what would have happened?"

"So you're saying no?"

"Rome, it's nothing on you. You're a handsome brother with to-die-for dimples."

"It's my life, huh? The shit I'm into is turning you off?"

"No, of course not. You were right about me being curious about your life. I find your life intriguing."

"Then what is it?"

"The rape," I responded softly. "I was raped in juvie, too." The look on his face told me that he knew already. "It's hard to let anyone close to me, let alone touch me intimately."

"I understand."

"Do you?"

"Yes, I do. I guess I thought you were over it after all these years."

"I don't think a woman ever really gets over being raped, especially by a family member."

"If he wasn't dead, I would kill him myself," he offered, clenching his fist.

I smiled and thanked him for his words.

"So since I can't have you as my girl, would you want to be in my crew?"

"Excuse me?"

"We need a lady's touch."

I laughed. "I'm sure you may think you do, but your boys might think differently."

"Well, it's what I want that counts. You in?"

"I might have to get back to you on that."

"The offer doesn't last long."

I searched his face for any indication he was joking about the offer. There was none.

"When is the deadline?"

"Tomorrow," he said, then got up and left without looking back.

Tomorrow came quickly. I was hard at work at the salon when Rome walked through the door with Wall Street.

"What's up, Shug'ah?" Rome asked.

"Not much."

"That's not what I'm asking."
"You want an answer now?"
"Yeah."

I looked around the room at all the ladies who were waiting for the next free chair. They were waiting for the false enhancement they thought would make them beautiful.

This environment really isn't me, but is being in Rome's crew the right move? Guess there's only one way to find out.

"I'll do it. I just need to know exactly what I'll be doing."

Rome made a quick scan of the room before replying, "We'll discuss that later." He then motioned to Wall Street, and just as quickly as they came in they left.

"What you and my brotha talking about?"

I looked at Tasha and thought, *Yeah, this place isn't for me.*

The next morning, Rome had me running laps at the local high school. He never really discussed right away what he expected me to do.

"Am I training to be a hit man or a boxer?"

"Don't get smart."

"I'm not, but damn, it's kind of cold out here and too early. It's not even four in the morning," I commented, frowning as I did my warm-up routine.

He laughed. "Shit, you don't know cold. You should spend a winter up northeast. I remember when I was thirteen and Pops sent me to Grandma's place for Christmas. It was cold as fuck."

"Where did you go?"

"Bridge-fuckin'-port, Connecticut. Come on. Shake off the cold. I need you in shape, and I need some sleep."

"Why?" I inquired.

"Why? Because this nigga is tired."

"I mean, why do I need to be in shape? Come to think of it, I'm not in too bad of shape."

"Let's just say I don't want anyone left behind because he…" He paused and glanced at me. "…or she needs to catch their breath."

"What about Tiny?"

He laughed again. "Tiny is a car seat warmer, but he handles his business, too. Are you ready for tomorrow?"

"What's tomorrow?"

"Christmas."

"I don't really care about holidays," I told him while taking in a few deep breaths.

He rubbed his chin and studied me for a second. "Okay, give me five laps and remember to exhale."

As I began running slowly, the cold air quickly filled my lungs and chest. My breath caught in my throat, and it felt as if I was going to pass out. I pulled my turtleneck sweater up to cover my nose and mouth. I slowed to a jog while passing Rome on my first lap. The warmth began to take over the coldness inside of me. That's when I picked up the pace and ran my remaining four laps without stopping. Breathless, I stood in front of Rome.

"Grab your ankles and breathe," he instructed. "Good for stretching out your muscles."

"How did I do, slave driver?" I asked while bent over.

He stood there and nodded his head. "You did well. As a matter of fact, you're ready."

"What do you mean, massa?"

"The test today wasn't really for you to run. I wanted to see if you would give up. I know what it's like to run in the cold. It's like a vice on your back and chest. You didn't give up, and for that, you're ready."

"Ready for what?"

He brushed the hair from off my face. "For Christmas."

"I told you I don't do holidays, Rome."

"We'll see. Why don't you call me Professor?"

"You and I both know you aren't that smart. I would rather just call you Rome. Is that alright?"

"Whatever Shug'ah wants to do is alright with me. Let's roll."

We drove home in silence. Well, I was silent, but Rome was on his cell with his employer. I heard him mention about something going down the weekend after New Year's. Then I tuned out the rest of the conversation.

Chapter 13

The house was still quiet when we pulled up. Thank goodness, because I was tired. After taking a long, warm shower, I went into Rome's bedroom where he was sprawled across the bed sound asleep. I pushed him over as gently as I could and laid down on the edge, clinging to it for dear life so I wouldn't fall off. Fighting for room, I sank my elbow into his ribs and woke him.

"What the fuck are you doing?"

"I'm trying to sleep. Now move your ass over."

"You need to hit the couch or something, because the only time I have company in my bed is when I'm fucking."

"I don't do couches."

"Fine," he mumbled before finally moving over.

I'm not sure how long we slept, but I was awakened by Rome pressing his body into mine. With his hand cupping my breast, he pressed his erection against my ass. I removed his hand from my breast and tried to squirm away, but he held me closer and kissed the back of my neck.

"Rome! What are you doing?" I asked, turning my head to look at him.

That's when I realized he was still asleep. I began to panic from feeling helpless. I reached down, grabbed his dick, and squeezed it like it was a Florida orange.

His grip on me loosened, and he pushed me off the bed onto the floor. When I looked up, I was staring down the barrel of his .45 automatic. He had one hand on his gun and the other on his dick.

"Are you crazy?" he asked and lowered his gun.

"No! Are you?"

"Damn, Shug'ah. I can't believe I had to pull my piece on you."

"Yeah? Well, I can't believe you were trying to get a piece of me."

"You lost me," he replied, looking clueless.

I stood. "You were touching me and trying to get…" I paused and pointed to my crotch area. "…a piece."

"Are you serious?"

"Yeah."

Without another word, he left the room, and I went to wash my face and brush my teeth because I had to get to work. I passed Rome on my way out of the house.

"Everything's cool, Rome. You were pretty much asleep, so I can't fault you for that."

"We're supposed to be working together, and if you can't trust me—"

"I do trust you. Don't sweat it. Like I said, everything's cool."

He sighed deeply and nodded. "Where are you going?"

"To the hair salon. It's Christmas Eve and Tasha's going to be busy as hell."

"You work for me now."

"Since when?"

"Since you agreed to it the other day. Or did you forget?"

"Sorry," I mumbled.

"Never—"

"I know. Never apologize," I said, cutting him off.

"Why?"

"Because it shows weakness."

"I see you're paying attention. Come on, let's go."

"Where are we...never mind."

Once in Rome's SUV, we headed to LA. During the ride, I told myself that I wasn't really going to miss going to the salon every day listening to all that female bullshit.

"Yo, Martinez," Rome spoke into his phone. "This is Professor... I'm good. Listen, how's the traffic up in there? Any shields?... That's good. I'm bringing in a new one... Pretty much all day... Right, right. I'll be there in a few minutes...Peace."

I could see from the corner of my eye that he was looking at me. I knew he expected me to ask him what was up, but I kept quiet. Whatever was going down involved me, so I would find out soon enough. Minutes later, we pulled into the parking lot of a shooting gallery.

"Are you ready to stomp with the big dogs?"

I smiled and gave him my deepest dog bark; he laughed. When we walked in, Rome scanned the room. I figured he was looking for the guy he had been talking to on the phone.

"Hey, handsome."

We both turned around to see a female standing there with a big smile on her face.

"How are you doing, Martinez?" Rome greeted her with a hug.

"I'm fine. Where's your new boy?"

When he pushed me in front of him, she seemed a bit surprised by my gender.

"I never thought you would have a chica in your crew."

"Neither did I, but Shug'ah is special. I just want to see if she has what it takes."

Her drawn-on eyebrows rose slightly. "Oh, really? Shug'ah, is it?"

She looked at Rome in a strange way and then her eyes went to me.

"Can we do this, please?" I asked her.

"Follow me. I have a booth for you."

I had seen shooting galleries on TV and in movies, but this place was tight.

Rome spoke up. "Some people are born to hold a gun, while others have to be trained. I wonder which one you are?"

"We're about to find out." Martinez handed Rome a .9-millimeter, and he handed it to me.

"One thing," he said, stopping me from putting in my left earplug. "Stand strong, because a nine-millimeter has a little kick. Just aim and fire."

Looking at the paper target shaped like a man, I asked, "Any particular spot you want me to aim for?"

I ignored Martinez's giggle.

"Aim at the chest and squeeze," Rome told me.

I put in my other earplug, made sure my feet were planted firmly on the floor, and aiming with both hands, I squeezed off two rounds. It was empowering. When I felt Rome's hand on my shoulder, I lowered the gun.

He took out my earplug. "Shoot between his eyes."

Hearing the praise in his voice, I didn't want to let him down. So, I got in position and fired. Rome instructed me to shoot a couple of more places on my paper enemy, and I obeyed.

Martinez hit the button to reel in the victim. "Well, well, well. It looks like you got a new member."

Rome studied the paper doll and smiled. "You were born to hold a gun."

"Naw, I think it's from all those years I played Duck Hunt on Nintendo."

Rome continued to make me practice shooting every moment he could. He even had me switch hands sometimes, saying I should be able to shoot with my left in case my right was occupied or injured. If we didn't go to the shooting range, he took me to an abandoned building to shoot cans and bottles. All the time we spent together shooting and weight training brought J and I closer. He was the only one in the crew who knew I was training to become one of them. After almost a month of Firearm 101, Rome made the announcement on the night they had a job to do.

"What the fuck are you thinking?" X shouted. "First, you bring in J fresh out of preschool. Now you want a bitch to roll with us? You're not thinking right." He pointed at me. "This right here is just for fucking, not for what we do."

Looking at the expressions from the other people in the crew, I could tell they were not pleased with Rome's decision.

"You through?" Rome asked X.

X drew in a quick breath as if he had more to say, but decided to swallow his other comment.

"Last time I checked, I was still the motherfuckin' boss up in here. Now, let's roll."

J and I ended up going with Rome and Tiny. We drove in silence to the meeting spot, and when he stopped, I broke the quietness.

"So what is it that you want J and I to do?"

Rome closed his door and glared at the two of us seated in the back. "Stay here and shut up."

"Yes, Daddy," I muttered while watching them walk away.

J simply laughed and started playing with the radio. I guess the reason we didn't see any action was because the rest of the crew had given Rome shit about having us there. This scenario of J and I sitting alone in the car played over and over again for the next few months.

Chapter 14

"I can't believe we did all that training for nothing," J said, while putting his gun on the dashboard.

Again, we had been assigned to the car. I adjusted the rearview mirror to get a better view. Rome and X had their backs to the car as they talked to Nine and three other guys who I'd never seen before.

"Well, I know how they feel about me. I just don't get why Rome is babying you."

J looked out the window. "He found out my age."

"We all know your age."

"No, you don't. I'm not even eighteen."

"Damn, playa. You lied to the head nigga in charge? No wonder you're sitting here keeping me company. Why did you lie?"

"There was a mark on me."

"No shit?"

"I'm serious. I got into it with this asshole in school and shit happened."

"Like what?"

"He said he was going to deal with me, so he got dealt with first."

I glanced in the rearview mirror at them again as a funny feeling crept up in me.

"What did you do?" I asked him.

"I got a piece from my cuz. Then we drove up to his house and called his ass out. As soon as he stepped outside, I popped him. His fam has gang ties, so I found out a few days after I killed him that I was marked. My only choice was to get protected."

"You could have left."

"Naw, I want to make a name for myself."

I smiled and looked at his determined baby face. "Roll on, Baby J, roll on. That's what I'm going to call you from now on–Baby J."

We talked shit and cracked jokes, but I was not feeling the scene. Something was up. A pair of headlights flashed about a hundred yards away, but I thought nothing of it. A few minutes passed, and I saw the flash again.

"Give me your cell," I told Baby J.

"Use your own."

"Stop playing and give me the fuckin' phone!"

I knew the crew would ignore my call, so I dialed Tiny from Baby J's phone. He seemed to be the only one who was cool with me. Rome gave him the night off so he could go check on his mom in the hospital.

"What's up, JJ?" Tiny said when he answered.

"It's not J, Tiny. It's Shug'ah."

"Hey, what's up, sweetness?"

"Are you still over at the hospital?"

"I'm leaving now."

"Is your mom okay?"

"Yeah. She has high blood pressure and has to go on a diet and shit, so she's pissed."

"Cool, cool. Listen, we're a few blocks from there. Rome had that thing tonight."

"Yeah, the meeting with a couple of Buchanan's guys.

What's up?"

"J and I are in the car, but something's not right. There's a car parked not too far away from us, and someone keeps flashing the headlights," I told him.

"I'll check it out. Don't do anything until I call you back."

I could feel my blood getting hot. Baby J grabbed his gun off the dashboard and made sure it was ready for action. Then we waited. Finally, the cell vibrated in my hand.

"Yo, Shug'ah," Tiny whispered. "I got two shitheads sitting in a car. One has some kind of high-powered shotgun. I think we're being set up."

"Can you take them out?"

"I'll take care of them," he said before hanging up.

I looked at Baby J. "Shall we dance, partner?"

"I got my dancing shoes on. Let's dance."

I'd been waiting for a chance to do something. I peered in the distance, wishing I could make out what was going on in the dark. Baby J and I walked calmly over to the guys with our guns behind our backs. When we got closer, I could see that Buchanan's guys looked nervous. I noticed Nine standing off to the side.

"Professor, do you always bring your bitch to your meetings?" one of them asked.

"Oh, I got your bitch right here," I informed him, pretending to reach for my gun.

Rome's jaw was tight when he turned to face us. "What the fuck are you two doing?"

X and Nine started in on us, as well. I looked beyond X's shoulder and saw one of the guys reaching for his gun.

"It's a setup!" I yelled.

I pushed a startled X with my shoulder, raised my gun, and fired, but the son-of-a-bitch fled. I took off after him, leaving the rest of them to deal with the other two guys. He ran into the adjoining alley. I stopped and held my breath, hoping to hear his. I did and it was too close. He snuck up behind me and shoved me against the wall.

"Drop it!"

I dropped my gun.

"I can think of a few things to do to you," he hissed in my ear while placing his hand between my thighs. I played along just to get him to loosen his hold on me.

"What do you want to do to me?" I asked, trying to hide my sexual paranoia.

It made me sick to hear him rattle off his list of ideas. Once he turned me around, I raised my leg up and drove my knee into his balls. When he went down, I picked up my gun.

"Bitch!"

"Yes, I am." I gave him a close up of my gun and his whole demeanor changed.

"Wait! Wait, please! I'm a cop!"

"Yeah, right."

"No, I'm serious. My badge is right here in my pocket."

"Don't you fucking move!"

He quickly stood to his feet and I heard something behind me, so I had no choice. I fired. He slumped to the ground. Checking his pockets, I found his badge. *Damn, he was a cop!*

"Shug'ah! Damn it, Shug'ah! Where are you?"

I ran towards Rome's voice. "I'm here."

"Let's go."

Baby J was in the driver's seat with the engine on. Rome and I jumped into the back, and Baby J sped off. The distant police sirens sang to the nighttime audience.

"Are you on that shit?" Rome asked me when we stopped at a light.

"What?"

"Are you on that coke shit?"

"I was thinking clearly. I had to run after that asshole."

"I'm talking about this." He put his hand on my left shoulder.

Shug'ah

"Fuck! Man, what are you doing?" I yelled in pain.

"You got hit, Shug'ah."

I looked at Baby J's eyes in the rearview mirror. "No, I didn't. I would've felt that shit."

"Right, and crack and coke heads can't feel shit. J, pull the fuck over," Rome ordered.

"Well, there's no better high than adrenaline." After I said that, the pain set in. The throbbing rhythm expanded and my arm became numb.

"Let me see," Rome said with a softer tone when Baby J found a place to park.

I pulled away from him. The pain was almost unbearable.

"Shug'ah, let him see," Baby J pleaded with me.

"J, hand me the box cutter from out of the glove compartment."

"What the hell do you think you're doin'?" I asked.

"I gotta cut your jacket to see how bad it is. I don't want you to move too much. You've already lost a lot of blood."

I couldn't see the blood on my black shirt, but I saw it on my khaki pants. As Rome cut my jacket, I turned away, but I could see his reflection in the window.

"Damn it!"

He stopped. "Did I cut you?"

"No. I just loved that fuckin' jacket."

He affectionately ran his hand over my head. "What am I gonna do with you?"

"You could stop treatin' me…" I paused and looked at Baby J. "Stop treatin' *us* like two children you babysit," I said, wincing in pain.

"One thing's for sure, you two won't be waitin' in the car anymore."

"Good. That's all I ask."

"Okay, Shug'ah. I need you to hold still. Hold on to something."

From the front seat, Baby J offered his hand, and I took it.

105

Rome lifted the sleeve of my shirt and gently pushed me forward.

"It went clean through. I think we should take you to Memorial to get looked at."

"And tell them what?"

Rome didn't answer. Instead, he took off his do-rag and tied it tightly around my arm. Baby J drove to his place over in West Rosecrans and promised he would check on me tomorrow. Rome told me to lie down in the backseat as he drove us home. The whole time, he yelled at Buchanan on the phone about being set up. Once we arrived home, he helped me inside.

"Come on. You got to take a shower. You're going to stink like the dead in a few hours."

Too weak to object, I stood there shivering as he undressed me.

"Your body is in shock. Try to relax."

Rome turned on the water and helped me into the shower. Then he stepped in fully dressed and started to bathe me.

"You're lucky it was a small caliber," he said, while untying the do-rag. "At first, I thought you needed stitches, but I think after a short time, you'll be good as new."

"Is it still bleeding?" My voice cracked.

"Just a little. I'll fix it up."

He wrapped a towel around me and told me to sit on the toilet. After looking through the medicine cabinet, he cleaned the wound with peroxide, rubbed some anti-bacterial cream on it, and covered it with gauze. Next, he carefully dressed me and led me to his bedroom. He made me a sling out of another do-rag.

"Looks like I'm going to have to buy you some more of these damn things," I told him as he slipped my arm through it.

"Don't worry 'bout that." He handed me a glass of water and a couple of pills.

Shug'ah

"Thank you," I whispered as he covered me with the sheet.

"No, thank you. If it weren't for you and J, the three of us would be in the morgue right now. You have proven yourself to me tonight. You're in for sure now."

"And Baby J?"

"*Baby* J, huh?"

"Yeah, he told me his real age. So are we both in?"

"Oh, for sure. Now get some sleep. I got to track down X and Nine."

"Don't forget Tiny."

"Tiny wasn't with us tonight, Shug'ah," he replied, then felt my head.

I guess he thought I was running a fever and hallucinating.

"I'm fine," I assured him, brushing his hand aside. "I called him to check out a car. Someone was flashing the headlights, and he went to check it out. He called us back and told us that two guys were in the car with high-tech weapons. He said he would deal with them."

"Alright, I'll call him, too. Now get some rest. I'll check on you later."

My eyes were heavy and closed within seconds. I was too out of it to entertain Melanie's subconscious screams for attention.

Chapter 15

"Hey, sunshine," Baby J greeted. "Talk about a Kodak moment. You're all crusty and shit."

I rolled my eyes. "Good morning."

"More like good afternoon. How are you feeling?"

"Hungry like shit."

"What do you want?"

"A flame broiled—"

"Double with cheese," he said, holding up a Burger King bag.

He helped me sit up. I glanced at my aching shoulder and saw the gauze was stained with dried blood.

"I have to change your bandage," Baby J said. "You want me to do it now or later?"

"Later, playa. I need to eat."

We both sat on the bed and ate our burgers.

"You scared me."

With my mouth full, I nodded in agreement. "I was scared, too."

"You didn't show it. I've always had respect for you, but I gained more last night."

His words meant a lot. "Did you talk to Rome?"

Imani Writes

"Yeah. He told me that you and I will still roll with him and Tiny, but we won't be seat warmers anymore."

"Where is Tiny?"

"Who do you think went to BK? Okay, I have to change your bandage now 'cause I gotta bounce."

I gripped the sheets as he removed the gauze. He meant well, but his bedside manner was much rougher than Rome's.

"Are you gonna have a problem with us rolling together?" I asked him.

"Not really. A playette protecting a playa is unheard of, though."

"No worries then. You're not much of a playa...Playa."

He laughed and continued to be my nurse. I looked at his baby face and knew no matter what, it was my job to protect his life. I needed to feel needed. It gave my life some kind of purpose, and if anyone needed me in this crazy lifestyle, it was Baby J.

"What are you thinking about, Shug'ah?"

"You."

He smiled, advertising his chipped front tooth. "You got a soft spot for a brotha?"

"More like a lil-brotha-who-is-destined-to-be-a-pain-in-my-ass kind of soft spot. But, on the real, I got your back. I'll always be there for you."

He smiled. "I got your back, too."

My cell rang.

"Hello?"

"Samantha?"

"Hey, Doc."

"Didn't you have an appointment with me today?"

I looked at Baby J and mouthed, *Oh shit*.

"Ms. Ruiz?" Doc asked impatiently.

"Um, yes, I did. I'm so sorry. I should've called you. I'm not feeling well today. Can we do this next week?"

"No. I have a few things planned and don't want my

schedule to get out of sync. So, I'll just see you in two weeks, young lady. Feel better."

"Thanks. See you then."

"Are you in trouble?" Baby J asked after I hung up.

"Nah, just the shrink."

At that moment, Rome opened the door. "You good?" he asked.

I stood up on weak legs. "I'm good."

"Then you two come into the living room. Now!" he shouted, then closed the door.

I looked at my boy. "Now that might be trouble."

When we reached the living room, everyone was there. Tiny winked at me when I entered. Not knowing the reason for the meeting, Baby J and I sat down on the couch next to Nine and waited for Rome to speak.

"Shit went down last night that never should've crossed my path. Almost all of you had a problem with Shug'ah and J joining up with us, but you're just going to have to get over it! X, you know what could've happened last night if they didn't step up? You, me, and Nine would be laying in the morgue right now, that's what. Y'all know I don't single out anyone." Rome looked my way. "But, Shug'ah and J really had our asses last night. We have another problem. Buchanan said he only arranged a meeting with two guys. What I want to know is who the fuck was the third nigga and who were the two fuckups in the car. We aren't taking any more jobs until we find out what the hell is going on. So, get to digging."

Nine shifted on the couch next to me. "I'm glad you're okay."

"Thanks."

One by one, they left the house, and I stood up to make my exit, as well.

"Yo, where do you think you're going?" X asked.

"I'm going to go help."

He shook his head. "You play hero one night and now

you want to do it again? You need to fuckin' relax."

"He's right," Rome stated, joining in on the conversation.

"But you said I was in."

"And you are, but you need more rest before you get out there again."

I didn't say anything. I simply walked to the bedroom while listening to them talk.

"That bitch is making you soft," X commented.

"No, she's not. And stop calling her a bitch."

"Whateva', boss. I think you better do a nut check, nigga."

I lay down, and just when I got comfortable, someone knocked on the door.

"Can I come in?" Rome asked.

"Yeah."

"Are you tired?" he asked, sitting down next to me.

"No. I've been sleeping for hours."

"Do you think you're making me soft?"

"I heard what X said and he's full of shit. He's just jealous, that's all."

"Why would he be jealous?"

"Because next to Tiny, X is your boy, and ever since Baby J and I came along, you've been spending a lot of time with us. I think X thinks he's being replaced."

"What do you think?" Rome questioned.

"About X? That nigga got some serious issues. I know the two of you have a special bond, and I'm not here to fuck with whatever you have going on with your crew."

He smiled. "Somebody has been noticing a lot."

I could tell Rome was wondering if I was going to give him an apology, but he wasn't going to get one. I held onto my left shoulder and tried to hide the pain as I sat up.

He rushed to the side of the bed. "Are you okay?"

"Yes. See, you need to stop hovering over me like I'm a damn baby."

"Fine," he replied with a clenched jaw.

"What else is bothering you?"

"Nothing." He got up to leave. "Oh, one more thing."

"Yeah?"

"What do you think about what went down last night?"

"It was fucked up."

"I know. What I'm asking is do you think Buchanan set us up?"

"Well, I never met the guy, but I don't think he would."

"The cop you killed was Buchanan's partner."

"Shit! Damn! I didn't know."

"No worries. This wasn't the first time we had to get rid of one of his partners. He was getting greedy and dipping in Buchanan's cash, so he had to get dealt with eventually."

"No shit."

"Yeah, I was supposed to erase his ass next week. You saved me a bullet," he said with a chuckle, then got serious. "What happened last night was really fucked up." Rome looked out the window, pressing his lips together like he didn't want to say what he was thinking.

I read his mind. "Your house is dirty."

He sat back down on the bed, and we talked for a few hours.

Chapter 16

"Are you ready yet?" Doc asked as I set up the checkers.

"Am I ready for what?"

"To talk about what's bothering you."

"I told you that topic is off limits."

"I'm not talking about your family."

"I don't know what you're talking about then," I said, shifting in my seat.

"Something has changed. You're acting a little closed off. You don't talk about anything with me anymore. I just want to make sure everything is alright with you at work and at home."

"Everything's cool. The reality of life slaps you in the face every so often, but trust me, I'm good."

The only thing good about my life was Baby J and the money. Baby J reminded me not to let the street game consume me completely. It had been a month since I got shot in the shoulder, and when I was with the crew, I loved to advertise my scar. Because I would get shooting pains once in a while and my arm was still weak, Rome suggested I exercise it to help the healing process.

Rome stopped paying attention to me like he did before our talk the day after I got shot. I just figured he wanted to keep peace in his house. We talked from time to time about the snake in our group. Although we didn't have proof, we both figured out who the fuck-up was. It would be just a matter of time before he got dealt with up close and personal Shug'ah style.

"Can you king me, please?"

"Huh?" I wasn't even paying attention to the game.

He glanced at me over the rim of his glasses. "You're going to have to come to my LA office for the next four appointments," he told me, while jotting down the address on a piece of paper.

I glanced at the paper. "Why do I have to go there?"

"I usually do a summer program for students who want extra credit, but I want to take the summer off to begin my private practice. Then, starting next semester, I'm going to cut back my classes. I'm getting a little old and worn out."

"I heard that. Okay, I'll see you in a couple of weeks. Same time, different station."

"One more thing, Samantha. Have a good birthday next week."

It felt good that he remembered. "I'll try. Thank you."

"Hey, Shug'ah. I have a B-day gift for you," Rome informed me the day before my birthday.

Baby J and I were playing a game on Playstation.

"I told you before I don't do holidays, and that goes double for birthdays."

"Well, you're going to like this one."

"What makes you so sure?"

"Remember Juanita?"

I paused the game and tossed the controller in Shabazz's lap.

"Rome...me and you...outside. Now." I said it softly so the others couldn't hear me.

We stepped outside and I looked around. A few neighbors were grilling and enjoying the 4th of July.

"I questioned you before about knowing a lot about me, and you had a pretty good explanation. But, how in the fuck do you know about Juanita?"

Rome knew he couldn't dodge the question. He licked his lips as if tasting the BBQ in the wind and sighed deeply.

"She was my cousin."

"Say what?"

"I never really talked with her because after my parents divorced, I went to live with my pops. She was my cousin from my mama's side. I saw her once in a while when I went to spend time with my mom during the summer. She was sent to juvie about nine months before you, and when I found out you were going to the same place, I asked her to look out for you. I had another female friend in there, too."

"Who?"

"Anita."

"I don't remember anyone named Anita."

"Long hair, quiet, but could throw a mean right when provoked."

"Coco Puff?"

Rome chuckled. "Yeah, that would be her."

"She and Juanita would exchange words every now and then, but she and I never really spoke."

"Coco was an acquaintance of mine. She and Juanita were from the same hood. No love there, trust me. Just respect."

"Coco worked for you?"

He smiled at my ability to see through his bullshit. "Yeah. I've always figured a woman could go places and do things in a crew that a man couldn't do. Besides, who would question a well-dressed, good-looking woman?"

"So you've been craving a woman's touch in your world

for a long time?"

"You could say that."

"I guess it was Coco who told you about…" I paused and cleared my throat. "…about me getting attacked on Christmas Eve?"

He nodded. "It was about that time when I started working for Buchanan."

Before I could ask another question, Tiny walked up the front steps. "How you want your steak, Shug'ah?"

"Well done."

"Boss?"

"I want mine the same way, nigga!" Rome said. "Stop acting like you know how to make steak any other kind of way. If I ask for rare or medium, it will come to me well done."

"Okay, damn, I get your point. Well done it is." Tiny adjusted his Kiss the Cook apron and went into the house to take everyone else's order.

As if knowing what my next question would be, Rome picked up where we left off in our conversation. "I was at that strip joint called Barbary Coast one night hustling, and some asshole tried to jack me outside. So, I did what any other nigga would've done."

"Killed him?"

"Damn right I killed him. Can't disrespect a hustler's hustle and get away with it. I was only nineteen and felt the world owed me. I was a bit of an asshole and not scared of a goddamn thing. Anyway, Buchanan was watching the whole thing. He flashed his badge and put me in cuffs." Rome stopped to light a joint and took a puff. "He put me in the backseat, but instead of taking me to the police station, he drove me to an abandoned warehouse where we talked about me working for him. At first, I refused, but then he started with his version of what he saw that night. He told me that he would embellish shit and make it where I would go down for murder."

"He blackmailed you? That's fucked up."

"True, but I still agreed to be one of his sellers. The money was good, and I eventually got over my anger completely. Our relationship really got deep when we had a misunderstanding with a few dealers over in Watts. That was my first time organizing a hit."

"What happened?" I asked, eager to know more.

"To put it simply, by the time the sun came up, we were the ones dealing in Watts. Buchanan made sure to take the spotlight off of me and my crew."

"Damn. I'm impressed. Was anyone from our crew working with you back then?"

"X was with me on that hit. So was Tiny, NIC, Lil' MC, and Scar Face."

"Lil' MC and Scar Face? Do they still work for you?"

"No. They didn't make it past that night. You never really get over losing someone in your crew. You always promise to have their back, but when they're gone, you can't help but blame yourself for their death. Feel me?"

I knew all too well what he meant. "Yeah, I feel you."

"Within a few months, Buchanan promoted us to protectors. He hired more dealers, and we were the ones to protect them. We looked out for his money because some of those dealers had sticky fingers. At times, we would just fuck them up, but sometimes, Buchanan would order them dead. Sometimes we had to kill the very ones we were paid to protect. When Buchanan started using us to kill people, we had to bring him evidence, such as fingers."

I laughed. "Sounds like some mob shit. Guess that explains the box cutters in the glove box."

"I know, right? It started to get crazy watching his dealers and cleaning up his mistakes, so I told him I needed more hands on deck. Wall Street and Shabazz were a package deal. Wall Street was avenging his father's death, and Shabazz was basically his sidekick. They grew up over in East Compton. Buchanan took them to the same warehouse for questioning, and next thing I knew, we had two more in the crew. Wall Street is a little interesting.

"His father was Asian and his mother is black. When he was about six, his mom ran off to New York with some poetry-writing cat. She left Wall Street in LA with his pops who owned a little grocery store. His father taught him the art of karate and his Chinese heritage. Three years ago, some young punks broke into the store and began vandalizing it. His father was in the back and came out to try to stop them, but unfortunately, he got killed. Wall Street still doesn't know who did it. He may never know."

"That explains a lot about him."

"What do you mean?" Rome inquired.

"I've never seen a brother so fascinated with knives and swords like him, and him being part Bruce Lee Roy explains that for me."

"Not to mention all of that meditating," Rome added. "All of you are my family, but he's a whole lot more to me being Malique's father and all."

"And Tasha still loves Wall Street to death."

"That's true."

"How did Nine get into the mix?"

"Nine and I go back to my basketball days. He was on a team we played against for years. I ran into him one night, and he and I began talking business. As far as your boy J goes, he's Scar Face's little brother. I would never willingly let him in this shit, especially at his age, but when he killed that kid, I had to protect him any way I could. Bringing him into my crew erased any mark he had on him. I knew how old he was, but I still took him in. I owed his brother that much. That was right before I found you at the supermarket."

Chapter 17

Rome was like the papa bear of the den. Without question, I knew he would jump in front of a bullet for any of us. It's just a shame a member of his crew had turned on him.

"You said you got me a birthday present, right? Where is it?"

"You're packing, right?"

"I'm always strapped."

"I'll take you to your present. Let's ride."

X pulled up just as we were leaving.

"Where y'all going?"

"To handle something right quick, nothing major. Tell Tiny to keep our steaks warm."

We drove in silence for about twenty minutes. Then his cell rang, but he ignored it.

"What does this have to do with your cousin Juanita?" I asked.

"Juanita really liked you. When she came out, she said she owed you a lot for convincing her to tell the truth and get out of juvie."

"But, she would still be alive if I never said anything."

"I can see how you feel responsible, but she enjoyed being out with her family, even though it was only for a short time. She and I grew closer, and she could never stop talking about you. She was even trying to get you out of juvie. She would call lawyer after lawyer hoping someone would take your case. She found someone and was going to tell you on her Christmas visit, but…well, you know."

"What really happened?"

"She was going to the mall to do some shopping, but she never even made it out of her car."

I fought the tears that were itching to escape down my cheeks.

"That fuck-up of a boyfriend she had put a hit on her. It wasn't your fault. If it didn't happen that day, it was going to happen another day. No one or nothing could have prevented that." He stopped the car. "However, revenge can be sweet like a slice of birthday cake."

"You want me to kill her boyfriend?"

"Oh, hell no! That nigga's dead. He died on the inside." He glanced at me with his eyebrow raised and a smirk. "It's funny how justice gets served."

I knew he ordered the hit.

"Shug'ah, in that house is the man who put a bullet in the head of my cousin and your best friend," Rome said as he put his car in park. "His name is Lamont. He sells weed out of the house, and he's a one-man show. There are a few guys in there with him, though. You'll be going in alone, but I'll be right outside waiting, and I have a few pair of eyes watching the house. You ready?"

I checked my piece. It felt good to be doing something solo. "Hell yeah, I'm ready!"

"Don't get cocky, Shug'ah. You're only there for one person and no one else unless they fuck with you."

"I got this," I assured him.

I walked up to the front door, slipped on my gloves, and knocked. When the door opened, the smell of some good-ass Chronic hit my nose.

"Can I come in? I need to see Lamont."

The skinny fool who opened the door ushered me in and led me to the living room where five guys were smoking weed and watching TV.

"What do you want?" someone asked.

"I need to see Lamont."

"I'm Lamont," one of them replied.

"No, you not, nigga. I'm Lamont," another one spoke up. "Hey, baby, you're sexy as shit."

They were playing this stupid game as if I was going to do a sexual favor to the one named Lamont, but I didn't have time for games. I pulled out my gun and cleared my throat.

"Let's try this shit again. Which one of you assholes is Lamont?"

I wasn't surprised when four fingers pointed to the guy on the couch with his hand down his pants. I quickly glanced at his four friends.

"You four, get over there and keep your hands where I can see them."

"What the fuck you want, bitch?" the real Lamont asked.

"I want you." Noticing one of the guys moving, I reached for my left gun. It was hard to ignore the pain that ran through my arm from the quick movement, but I didn't flinch. "Uh-uh, playa, don't move. I'm only here for him. Don't make me kill one of y'all, too."

Lamont stood up quickly. I pressed my gun against his forehead and guided him back to his seated position.

"I never did anything to you. I don't even know you," he babbled.

"You killed my best friend a few years back right before Christmas."

He thought for a moment. "I was paid to kill her. That was business."

"Well, this right here…this is personal, motherfucker!"

I fired one shot between his eyes. Blood squirted on the

wall behind him; his body slumped into the chair. The gunshot blended in with someone setting of premature fireworks.

"I want all of your cell phones on the table. Now!" I said as I snatched Lamont's cell off of his belt. I tucked my left piece in the waist of my jeans before pulling the cord from the house phone out of the wall. "Empty out that bag right there on the table," I instructed one of them.

Money tumbled out.

"I want all of your cell phones in the fuckin' bag. Now, for the next three months I want you to pay the bills for these phones. If your phone gets disconnected, I'll take that as a sign that you talked about what happened here today, and then I'll have to blast you just like I did your boy Lamont. If you're the type of nigga that pays your bill late, I suggest you pay in advance." I turned to walk out. "By the way, please be so kind as to give me thirty minutes before you move a muscle. I have someone watching this crib, so don't do nothing stupid." I then ran to the car and jumped in.

"So what happened?" Rome asked as he sped away.

"Happy birthday to me."

With those words, I felt a shiver run through my body. I guess it was at that moment the rest of my heart turned stone cold.

"There's one more stop before we head back," Rome told me.

We ended up in a nice neighborhood in Inglewood.

"Come on. He's waiting."

While walking up to the front door, I didn't know what to expect. The door opened.

"Happy Fourth, Professor!"

"Right back at you, Buchanan."

When I heard Rome call him Buchanan, I was surprised. I was meeting the man in charge. He stood at least six feet tall and seemed pleasant, but I knew the real deal. He had a

Hollywood smile plastered on his white face. I just figured it was for his neighbors' benefit.

"Come on in, you two," he offered quickly.

Just like I expected, the smile disappeared as soon as his front door closed. A small glass of Scotch adorned his hand as we followed him into his kitchen.

"Who did you bring to my fuckin' house?"

"This is Shug'ah, my latest and last addition to the crew."

I just nodded and tried to avoid looking into his cold, dead eyes.

"I told you I didn't want a female in my mix."

I couldn't believe they were talking about me like I was in the bathroom taking a piss.

"She's in," Rome said, standing his ground. "Shug'ah is the one who saved my life the other night *and* she took a bullet."

Buchanan came over and looked me up and down. "She's pretty." He glanced at Rome. "Do me a favor and get me a drink." When Rome left, he looked at me again and asked, "Are you fucking Professor?"

My jaw clenched and I bit my tongue.

He leaned in close to me. "I'm not going to pretend I like you. You being in my business is a fucking mistake."

He touched my face and trailed his finger down my chest. I swatted his hand away.

"Don't fuckin' touch me," I warned him through clenched teeth.

"Everything okay in here?" Rome asked.

"She's a wild one. Keep an eye on her. One fuckup and end of story for the both of you. Now, take this over to my brother's house and enjoy the rest of the holiday."

Rome took the package from Buchanan. I could tell from his body language that he didn't like being threatened.

"New York tomorrow?" Buchanan asked.

Rome turned to face him. "Yeah, everything is set."

Hollywood Buchanan appeared again. "Have a nice flight."

When we got to Buchanan's brother's place, I was prepared to wait in the car, but Rome told me to join him. His brother was a skinny, jumpy-ass white boy who barely spoke two words and hardly looked in my direction. I found out on the ride home that his nickname was Snow Man because he had an appetite for cocaine. He laundered most of the money Buchanan got through a bank where he worked, and Buchanan paid him in blow. They were a dysfunctional family to say the least.

Tiny greeted us with steaks that were hot off the grill when we walked through the door. While eating, I could feel X watching me. I glared right back. I was really beginning to hate his ass.

Chapter 18

The next day, I woke up to Rome packing a duffle bag.
"Morning."
"Hey, birthday girl. Here." He handed me a little box.
"Didn't I tell you—"
"Shut up and open the damn thing."
Inside it was a white gold chain and a pendant with the initial "S" surrounded with ice.
"I love it, man! Thanks!"
"Don't thank me. I gave you my gift yesterday. That's from J. He asked me to give it to you because I sent him on a run. Now, I need you to run me to LAX."
I took a shower and got dressed. My birthday gift looked good around my neck. Baby J really came through. I gave him a video camera in May for his birthday, and he promised to give me a sweet gift for mine. Wanting to thank him, I called him.
"Yo, what's up, birthday girl?"
"Not much, playa. Fixin' to run Rome to the airport."
"Do you like it?"
"I love it. Thank you."
"It's not too girlie?"
I laughed. "Naw, it's cool."

"I'm glad you like it. Hey, let me holla back at you."

"Do your thang. I'll catch you later."

The ride to LAX was more like Rome's "what-to-do-while-I'm-gone" seminar. Then in the middle of a sentence, he said something that made me swerve into the other lane.

"What?!"

"I said I love you."

"That's what I thought you said. Why did you say it?"

"I know you and I will never be intimate."

"You got that right," I responded softly.

"I've been infatuated with you from the moment I saw you in school many years ago." He sighed deeply. "But, like I told you before, you and my boy Kareem were kicking it. So, I couldn't step to you. I guess you can say I feel for you the same way you feel about J."

"Yeah, that kind of love is cool because you know I got mad love for Baby J. I would protect him no matter the cost, even if it means my life for his," I expressed while pulling into the terminal.

"Then I don't need to explain how I feel about you."

I smiled. "No, you don't."

After getting out and grabbing his bag, he walked up to the driver's side. "I know you and X have a little thing goin' on. Just remember to keep a low profile with him. We still have to get to the bottom of this whole betrayal business. I'll be back in a few days. I'll call you the night before so you'll know when to pick me up."

As he walked into the terminal, a few females turned to look at him. Rome was superstar material. Many looked twice; I'm sure they were wondering if he was someone famous. I never saw the man a step below well dressed. I hit Pacific Highway 1. I knew what he was going to New York for. During one of our late-night talks, he told me that Buchanan had connections on the East Coast, so I guess one of them fucked up and needed to be dealt with. I never wondered if Rome had gotten soft. Truth is, he had more of the one thing the rest of us wished we had more of—heart.

"Any plans for tonight?" X asked.
"No. Why?"
"Just wondering if you were hungry."
"Kind of. I wouldn't mind getting my grub on."
"How about Roscoe's?"
"Hell yeah! That sounds good right about now. Hold on. Let me get my best friends," I told him, referring to my guns.
"Naw, don't worry about them. Professor told us to keep a low profile."

I wasn't sure what he was up to, but I went with it. We drove to Central Avenue pretty much in silence. My woman's intuition started kicking me in the ass. Something wasn't right. X had hardly spoken two kind words to me, and here we were about to have dinner together. I had to watch my back.

"I know you and I haven't really been feeling each other, and I want to fix that. I mean, we are on the same side, right?"

Now that was the question of the day, which I was able to avoid answering because our food was placed in front of us. He and I continued our forced conversation during our meal. I guess a part of me wanted to believe he wanted to be friends.

After eating, I was ready to go home, but X wanted to hang out at a bar.

"Sorry, but I don't drink. I hate alcohol."
"For real? Let's go shoot some pool then."
"Okay."

We stopped at a spot on Crenshaw and played a few

games. Soon, X and I were the only patrons in the establishment. Three guys walked in and the owner locked the door after them. Before I realized what was happening, I was being punched like a fucking man. At that moment, I became mad with myself for letting that bastard talk me out of bringing my two friends along. I tried to throw punches back, but they overwhelmed me.

"Don't hit her in the face anymore!" X yelled. "Just her body!"

However, my body couldn't take any more. A blow to my stomach sent me to my knees. I could barely breathe. That's when I grabbed my pool stick from the floor. I swung at the closest one as hard as I could and kept hitting him until he stopped moving. Feeling a burning pain in my side, I turned to see one of them with a knife. I looked down at my side and saw the blood soaking my shirt. He had sliced me like a fucking turkey. He then lunged at me and stabbed me between my breasts. The pendant saved me from being penetrated by the knife, but the point of the blade slipped off the pendant and nicked me. Remembering the move I learned in juvie, I shoved my hand under his nose as hard and as fast as I could. He dropped the knife and squealed in pain like a pig. Swiftly, I knelt down, removed my gun from my ankle holster, put him out of his misery, and aimed at X.

"You know you fucked up, right?"

He sat there with a smirk on his face.

"You think this is a fuckin' joke?"

"No." He stood and was a foot away from the receiving end of one of my bullets.

I tried to control my breathing and the pain. "Give me one fuckin' reason why I shouldn't pull this trigger."

He raised his gun toward me and we were at a standoff. He fired. I glanced over my shoulder. I had forgotten about the third guy.

"That's a good reason," I told him and lowered my gun.

X checked the one I beat with the pool stick. "He's dead. Come on. We got to go."

He placed some money on one of the pool tables and we rolled out.

When I got home, I showered and inspected my new battle scars. The cut on my side was painful, but felt worse than it really was. The small nick between my breasts was equivalent to a paper cut. I found a few big band-aids and nursed myself. I knew I would have one hell of a black eye in the morning. I was sore and tired, but I knew the pain would only get worse.

Samantha, come play with me.

Melanie's taunting kept me tossing and turning for hours. I eventually passed out from sheer pain and exhaustion. Around four in the morning, my cell rang. I ignored it, but it kept ringing repeatedly.

"Who the fuck is this?"

"Shug'ah? What's wrong with you?"

"Nothin', Baby J. What's up? I just got to sleep."

"I need you to pick me up."

"You're joking, right?"

"This is serious. I need to get away from this crazy-ass girl Tiffany. She's over here trying to get me to tell her I love her and shit."

"I love you, too, but I'm too tired, playa."

"Come on, Shug'ah. I would do it for you."

"No, you wouldn't, because I wouldn't be in your situation."

"Come on. Please?"

I looked down at the shimmering pendant that saved my life—the pendant Baby J gave me.

"Alright, damn! Where are you?"

"Avalon."

"You can walk from there."

"True, but I need another favor."

"I really don't need this right now, Baby J."

"I want you to pretend to be my jealous girlfriend. I really need to break it off with her."

"Fine," I replied with a huff. "Give me her address."

I put on my jeans, a black wife beater, but no shoes because I wanted to appear crazy. I parked down the street so she wouldn't see my ride.

"I can't believe I'm doing this," I whispered to myself before banging on her door and ringing the doorbell. "Joe, I know you in there with that bitch!"

I yelled a few times just to make my presence believable. The door flew open.

"Who the fuck are you?" Tiffany demanded.

"Don't worry about who the fuck I am. You need to worry about what I'm gonna do to you because you're fucking my man." I crossed my arms and tapped my bare foot on the cool concrete. "Joe? You better get your ass out of this trick's house!"

Looking over her shoulder, I could see him gathering his stuff while smiling the whole time.

"You have no right to come here and do this shit."

"Oh, he didn't tell you about me?"

She shook her head.

"Joe, I'm going to kick your ass. I'm so sick of this shit. Got me driving around looking for your trifling ass."

"He's my man!" Tiffany yelled.

Without a warning, I slapped the shit out of her. Joe eased past his now stunned ex-fuck buddy. When I turned to walk away, she grabbed my hair. Big mistake. Turning to face her, I got a firm grip on her throat and shoved her against the doorframe.

"I had a really fucked-up night. Are you sure you want to dance with me like that?"

She looked at me, her eyes wide with fear. I loosened my grip, and she disappeared into her house. Baby J had walked ahead, missing my final performance. I ran to catch up to him.

"You're not dropping me home?" Baby J asked as we pulled up to Rome's house.

"Walk. I'm tired."

"That's cold."

"You dragged me out of bed to get you. I did my part, and now I'm going back to sleep. You can stay if you want."

Before getting into bed, I stepped in the shower and washed my feet. By the time I walked in the bedroom, Baby J was already comfortable with his eyes shut. I closed the curtains so the morning sun wouldn't disturb us, and then I lay next to him.

"Why do I put up with you?"

"Because you wuv me," he said, smiling without opening his eyes.

"Yeah, I wuv ya." I agreed with a yawn. "Night, playa."

It was a little before ten when I opened my eyes and saw Baby J staring at me.

"What?" I asked while stretching, which I shouldn't have done because all my bodily pain screamed good morning.

"Did Tiffany get a swing in?"

"Hell no. That bitch didn't touch me."

"Then explain the black eye and these." He threw the band-aid wrappers at me.

I sat up wincing in pain and he pulled up my shirt.

"That's about a five-inch cut, Shug'ah. How the fuck did that happen?"

Baby J was the one person I could never lie to. So, I told him what went down as he paced around the room.

"X is going to pay for this shit."

"You can't do anything."

"Why?" Baby J asked. "Because he's a fuckin' senior member? Fuck that shit."

"You can't go to his place to do anything. You'll give him a reason to fuck with you."

"The same way he did with you? I don't think so."

"And what the fuck is that supposed to mean?"

He took a deep breath. "Nothing. Forget it."

"Naw, naw, I'm not going to forget it. You think I got played because I'm a woman? I never expected that from you."

"I didn't say that."

"You didn't have to. Look, I don't need anyone to protect me."

"Yes, you do. And the minute you start thinking you don't, shit happens."

I thought about what he said, and he had a point.

"You want some Fruit Loops?" I asked, feeling the need to change the mood.

"No, thank you. I'm a Corn Flakes kind of guy."

I got up and we both went into the kitchen. I was surprised to see X sitting at the table and even more surprised when Baby J punched him.

X massaged his jaw, but said nothing.

I turned to Baby J. "Can you give me some time to talk to him?"

"Not a chance."

"It'll be cool. I promise."

He leaned in closer until the two were face to face. "If you ever put Shug'ah in harm's way again, I'll kill you."

"Talk to me," I told him when Baby J left.

"It's simple: I killed two birds with one stone. Those three were guys who Professor told me to deal with while he was gone."

"So why did you throw me in the mix?"

"Back in the day, any new member in a crew—"

"Had to be jumped in," I said, interrupting him. "Yeah, I know. There's one difference, though. I was already in."

"Not in my book. I didn't think you had the balls to be in the crew, but I do now. You handled yourself well last night. It takes a lot to impress me, and you did."

X was as street as they came. I could tell from the sound of his voice and the way he looked at me that he had a newfound respect for me. However, I still was going to watch my back around him.

My cell rang.

"Yeah?"

Rome was on the other end. "I'm in Texas. I'll be in LA around two, and I'm not alone."

"I'll be there." I closed my phone and looked at X. "He's coming in around two."

"Are you going to tell him about last night?"

"I wasn't planning on it."

When X left, I ate and then went to make the bed. Afterwards, I changed the bandage on my side and inspected my eye. There would be no way of hiding it from Rome.

Chapter 19

I arrived at LAX late, and, of course, Rome was mad as he stood there waiting with a woman.

"Did I not tell you that I would be here at two?" Rome asked, while closing the car door.

Remaining silent, I looked at my passenger in the backseat as I pulled away from the curb. I adjusted my shades, and she cocked her right eyebrow before looking out the window.

"Oh, so now you're quiet?"

His cell rang. *Thank God.* I ignored his ranting on the phone. I figured the mystery lady was someone who knew about our life, because Rome didn't shield his words.

"Hurry up. I need to get home," he instructed when he ended the call. "Something's up. I don't have time for this fuckin' shit. I'm tired as hell and now I have to meet with Buchanan in a few hours. Shug'ah, this is a friend of mine from New York, Blaque Ice. Blaque Ice, this is Shug'ah."

"Cool," I said, no pun intended.

"Likewise," she replied.

We drove the rest of the way in silence. X was sitting on the steps when we pulled up. We glared at each other as I walked by him and went into the house. Blaque Ice followed me and planted herself on the sofa. Thinking she was the flavor of the week, I smiled to myself.

I went to search the bathroom cabinet for painkillers. I figured it was time to buy stock in Tylenol because I was popping so many. After chasing the two little pills with some OJ, I lay down on my bed.

"Are you fuckin' crazy?" Rome yelled at me, bursting into the room and kicking off his shoes. "I swear to God y'all are going to stress me the fuck out!"

"What are you talking about?"

"What the fuck were you thinkin' going on a hit with X? You've lost your damn mind!"

"Say what?"

"I know you can't wait to get all up in this business, but you don't have to beg to go on a hit."

"Yo, hold up! I didn't—"

"Whatever! It's done. Here."

I looked at the bills in his hand.

"Take it."

"What's this for?" I asked, taking the money.

"A duce apiece."

I stood. "You lost me."

"Four g's. The job was two grand a head; X told me that you got two of them." He placed his hands on my shoulders and looked deep into my eyes. "I know you got what it takes, so you don't have to prove anything to anyone, especially X. Feel me?"

I nodded.

He dug in his bag and pulled out his deodorant and favorite cologne. "Damn, Shug'ah, there isn't enough sun in LA for all these fuckin' shades. I can't even find a spot on my dresser for my shit."

I didn't sweat his attitude about my personal stuff. I knew he was just upset about me getting caught up with X.

"Put some of your stuff in a box or something. Now I

have to take a shower and get to this damn meeting." He started undressing, and I turned to leave. "I need you to stick around. No more dumb shit, okay?"

I smiled. "Got it. I know it's none of my business, but who's the skirt?"

"Just someone who makes me feel welcome when I go to the NYC. She has a little business to take care of here, so I'm going to make her feel welcome in LA."

When he went to shower, I went into the kitchen where X was gulping the rest of the OJ. I drew my piece, kicked the refrigerator door closed, and hit the carton from his mouth. He backed up against the stove.

"You're stepping to me like that? Putting a nine in my fuckin' face? Why don't you step to me like the man you are, Shug'ah?"

"Nigga, please! Do I look stupid? You're two hundred pounds of muscle. I'm not trying to hit your ass." I lowered my gun.

X folded his arms across his chest. "Two-thirty to be exact. Why you flippin'? You got your share of the money."

"I don't need your guilty conscience to pay me off. You lied to cover your own ass."

"And? If you're not happy, then give me back the money."

"Fuck no. I earned every motherfuckin' dime of that shit."

"Yes, you did. So we're good now?"

"I wouldn't say that." I put my gun back in its place. "We a'ight."

X eyed our one-woman audience up and down before he left.

"Can I help you?" I asked her.

She sighed deeply. "No. I'm just wondering what's going on."

It was my turn to mentally scan her. She was the kind of woman you looked at twice to make sure you saw her right the first time. Her beauty could entice a man to do or say anything. I wasn't much on designer fashion, but she clearly had a taste for the finer things in life. Ice dripped from her earlobes to her ankles. Her eyes were almost deer-like and darker than midnight. That's probably why they called her Blaque Ice. She might even be stone cold on the inside, but let it be known, I was the head ice bitch up in there.

"Blaque Ice, is it? Don't go noticing too much."

She laughed. "You sound just like Professor."

"How long are you in town?"

"This is just a short trip. I fly out tomorrow."

"Those are always the best," I responded with a smirk.

Bored and in need of a distraction, I stepped outside to get some fresh air. With nothing going on that night, I needed to call my boy. So, I dialed his number.

"Baby J, what are you up to tonight?"

"I'm just going to play some poker with the guys."

"The crew?"

"Naw. Some guys I went to school with."

"That sounds like fun. Do you think they would mind a pussycat playing with them?"

"You want to get dealt in?"

"Hell yeah! That will give me a chance to put your pointers to work."

"We play for good money."

"Oh, yeah? Well, I got a pocket full."

"I heard that. Come on by my place. We don't start playing until eight."

"Okay, but I'm going to come through now, if you don't mind."

"Everything cool? X isn't messing with you again, is he?"

"Naw. He and I came to an understanding. It's over and done, I promise. I'll tell you about it when I get there. Do you need me to bring anything?"

"Drinks, chips, nuts, maybe some chicken."

"Do I look like a fuckin' catering company?"

"Shit, you're the one who asked."

"Yeah, but I said anything, not *things*."

He laughed. "Bring whatever. I'll see you later."

The night at Baby J's was just what I needed: hanging out with people I didn't know. I brought all the things he requested and then some. I felt free because I didn't have to pretend to be a hard ass. On our first hand, I lost a grand but made it back on the third. I was a great bluffer, so by the end of the game, I added two and a half grand to my pocket. Baby J and I finally crashed around two in the morning.

The first to wake up, I rolled over and stared at him. He was snoring away without a care in the world. It killed me to keep the fact that we had a dirty player in the house from him, but Rome told me not to tell anyone. So, I had to honor his request. When Baby J started to snore louder, I pinched his nose closed. He brushed my hand away.

"You know people are going to talk?" he said after a yawn.

"About what?"

"They're going to think we're creeping on the side."

"Nobody's going to talk."

"How do you know?"

"Everybody thinks I'm a lesbian."

Baby J cracked up, laughing so hard that the bed vibrated. "You ain't, though, right?"

"Not to my knowledge. I just don't like to be intimate with a guy."

"Because of the—"

I cut him off. "Yeah, because of that."

"But how can you chill with me like this?"

"You and I don't have feelings like that. I love you like family."

"No offense, but you're like one of my boys. Not that I would be lying up in here with one of them or anything."

141

"I know that's right," I said as we laughed. I held my side because it hurt to laugh. "On the serious side, whatever it comes to, I got your back."

"I got yours, too."

I lay there and closed my eyes. The image of Melanie's face flashed in my mind as if she was right there with me. I jumped out of bed so fast that it felt like my side was ripping open. Melanie didn't even wait until I was in a deep sleep anymore before making her appearance. I wished she would get out of my head. I also wished Rome's houseguest would be gone by the time I got home.

Chapter 20

Christmas Eve, 2002

As I said before, I don't do holidays, but Rome told me it was time I got a pimp ride. So, he took me along with him to buy one as a Christmas gift. He said he had it ordered and ready to go.

"Manny, do you have Shug'ah's car ready?" Rome asked as Manny welcomed us to his car dealership.

"Sure," Manny replied, smiling. "Hey, Mike! Bring the car around."

I froze in disbelief as Mike pulled up in a pink Caddy like I sold Mary Kay cosmetics or something. Rome, Manny, and Mike saw my disgusted expression and fell out laughing. It was Rome's idea of a joke, but I didn't find it funny.

"We got her good!" Rome laughed. "Alright, bring out the real one."

Mike left and returned with a fully-loaded black Cadillac Escalade.

"How do you like your truck?" Rome asked as we chilled on Crenshaw later that night.

I climbed up on the hood. "I love it! Thanks."

"No need. You've been working overtime to find the one that betrayed me. I can't wait to bring him down tomorrow."

"Me, either." I zipped up my coat.

Tiny, X, and Baby J spotted us.

"Nice wheels, Shug'ah," Baby J said, joining me on the hood. "Now I might have to upgrade my ride."

"Uh, no! You're not fixin' to get a ride like mine." I gave him a playful shove. "Crenshaw's jumping for a Tuesday night."

Baby J stared at a big booty girl as she walked by. "It's Christmas Eve, baby. Nobody's doing shit tomorrow, so they're hanging out tonight."

"Anybody want some food?" X offered.

"Yeah," Tiny answered. "I want some wings and fries."

"I'll get it," X offered, glancing at his watch. "Anybody else?"

Since nobody else wanted anything, X left to get Tiny's food, while Tiny wandered across the street to talk to a girl that was close to his size. I shuddered at the thought of the two of them fucking.

"Hey, I got to hit the head," Rome announced.

"Too much info, nigga," Baby J joked.

We laughed as Rome went across the street. It was a good moment for us. Everything was cool. By the same time the next day, our house would be clean and we'd have no more worries. I sighed and looked up toward the smoggy heavens. My daze was broken when I saw Rome coming back across the street. Suddenly, I heard shots and then Rome fell to the ground. I could see people screaming and running, but I couldn't hear anything. I slid off my ride, grabbed my gun, and fired at the car the shots came from. There were so many cars trying to pull away that a traffic jam formed.

The car where the shots came from was one of the vehicles trapped. As it skidded to a halt, Baby J and I ran up to it with our guns loaded and ready. Without any hesitation, I shot the guy on the passenger side, and Baby J killed the shooter seated in the back. The driver got out and tried to blend in with the crowd. Tiny stood there in shock. I knew what he was thinking; it was his job to protect Rome.

When I turned around, I saw X standing over Rome. I ran over and pushed him out of the way. I fell to my knees next to Rome and looked at the blood gushing from his body. Sound came back to me like a tidal wave as I beat on his chest.

"No! No! No! You're not going to die on me! Just hang on!"

I was lying to him. I knew death was ready to claim him, so I had to "clean" him. I took out my blade and cut his holster off. I also grabbed his cell phone. Looking around, I saw all the people staring at Rome gasping for air like he was a dog who had been hit by a car. I stood with my gun raised and Rome's holster and guns in my other hand.

"Stand the fuck back!" I yelled.

"Shug'ah, what are you doing?" Baby J asked.

"I can't let him go like this! I don't like all these people looking at him and shit! He doesn't deserve this."

I knew what I had to do. I looked at my crewmates but couldn't find the words to ask their permission. I knelt down beside Rome; his eyes gave me the permission I needed. I kissed my fingers and then softly touched his forehead.

"I'll miss you, my friend," I whispered as he still fought for a breath.

I closed his eyes, stood, and looked down on him. Tears blurred my vision as I aimed and put my mentor out of his misery. I then turned and faced the crew. Tiny looked past me at Rome's body. X stood there staring at me in disbelief.

"I can't believe—"

"Now ain't the time," Baby J said, silencing him. "Let's get out of here. Meet up at the house."

The approaching sirens were always our cue to leave. X and Tiny went in different directions. I gave Baby J the keys to my ride, and we were able to get out of there before the police showed up. It sickened me that we had to leave Rome's body lying there in the cold street. I swallowed the nausea brewing within me.

Baby J broke the silence. "You had to, Shug'ah. No one can fault you for that. There was no hope for him. He wouldn't have made it."

I couldn't speak.

Tiny was already there when we got to the house.

I looked at Baby J and told him, "Give me a second before I go in."

I sat there thinking about as many moments as I could about Rome. Minutes later, Tiny tapped on the window. He was one of the men who had been with Rome from the beginning.

"Open the door, Shug'ah."

I got out slowly. He opened his arms for me and we held each other. For the first time in a very long time, I cried.

"Shhhhhhhh," Tiny said, comforting me. "I loved him, too." His voice wore pain and guilt. "Let's go inside."

Before we could open the front door, we heard Tasha scream.

"What happened?" she asked me as I entered the house. "Shug'ah, what happened?"

I had no clue how to comfort her when I couldn't even comfort myself.

"Don't wake the baby," was all I could say. "Don't wake the baby."

X came in and sat on the couch. Nine shortly followed. We didn't want to repeat the story, so we waited until Wall Street and Shabazz showed up. Before they did, I went in Rome's office, removed the chip out of his cell, and placed his gun and holster in the cabinet.

Finally, everyone showed up and gathered in the living room. While I went over what happened, I studied their faces.

Shug'ah

The dirty son-of-a-bitch sat on the couch with a fake-ass somber look on his face. I knew he was behind Rome's death, and I couldn't wait to put one of my bullets in his skull.

The police called to inform Tasha that her brother had been murdered. She and Wall Street took Malique to his grandmother's house and then they went to the hospital.

"X, can I talk to you for a minute?" I asked after the rest of the saddened souls drifted throughout the house.

He stood and shook his head. "I can't do this with you right now."

"Give him time, Shug'ah," Nine said softly. "He'll come around."

"He's upset because of what I did."

Nine cleared his throat. "From what I understand, you did him a favor. No man wants to lie in the street staring death in the face and wondering when his moment will be up."

"Thanks, man."

"No problem. That was my boy from way back when. If I was there, I would've done the same thing."

He held out his hand, and I shook it. Nine was a man of few words, but when he did speak, he knew exactly what to say.

"Shug'ah, let's get out of here and go clear our heads," Baby J suggested.

"Naw, I need to be here for Tasha and Q."

"You sure?"

"I'm sure. Can you help me with something, though?"

"Yeah. What do you need?"

"Help me pack up Rome's shit. I don't think Tasha should do it."

Wall Street brought Tasha home a few hours later. They told us the police questioned them as a standard procedure. I was happy Wall Street decided to spend the night with her while Baby J and I finished packing all Rome's stuff in the garage. We ended up in his office, where I took a seat at the

147

desk.

"That suits you."

"What?" I asked.

"You look good behind that desk," Baby J told me.

"Get that idea out of your head. I don't want to be running things. Besides, I think this crew is dead in the water."

"Why do you say that?"

"Rome was the backbone. Buchanan only dealt with him. I seriously doubt he's going to appoint anyone in here to take his place. Shit, he hardly knows any of us." My cell rang and I answered. "Hello?"

"Shug'ah, what happened tonight?" Buchanan asked.

He must have this place bugged, I thought as I signaled to Baby J that it was him. He left the room so I could talk. I took my time and explained to Buchanan what happened. Then I explained my plan to deal with the one who was responsible. He confirmed my fears—the crew was dead. He didn't want to continue without Rome. However, when I hung up, I had a feeling our crew was very much alive and well. I just had to persuade Buchanan to feel the same way.

Chapter 21

"Samantha! Samantha! Sam! Wake up, silly!"
"Melanie?"
"Samantha, come play with me."
"Where are you, Mel? I can't see you."
"I'm right here next to you."
I looked around, but she wasn't there. "Melanie, come out and stop playing."
"Why, Samantha? Don't you want to play with me?"
"Of course I do, love. I just can't see you."
"See me now?"
I felt something hit my head, and I sat up in bed breathing heavily.
"Momma said to get up now." It was Malique all dressed up.
It took me a while to catch myself because not only was it early Sunday morning, but it was the day of Rome's funeral.
"Thanks, Lil' Man. You're looking kind of sharp. Tell your mom I'll be right out. Okay?"
"Okay."
Tasha came in while I was showering and laid a dress on the bed with a pair of pantyhose and dressy high heel shoes. I put on my bra and panties, but a dress was not an option.

Instead, I slipped on a pair of black pants and a long-sleeve white blouse, but I did wear the shoes she gave me. I brushed my hair into a ponytail and put on some makeup.

"Uh-uh, Shug'ah! Wear the dress," Tasha protested when I walked into the living room.

"Tasha, I love you, but I don't do dresses."

"Well, at least you put on the shoes. Come on. We're running late."

"I'll be right out. I forgot something."

I went into Rome's office, opened his treasure box, and took out his pearl-handled chrome .9mm, slipping it in my shoulder holster.

"Why are you wearing Professor's piece?"

I turned and faced Wall Street. "I got some shit to handle today," I responded, then slipped on my coat.

"Not today," he said with a warning tone.

"Yes, today! It's been a long time coming, too." I walked past him and didn't offer any other explanation.

The service was beautiful despite the cold rain. Everyone was there, including Blaque Ice. The cemetery brought back memories of the only other funeral I'd been to, which was my father's. My mother had refused to allow me to attend my sister's funeral. After the final prayer and the lowering of the casket, everyone started to depart.

"I need y'all to stay here for a minute," I announced.

X seemed agitated. "Fuck that. I got to go."

"Keep your ass still, Xavier!"

He pulled out his cell, and I walked up to him and snatched it out of his hand.

"Who the fuck do you think you are?" he yelled.

Shug'ah

"Tasha, get Q and go home."

"Come on. I'll take you," Wall Street said.

I stopped him. "Sorry, bro, but I need all the crew here."

"What's going on, Shug'ah?" Baby J asked once Tasha and Q left.

"I'll tell you what's going on," X answered. "She put a bullet in my boy's head and now wants to be in charge."

My blood ran hot. "You act like I killed him!"

"You should've waited!"

"Waited for what? For the doctor to pronounce him dead? Rome knew he was gone. I gave him peace."

"You act like he was a fuckin' racehorse with a broken leg. He could've lived. You know what? I don't want to hear whatever it is you have to say. I'm out."

I had no choice but to pull out Rome's gun. "I don't think that's a good idea."

X turned. "Oh, so we're here again?"

"I guess we are."

Tiny took a step towards me. "Shug'ah, talk to me."

"One of you ordered that hit on Rome, and I need to put an end to this shit right now. I need all of you muthafuckas to put your hands where I can see them and get over there."

Like a shepherd leading its herd, I guided them into a semicircle in front of Rome's grave. From my left to right stood Tiny, Baby J, Shabazz, X, NIC, Nine, and Wall Street. They all looked at me in disbelief.

"You're fuckin' crazy," X announced.

"Am I, X? Too many things don't add up from that night I got shot and the night I got sliced because you wanted to test me. I wanted to give you the benefit of the doubt, but I'm not sure about your loyalty. Where were you when Rome got shot?"

"Oh, hell no! I know you're not trying to say I had something to do with all this shit!"

I aimed the gun in his face. "Not too long ago we were

151

right here, weren't we? I wanted to kill your ass that night you had me jumped, but I didn't have proof."

He swallowed hard.

"What proof?" Tiny asked. "X would do anything for Professor. You know this."

Wall Street, Shabazz, and NIC put in their two cents pleading for X. Baby J remained silent.

"Rome and I have been working to get the proof, and we got it. You were jealous of him. You hated the fact that he and I were close. You wanted this shit for yourself."

"Bitch, you crazy!"

I got the signal, pulled the trigger, and fired into the one who had betrayed us all. Afterwards, I smiled.

"I didn't scare you too much, did I?"

X put his hand on his stomach and slid it up to his chest. Then he looked at the body on the ground to his left.

"You thought you would get away with it, you sorry excuse for a man?"

He squirmed in pain.

"Who made you do it? Who do you work for?" I yelled.

He wouldn't talk, so I shot him in his knee.

"Maybe you didn't hear me. Who is in charge?"

"Me," he whimpered.

"Huh? I didn't quite get that."

"Me, bitch! You made sure of that the night you killed my boss."

"Come on, I'm no Girl Scout. I've killed more than one nigga. Be specific."

"The night in the alley."

"The cop in the alley was your boss?"

Rome and I never made that connection.

"Yes. I should've killed you when I had the chance."

"It was you who shot me that night, wasn't it? And the car was signaling to let you know you were in the line of fire because Rome and X were to get hit that night. I remember you backed up further every time the lights flashed. You've been plotting against him for months."

"Years," he said, correcting me.

"Tell me the driver's name. Now!"

"Fuck you."

"Awww, Nine, you got it wrong. You're the one who's fucked. We could find out, but you would be saving us a lot of time."

"Why should I tell you? You're still going to kill me," he said, spitting blood.

"You should tell me, not unless you want me to shoot you in the other knee! What's his name?"

"Bones."

"Bones? Nigga, half of LA goes by the nickname Bones. What's his real name?"

Nine started coughing uncontrollably but finally managed to reply, "William Trent."

"Why did you do it?"

"Professor killed my brother that night in Watts."

"So, tell me, Nine, do you see death coming?" I turned to Tiny. "Do me a favor and drag his punk ass over there by that tree. He's fuckin' up our boy's final resting place."

Tiny dragged him and we all followed.

I took my stance over his body. "I'm the face of your death, the last muthafuckin' thing you'll see. May you NOT rest in peace."

Rome's killer paid the price for his crime with two shots from Rome's own gun. I took pleasure in blasting Nine to hell.

"Find this nigga named Trent," I told the others while putting the gun away. "I got a look at him that night. He has three tears tatted under his right eye and a long, bitch-ass ponytail. I need to know where he is. I need to know yesterday!"

Later that night, X and I had a much-needed conversation

as we ate.

"How did you know it was Nine?" X asked.

"Well, have you ever heard the saying 'Quiet dogs bite hard'? I just figured a nigga that quiet had something to hide."

"So Professor never suspected me?"

I looked up from my ham and macaroni and cheese. "I played the King Solomon card."

"The what?"

"King Solomon from the Bible."

X still looked confused.

"You know, two women went before him each claiming to be the baby's mother. So, King Solomon decided to cut the baby in half and give each woman a half. One told him to do it; the other begged him not to and to just give the baby to the other woman. That's how the king knew she was the real mother."

"Yeah, I remember that story, but what does it have to do with me?"

"It didn't take me long to find out you would lay down your life for Rome. He knew that, too. Never once did he suspect you, and neither did I. We figured out it was Nine a while back; I just wanted him to show his hand. So, when everybody else was pleading your case, he was smiling like he had gotten away with it."

X's shoulders rose a little as if everything going on was weighing him down.

"Don't get me wrong, I think you're a fuckin' pain in the ass," I told him.

"Likewise, but I can live with that." He looked down at his plate. "I'm sorry for getting on your case about shooting Professor." He looked at me. "I do understand why you did it."

That felt good to hear, because X was the only one in the crew who felt I was wrong for doing what I did. I figured it was his grief controlling his thoughts, but I needed him the most for my plan to put Buchanan on check.

"Buchanan is pulling the plug on our crew."

"Are you serious?"

"Yeah. He told me the night Rome died." I paused and looked at my cell. It was Baby J calling. "What's up?"

"We got him."

I stood. "No shit? Where?"

"We trailed him to the Barbary Coast."

"You sure it's him?"

"Yeah. I bumped into him before he went in. He got the three teardrop tats and long hair."

"Keep an eye on him. We'll be right there."

"We got him?" X questioned.

"Yes, we do. When's the last time you got laid?"

Chapter 22

X looked at me like I was crazy. "Why do you want to know the last time I got some?"

"Just answer the question."

"I got some pussy last night. Why?"

"Because we're going to the Barbary Coast, and I don't want your dick leading you in the wrong direction. I'll be right back."

I went through some of the clothes Tasha gave me and found a short leather skirt and a blouse that zipped up the front. I slipped on the shoes I had on earlier and released my hair from the bonds of the ponytail. Then I applied some of Tasha's eye makeup and topped it off with red lipstick.

"Okay, I'm ready." I put on my coat and gloves.

X eyed me up and down.

"Are you enjoying the view?"

"I can't believe there was a woman under all of that bullshit."

"Oh, shut up."

Baby J met us outside the Barbary Coast. "You look nice, Shug'ah. Real nice."

"Not you, too. Just tell me one thing. You got my back, right?"

"Always. Why do you ask?"

"Because I don't want to be caught dead looking like this."

A big guy at the door met us. "Ten dollars," he said.

I looked at his shirt. "Big Ron, is it? Why do the ladies have to pay?"

"Male or female, if you want to get through those doors, you need to pay."

"All these guys come in here to see tits, ass, and sneak a peek at some pussy, right?"

"What's your point?"

"Well, I could go home and get naked…" I paused and unzipped my shirt just a little. "For free."

His eyes roamed from my face down to my cleavage. "Go on in."

"Thank you, baby."

Monifah's song "Touch It" started playing as I made my way through the crowd. A few assholes tried to actually touch me, but I kept my focus on searching for my target.

"I see him!" X yelled above the music. "He just went in the back!"

I thought he would jump at the chance to kill the guy, but him telling me that he spotted the mark was his way of giving me permission to do it. When I reached the back, I saw him in the room getting a private dance. His head was tilted back and his eyes were closed. I tapped the dancer on her bare shoulder and she turned to face me.

"Oh no, bitch! Get your own nigga," she said, then went back to grinding on his lap.

I tapped her again, but this time with a hundred-dollar bill. She left without a word, and I picked up where she left

Shug'ah

off. I straddled him and started gyrating on his lap. He was so fucked up that he didn't even realize the switch. I unzipped my shirt more and he rubbed my cleavage in his face. Since I was in total control, I didn't feel anxious about the sexual contact.

I carefully slid my gun out from its leather holster. "Does it feel good, baby?" I asked.

"It feels so fucking good."

I pressed the cold steel against his forehead. "And how does this feel?"

His eyes flew open. I hit him in the mouth with my gun.

"Hello. Remember me, asshole?"

I grabbed the cushion from the other chair and put it over his face. Before he could move or remember what he ate for breakfast, I let off two shots and exited the backroom. X and Baby J were at the bar waiting. I signaled them it was time to leave. As I walked out the door, a hand grabbed my shoulder from behind.

"Leaving so soon?" Big Ron asked.

Monifah's lyrics, *Do you really wanna fuck with me tonight,* could still be heard.

"Yeah, my pussy is cuter than theirs anyway," I replied without turning around. I heard him chuckle as I walked away.

The three of us left without incident and later stood under a nearby streetlight. Baby J stared at my chest. There was blood on my chest and the pendant he gave me.

"Damn! It must have splattered on me when I hit him with my gun. Just a little blood on the Shug'ah, baby." Unbothered, I zipped up my shirt.

With all the parties responsible for Rome's death dealt with, we could focus on saving our crew. A part of me figured it would be a good idea to leave all the shit behind and use the money for a fresh start on life. However, the crew had been my life for two years. They were my family. Plus,

159

Imani Writes

like Rome always said, the money was good and the power that came with being a hired gun was priceless. For those reasons, I felt that I had no choice but to fight for my crew. My family.

The plan was to lay low after we killed Trent and make Buchanan believe we were obeying his orders. In February, we hit a few of his dealers and robbed some of them, too, just to prove the importance of our roles. We even hired a few guys to break into Buchanan's house and steal some stuff. Unfortunately, he was home, so he got a severe beat down. By mid-March, we got the call that we were back in business. It was nice our unfriendly persuasion put us back in business. Instead of appointing another leader, we all agreed to look out for each other. Nevertheless, X and I seemed to be the only two who Buchanan would contact when he needed us to do a job.

At that point, I started to let myself go. I kept my hair braided, and jeans and T-shirts became my wardrobe. Makeup was a thing of the past. Let me not mention how Tasha had to wrestle me down to braid my hair when it got too fuzzy.

Per Buchanan's orders, I went to New York a few times to clean up some East Coast bullshit like Rome used to do. It was always nice to get away for a day or two. Buchanan still had a problem with me, but he learned to hide his concerns. His money was flowing, and that was good for us. I stopped keeping count of how many bodies were tied to my guns. Honestly, I didn't give it a second thought. I would get my orders and carry them out.

I still went to my sessions. I had missed a few over the past year, but Doc exercised patience with me, especially after Rome's death. I wanted to trust him with the things that were going on in my life. It would have been nice to talk to someone other than my boys. However, I felt he would treat me differently if I did, so I kept silent on my personal life.

Chapter 23

April, 2004

I went over to X's place to pick up my guns that he promised to clean for me. I was in his room seeing what CDs I could borrow, when I heard loud voices coming from the living room. I went out to see what was going on.

"What's up, X?"

"My cuz is up here trying to set a nigga straight."

"Well, it looks like he needs to get dealt with," I replied, but when I turned to see his cousin, my mouth dropped open from shock. "What the fuck? Is everybody somebody's cousin up in this muthafucka?"

"Well, well, well, if it isn't Samantha Ruiz."

"Don't, well, well, well me like I owe you money or some shit."

It was X's turn to look surprised. "You two know each other?"

I looked at the face of the man who I loved so many years ago. Time had been good to him.

"Yeah. Kareem and I go way back."

"What are you doing here, Samantha?" Kareem asked. "You and Xavier kickin' it?"

"Hell no! We just work together."

"You're caught up in this life, too?"

"Yeah, and stop calling me Samantha."

"Why?"

"Because I go by Shug'ah now."

"Why are you in this life?" Kareem questioned.

"None of your fuckin' business. Now move. I got to go," I told him, taking my guns from X.

"Not until you answer my question."

My cell rang. It was Buchanan saying he needed to meet with me for a job.

"I have nothing to say to you," I told Kareem after I hung up.

"What happened to you?" he asked as I walked by him.

"What happened to me? Five years is what happened to me, you self-righteous son-of-a-bitch! I sat in juvie for five long fuckin' years. That's what happened to me. You wanna hear about the beatings and how I got raped in there, too? What happened to me? You got nerve, man."

"I'm sorry."

"Shut the fuck up! Don't act concerned for me now, momma's boy. If you were concerned, you would've kept writing me."

"I did write you."

"In five years, you wrote me twenty-three times. I know exactly how many letters I got from you, because when I realized you stopped writing me, I would reseal the fuckin' envelopes and pretend they were new ones. I held on to the hope in your words that you would be there when I got out. You told me that we would make a life together filled with love and happiness, but you never gave me a second thought when you flew off to Paris to go to your snobby fashion school. It's cool, though." I pasted a fake grin on my face. "I got a life now, too. It may be filled with death and pain, but I'm living. No thanks to you."

"I'm sorry."

"Stop apologizing. I don't need it. And don't bring your ass around here again."

"I can't do that."

"Why not?"

"I will only stop coming around if you let Xavier go."

"Let X go?" I looked at X, who seemed to be enjoying our banter. "X, are you here against your will?"

"No, ma'am!" he answered.

Kareem's jaw tightened. "Let him go or else I'll—"

"You'll what?"

"Don't forget I used to run these streets, too."

"What are you trying to say, Kareem? You're going to go toe-to-toe with me?"

"If that's what it comes to."

Hearing Kareem wishing me harm stabbed into my soul. "Watch yourself, Mr. Hotshot Designer. I don't do well with threats."

"Well, my aunt isn't doing well without her son."

"Then talk to him. I have nothing to do with that shit."

I left him standing there wearing a frown. As I drove away, I never thought I could feel anger towards him. Even when the letters stopped, I made excuses for him. I always knew I would love him for life, but right then, I wasn't so sure.

Two months later

"You sure you're okay?" Doc asked.

I stared out the window of his LA office. The June heat was lurking outside looking for a way in.

"I guess I'm okay."

"Then can you stop wiggling your leg, please?"

I didn't even hear him. My thoughts were centered around Kareem. I couldn't think about much else after having seen him several weeks ago.

"Who the fuck does he think he is? He shows up after nine years and expects me to roll over and take his shit? That's not gonna happen."

"Who is he?"

"Kareem. He was my boyfriend in high school. He's the one I was out with the night of…the night..."

"The night Mel died?" Doc finished my sentence.

I leaned back in the chair, and for the first time, I opened up to Doc about that night.

"I wanted to go out with him, but I needed to protect Mel. Mom told me that she would be home, and I believed her. After the movie, we went to the Chicken Shack where my mom worked part-time. I was mad at her when I saw her there working. I guess a part of me always knew if he could rape me, then he could do the same to my little sister. So, I had to protect her, but I didn't that night." Tears welled in my eyes. "He killed Melanie, so he had to die. Melanie was my life. Now she's gone because I went on a date and wasn't there to protect her."

"Who do you think is to blame?" Doc asked softly. "Your mom? Kareem?"

"No, I'm to blame, and Melanie never lets me forget it."

"What do you mean?"

"She comes to me in my dreams and sometimes even when I'm not sleeping. She taunts me and blames me for her death."

"I don't think it's her, Samantha. I think it's you. You blame yourself for her death."

"That's because it's my fault. If I'd told someone, Jackson would've gotten arrested and Mel would still be here.

I would still have my family. Now Kareem shows up out of the blue and tells me that I'm living wrong because I'm a hired gun. He promised me we'd live together happily ever after, but he broke his promise."

Doc's expression didn't change. When he didn't say anything, I continued to free myself.

"I've been working for this dirty cop for years and doing things I'm not proud of. I don't feel human, Doc. I can take a life without thinking twice about it. What's wrong with me?"

"You gave up on life, plain and simple. You lost the ones you loved at such an early age, and as a result, you forgot about living for you."

"That's because I died the night he killed my sister," I expressed, feeling as though I was chocking on the words. "I loved her so much."

"You still can love her memory."

"What memory? She entangles herself in my dreams at least four times a week. At times, I hate her for blaming me for her death. I don't need her reminding me of my fault."

"Tell me about the dream?"

I told Doc from beginning to end the dream that haunted my mind.

"I don't think that's the end of the dream," Doc told me once I finished.

"Fuck that! It's the end for me."

"I want you to dream the dream all the way through."

"Are you crazy? As soon as I start dreaming, I fight to wake up. I can't get the image of that knife in her chest out of my mind. Even worse, she points at me and tells me it's my fault."

"Dream it through," he repeated.

"I can't promise you that."

"I think you should try it."

"Look, I said no promises. Okay?" I yelled and knocked the hourglass off his desk. It shattered and the sand spilled onto the floor. "I didn't mean to do that. I'll buy you a new one."

"It's alright," he said calmly. "I'm just happy you finally opened up."

"I have to leave," I told him when he returned from getting the broom and dustpan.

"I'll see you in two weeks, Samantha. Please be safe."

Although it saddened me to relive the night Melanie was killed, I felt a weight lifted off of me. *Doc could be right,* I thought. *The dream is me blaming myself. I need to get out of this life. I need to do what Doc said and live for me, not my past.*

I stood on the sidewalk for a few moments to collect my thoughts. I had to make a decision that could change my life once again—hopefully for the better this time.

"Hey, you!"

I didn't recognize the voice over my shoulder, so I kept walking to my truck.

"Will you stop?" the voice said angrily.

When the person grabbed my elbow, I reached for my gun. "What the fuck do you want?"

Turning around, I saw it was Kareem.

"Look, we need to talk about X."

"We talked about him before, and I'm all talked out right now. Hit me up later."

I got in my ride, but before I could pull off, Kareem opened up the passenger side and got in. I shook my head in disbelief.

"Get out my fuckin' truck." I told him.

"No."

"No, huh?" I said, leaning over quickly to the glove compartment.

"You're going for your gun to shoot me? That's fucked up. All I want to do is talk."

"Last time we talked. When you threatened me,

remember?"

"I was upset and shocked to see you. Please, I really just want to talk."

I started my truck and pulled away. "Okay, talk. And get to the point…quick."

"I want you to let him out. His mother is scared he's going to end up dead running with your crew."

"It's not *my* crew. You're giving me too much fuckin' credit."

"Look, he's my family, and I don't want anything to happen to him. How would your mom feel?"

I looked at him like he had lost his damn mind. "My mother? You got jokes today. You know my mom crossed me off her Christmas list when I killed her man. I'm dead to her, and she's dead to me."

"I'm sorry."

"Don't be. Shit happens."

"But it's not your fault," Kareem said sympathetically.

"Now you sound like my fuckin' shrink."

"You're seeing a psychiatrist?"

Damn. I gave him too much information. "Yeah, it's part of my probation deal." As soon as the words left my mouth, I knew it was something else I should have kept to myself.

"Probation? Now that's funny."

I pulled the truck over quickly and shifted in park.

"And just what do you mean by that?" I got out and slammed the door.

Kareem got out and followed me to the edge of the cliff. "I mean, I know you've been running drugs and killing people."

I wasn't listening to Kareem. My thoughts were elsewhere as I looked down at the waves of the Pacific caressing the large jagged rocks.

Chapter 24

"Do you know what I do every time I drive back from the city?" I asked.

Kareem shrugged his shoulders. "What do you do?"

"I pull over right here, walk to the edge, and try to convince myself to jump."

"Why don't we get back in the car, Samantha?"

I winced when he said my real name. Doc and Kareem were the only two people I allowed to call me that.

"I'm not ready to go."

"Well, at least step away from the edge."

His voice had a tone of concern. Maybe a part of him did still care about me. Doing what he asked, I took a step backwards and heard him sigh deeply.

"I joined the crew for power. I wanted people to cower when they heard the name Shug'ah. Being the only woman running with a male crew has been hard. Truth be told, X and I are cool, but we're not tight. I have the respect of the crew and have made a name for myself, though."

"Yes, you have," he responded sarcastically.

"The thing is, I don't want that name or that title anymore. I come here and try to convince myself to end it so I can fly before I die."

"What stops you?"

"I don't know. I always get to the edge and tell myself to do it, but then, I find myself in my ride heading back to Compton. Funny, isn't it?" I chuckled.

"What is?"

"I have the power to pull a trigger and take someone else's life, but I don't have the power to end my fucked-up life."

"I know things seem bad, but damn, nothing is worth killing yourself."

"I killed my sister," I told him, while staring out at the Pacific. "I guess that's my ticket to hell."

"No, you didn't."

"Yes, I did. I should've never gone out with you that night. If I didn't, she would still be here."

"Now you're blaming me?"

"Of course not. It's all on me."

Kareem held onto my shoulders and turned me to face him. "It's not your fault at all."

"It's how I feel," I said, looking deep into his eyes. "I'm haunted almost every time I close my eyes. Sometimes when I sleep, I dream of Melanie telling me it's my fault." I paused and frowned. "Why am I telling you this shit? It isn't any of your fuckin' business. X is your business."

"I still care about you."

"Squash all that mushy bullshit. What I want to know is why you're wasting your time on X? That muthafucka doesn't want out! Why is that so hard for you to see? You are so driven about getting X out that you don't even see that someone else is aching to leave all this shit behind."

"Yeah? And just who the fuck wants out of your cushy crew?"

I took a deep breath, looked over the cliff, and turned to look at him. "I do," I said softly. "I want out."

Kareem didn't say anything; he didn't have to. He opened

Shug'ah

his arms, and I quickly stepped towards him before he changed his mind.

"I didn't know," Kareem whispered as he held me closer. "I didn't know."

After a timeless embrace, he held my face. I could see in his eyes that he saw the real me just like he did when we were younger.

"Let me have the keys, Samantha?"

"They're in the car."

"Come on, let's go." He actually held the door open for me.

"Don't fuck up my ride."

"I wouldn't dream of it," he assured me with a smile.

My stomach felt funny. For a split second, I thought of the butterflies he always seemed to give me when he smiled. Then I dismissed it as just being hungry. I put on my seatbelt and got comfortable. I studied Kareem; he was still a fine-ass brother, and the goatee he sported made him look more distinguished. He had his life together and was doing the fashion thing with his clothing line, Another Level Up. It was growing fast, but success hadn't changed him. His eyes were always kind when they gazed into mine. I smiled slightly.

"What are you thinking about?" he asked.

"I'm thinking about Denzel."

Kareem's smile turned into a hearty laugh. "See, you know you're wrong."

"So you remember our date?"

"Of course, I do. You had a thing for Mr. Washington, and I see you still do."

"Yeah, but you know a part of me will always have a thing for you, too."

"I'm truly touched."

I smiled and looked into his boyish eyes, feeling like a teenager again. The only part of "that" night I allowed myself to revisit were the hours I spent with him. Sitting in the car and laughing seemed to melt away the years we were apart. Kareem didn't know how much he was quieting the silent screams inside my head.

"Where are we going?" I asked when he slipped the truck's gear into drive.

"Don't you want to go home? I can have X drive me back to my place. I really want to talk with him and hopefully get through to him."

I knew X wasn't ready to release the power he had on the streets, and I didn't feel like facing him after such a nice afternoon with Kareem.

"I don't want to go home. Take me to a hotel or something. I'm not in the mood for anything tonight. I just want to eat and chill."

"I can take you to my place, if that's okay with you."

I sighed and closed my eyes. "Yeah, that's cool."

Chapter 25

"Wake up, Samantha," he said, gently shaking my shoulder. "We're here."

"Okay, okay, hands off! I'm awake."

"What do you think you're doing?" Kareem asked when I reached for my guns.

"These are what I call my American Express cards. I never leave home without them."

Kareem took in a deep breath. "I don't want your guns up in my house."

"Nigga, please. Don't be a hypocrite. You're trying to tell me that you don't have an American Express card or two? Hell, I know you got heat up in your crib."

"Of course, I do, but I applied the right way for my credit."

"Cute…very cute." I paused, looked out the window, and laughed. "And what a crib it is. You live in a project?"

"It's a condo," Kareem replied, correcting me.

"Baby, the rent may be higher and the place may be spotless, but you're still living on top of each other. You say condo; I say projects."

"Whatever. Are you coming in?"

"It depends on if I can bring these," I said and raised my guns.

Kareem gave in. "Fine. Just make sure you keep your shit out of sight and unload them."

"Yes, sir." I secured my guns in the holsters.

His place wasn't anything like the projects. It was quiet and peaceful, and those were things I wasn't used to. I figured I would either like it there or lose my fucking mind.

"Make yourself at home."

I looked around his small place. "Home? Looks more like a sardine can to me."

"I don't buy what I can afford; I buy what I need."

"Meaning what?"

"Meaning I can afford a five-bedroom, four-bathroom house with a big-ass kitchen and so on, but I refuse to."

A house like that sounded like heaven. "In other words, you're stingy."

"You know that's not true. I'm just careful with my paper."

"The hell with being careful. I always say if you got it, spend it."

"And I always say if you got it, save it."

I knew what he meant because I had my stash, too. "What about when you go?"

"Go where?" he asked.

"When you die."

"I don't know about you, but I plan to be around for a while. Are you hungry?"

"Kind of. But, if you're cooking, then I might have to pass."

"Why?" Kareem struggled to keep a straight face.

"Honestly, you can design clothes with your eyes closed, but I doubt you have cooking skills."

"I take you out the hood for a minute and you get a sense of humor all of a sudden. It just so happens that I have some takeout left from last night."

"See, no cooking skills." I sighed and sat down on the couch.

"Excuse me, miss, but you're not the queen bee up in my joint. You better help me."

I reluctantly left the comfort of his sofa and went into his small kitchen.

"All you have to do is set the table."

"What? The last time I set a table I was sixteen."

"Well, the concept hasn't changed; plate, fork, knife, drinking glass. It will come back to you, I promise."

"You think you're so funny, don't you?"

He smiled and gave me quick instructions on where everything was in his small kitchen. I then set the table for two.

"What would you like to drink?"

"Do you have Kool-Aid?"

"Do you know any black folk that don't have it? Let's eat." He placed the plates on the table and smiled. "I'm impressed with your table setting."

"And I'm impressed with your takeout. Smells good."

"Well, you know what they say. Chinese food tastes better the second time around."

"A lot of things are better the second time around," I said, hoping he would know what I meant.

I think he caught on to what I was saying because our eyes locked, and for a moment, I allowed the butterflies in my stomach to exist as butterflies. There was no denying them.

The ringing of my cell phone broke our silent conversation. I pulled it out, rolled my eyes at the number, and turned my phone off.

"Who is it?"

"None of your fuckin' business!"

As soon as I snapped at him, I regretted it. Just knowing X was looking for me destroyed my mood. I knew we had to

175

meet with Buchanan that night about some firepower he wanted us to move for him, and it could be dangerous if I didn't show up.

"Samantha, let me lay something out for you. I am not one of your lil' niggas that kisses your ass every time you tell them to. So, I would appreciate a little respect in my house."

"Respect is yours. I apologize." I frowned and pinched the bridge of my nose. "We have some shit to handle tonight. That call was a reminder."

"Do you want to go and handle your shit?"

I should have gotten up and drove as fast as I could away from Kareem. However, the longing of 'what if' lingered in my thoughts. I wanted to stay. My eyes went from my plate to the eyes of the man who still held my heart.

"Nah, he can handle it without me."

"You mean X, don't you?"

"Do we have to do this shit again now?"

"Just answer the question, *Samantha*."

I hated how he put so much emphasis on my name, as if trying to resurrect a part of me that had been dead for years.

"Fuck this shit! You act like X is a motherfuckin' choirboy. He was in the crew long before I was, so don't act like it's my fault he's doin' what he wants to do. If I don't pull the trigger first, he does. X is as cold as a man can get, and he's just as fucked up as I am."

"I think we should just drop it and finish eating."

I wanted to get up from the table and take a walk outside, but the grumble in my empty stomach won the bid to stay. We ate in silence. Kareem's jaw clenched with each bite. After dinner, we cleaned up the dishes.

"I'm sorry," Kareem quietly said.

I wasn't sure what he was apologizing for, but I went with it. "It's cool."

We both sat on the couch, and Kareem flipped through the channels. We watched some old comedy reruns and shared a few laughs. I looked at my watch; it was almost ten. X and I were supposed to meet Buchanan at midnight.

"Have a hot date?"

"I thought I was on it," I replied lightly, trying to put both of our minds at ease.

He smiled and stretched, which turned into a yawn. "I'm tired."

"Me, too. We have to figure out the sleeping arrangements because I don't do couches."

"You're a guest in my home and claiming my bed?"

"Yes, and without you in it."

"I had no thoughts of that, trust me. You're welcome to sleep in my room, and I'll take the couch. The bathroom is right next to the bedroom. You can get to it from the hallway or the bedroom. Look in my dresser for something to wear."

"Okay. I'm going to take a shower."

Closing the door behind me, I looked around his room. Everything was so damn neat. There wasn't even one wrinkle on the bed. I took off my holster, removed the clips, put them back in my belt, and pushed it under the bed with my foot. Then, without even checking them, I put my phone and pager in the closet.

The bathroom was no different from his bedroom. Nothing was out of place. It was a lot different from what I was used to. After undressing, I stared at the stranger in the mirror. I ran my fingertips over the scars I had acquired over the years and massaged my left shoulder. The bullet wound left such an ugly scar. Stepping into the shower, I let the warm water massage my physically and emotionally tired body.

A soft knock on the door startled me. "What?"

"Are you going to be in there all night?"

"No."

"Good, because I can't go to sleep without taking a shower."

"Oh? And here I thought you liked being funky."

"No, baby, that's your department. Are you done?"

I turned off the shower. "Yeah, just one second."

I wrapped a towel around myself, gathered my clothes, and headed back to the bedroom, where I threw on a wife beater and a pair of his sweatpants. Not long after I got in bed, there was a knock on the door.

"Samantha, I don't have any clothes. Can you unlock the door, please?"

I let him in and there he stood adorned in only a towel. While doing a quick scan, I realized he was doing the same, only he was looking at the scar on my left shoulder.

"What happened?" he asked gently.

"I was injured on the job," I responded sarcastically while climbing back into bed.

He nodded and retrieved his sleepwear. "Good night."

I pulled the cool sheets up to my chin. "You, too."

He left, and I turned off the lamp and focused on the light coming from under the bathroom door. I could hear him brushing his teeth and wondered what he was thinking.

A few minutes later, the light under the door went off. I lay there in the dark and tried to keep my eyes open. It was too damn quiet. My eyes closed, inviting Melanie to my subconscious.

I woke up gasping for air. This dream was different because Doc was there holding my hand and forcing me to face Melanie. I rubbed my eyes and looked at the clock on the nightstand. It wasn't yet midnight, so I could still make the meeting. I'd be late, but at least I'd be there. I quickly got dressed, then grabbed my guns and phone. I wasn't surprised at the twenty-two missed calls. I listened to a few of the voicemails as I tied the shoestrings of my Timbs. All of the messages were from X, who sounded more agitated with each one, so I erased the rest of them.

I walked quietly past the couch where Kareem looked so

damn uncomfortable. I put on my coat and went in the kitchen to get my keys where Kareem left them. I thought my eyes were adjusted to the darkness, but the sound of a glass shattering on the floor proved me wrong.

"What the fuck?" Kareem said loudly as he jumped off the couch.

The light he turned on blinded me for a few seconds. "I didn't mean to wake you."

"Well, I am. Where are you going?"

"I have to roll. Where are my damn keys?"

Kareem pointed to a key holder on one of the cabinets. "Aren't you forgetting something?"

"No."

"You're not going to clean up your mess?"

I grabbed my keys, glanced at the broken glass, and walked to the door without a word.

"Coward."

That one word caused me to tense. I turned and faced him with every intention of exploding with anger. Nevertheless, I just cleared my throat and shook my head.

"I'm not a coward."

"Prove it then," Kareem challenged. "Stay here. Stay as long as you want."

"That's not a smart move on my part. I'm not being a coward; I'm just being smart."

"I disagree."

"You don't understand, Kareem."

"Make me understand."

"Brotha, please. The less you know about my life, the better for you."

I unlocked the door and walked out. Even though I wasn't facing him, I could picture his expression. I had to go to that night's meeting and all the meetings for nights to come. My life was in jeopardy, and nothing Kareem could do or say would convince me to stay.

"Baby, please stay."
Well, maybe that could make me stay...maybe.
He closed the door behind me, turned the deadbolt on the door, and slid the chain back in its place.

Chapter 26

"Thank you," he said softly.

I sat on the couch. My elbows dug into my knees as I held my head in my hands and rubbed my temples with my thumbs. The decision I'd made to stay gave me a headache. Maybe I was aching from the thought of what would happen when I did go back.

"Here you go." Kareem handed me a painkiller and a glass of water. "Be careful with that glass. I seem to be losing the set tonight."

He was trying so hard to lighten the mood, so I gave him a little smile for his effort. My cell rang, and without hesitation, I dropped it into the water, drowning the ringing. Kareem rose to his feet and extended his hand to me, which I accepted. He held my hand until we got to his bedroom. We sat side by side on his bed, and he lifted my legs to untie my shoes. Next, he helped me out of my jacket and hung it in the closet. Then he held out his hands. Knowing what he wanted, I handed over my guns. I watched as he removed the clips and placed the belt and guns in the closet with my jacket.

"Try to get some sleep," he suggested before leaving the room.

"Kareem?"

"Yeah?"

"Don't leave me in here alone."

"You need to sleep, and I have an early start in the morning."

"It's hard to sleep because she haunts my dreams."

"She who?"

"I'd rather not talk about it. Just stay with me."

A smile swept across his face.

"No, not like that. You on one side, and me on the other," I said while lying down.

Sleep must have come quickly, because when my eyes opened, it was ten in the morning. Next to the clock was a piece of paper with my name written on it.

Good morning. I told you I had an early day, so make yourself at home. I meant what I said last night. You're welcome to stay as long as you need to. Be careful in the kitchen. The broken glass is still on the floor. House rule: you break it, you clean it. See you after six.

K.

His letter made me smile. I stretched out on the bed and enjoyed the quietness around me. I knew I had to call X, but I decided to call Shabazz's cell after I threw my clothes in the washing machine. He wouldn't think twice about checking the number.

"What's up?"

"Yo, nigga, where the fuck you at? X was looking for your ass last night."

"I know. Where is he now?"

"He's sleep. Bitch-ass Buchanan never showed up last night. X rolled in around three in the morning mad as fuck. Where you at?" he asked again.

"Just tell him I called. I'll call in a few days."

"A few days? You got heat on you?"

Shug'ah

"Naw, nothing like that. I just need a few days," I said, then hung up before he could say anything else.

I was so relieved the meeting went south. Buchanan would never know I wasn't there. Still, X knew, so I knew I would still have to deal with his shit. Completely forgetting about the glass on the floor I walked into the kitchen to get something to eat. I was quickly reminded when a piece of glass pierced the bottom of my foot.

"Fuck!"

I sat and pulled the glass from my foot. Then I grabbed a few paper towels and stopped the bleeding before cleaning up the glass. Instead of eating, I went into the living room to watch TV. I flipped through the channels and found *The Price Is Right*. I couldn't believe that show was still on the air and Mr. Bob Barker was still doing his thing. After the first big spin off, my stomach rumbled. So, once I put my clothes in the dryer, I ate chips, a Snickers, and had a soda. I laughed when the final contestants overbid. Both got nada. The ringing phone interrupted my laughter.

"Hello?"

"Why are you answering my phone?"

"Because you called."

"How are you doing?"

"I cut my damn foot." Kareem cracking up didn't amuse me.

"Woo! I told you to clean up," he said and finally stopped laughing. "I need a favor. I took out some chicken and put it in the sink before I left. Put it in the fridge, and I'll cook when I come home."

I smiled. *He is so domesticated.*

"Anything else, Jeeves?" I asked.

"Yes. Don't dirty up my place."

"I won't," I promised, then looked at the chip crumbs on his sofa, the Snickers wrapper on the floor, and the watermarks on his glass coffee table. "This place is spotless."

"I don't believe you. I better go. I have a meeting in a few minutes."

"Knock 'em dead or whatever you do."

"Hey, thanks for sticking around," he said and hung up.

Not the one to return pleasantries, I was glad he got off the phone. The game shows were taken over by soap operas. My life was complicated enough. I didn't need the extra drama, so I turned off the TV and cleaned up my mess. Before I put the chicken breasts in the refrigerator, I decided to season them for Kareem. However, upon searching the cabinets, I only found salt and pepper. So, I did the best I could with what I had to work with, which included a few cloves of garlic that I chopped up and put on the chicken. Afterwards, I cleaned the kitchen and took a long, warm shower.

Before I got dressed, I lay across the bed and had an unexplainable feeling sweep through my body, which was probably contentment. I took a nap, got dressed, and went to get something to eat, but Kareem's refrigerator was empty. Staring at the chicken, I decided I might as well cook the damn things. I would starve if I had to wait until he came home before dinner. I needed something to go with the bird, so I decided to turn the oven on low and slip out to the store.

When I pulled up to the store, I remembered I left my guns in Kareem's closet. That was the first time in four years I had gone anywhere without them. It felt nice.

I received many stares while in the store, probably because I didn't fit in with everyone in Malibu. Not wanting to return to where I came from any time soon, I made up my mind that I was going to take a mini-vacation from my life. So, in addition to the rice, frozen corn on the cob, and packets of Kool-Aid, I tossed a comb, brush, shampoo, conditioner, and a handful of makeup products into my basket while slowly walking down the beauty aisle. The cashier didn't even blink when I tried to discreetly pull out my thick roll of money to pay for the items.

When I pulled up, Kareem was walking towards the stairs. I honked my horn, and he turned and walked towards me.

"Hey," he greeted me.

"Hey yourself."

"I thought you were gone."

"Like you would miss me." I grabbed the bags from the backseat. "Are you going to help?"

"My hands are full with these bags. What did you buy?"

I glanced up towards his apartment and saw no smoke. "Stuff for dinner. And you?"

"Stuff for you."

I smiled. "I think we should get inside."

"Why? Are you scared people will see you smile?"

"Um, no. Scared your place might catch on fire. I left the oven on." You would've sworn I told him I placed a bomb in his pad the way he ran up the stairs. "Is it safe?" I inquired, looking at him inspect the chicken.

"It's safe," he said with a deep sigh. "Don't ever do that again!"

I frowned.

"Please," he said in a softer tone when he saw my expression.

"I won't."

A smile formed on his lips. "So the all-mighty, all-powerful Shug'ah cooked for me? Now what did I do to deserve this?"

"Nothing. I was hungry and wasn't going to wait for you," I said, handing him a pot. "Can you boil water?"

He laughed and filled the pot with water. Once I got the rice going, he took my hand and led me to the couch. I completely forgot he had stuff for me.

"Now I guessed on the sizes, so I hope everything fits," he told me, handing me the bags.

He had bought me underwear, bras, shirts, and pants. My favorite was a pair of purple fuzzy slippers.

He lifted up my foot and smiled. "Is this where you got an owie?"

I rolled my eyes and pulled my foot away from him.

"I have a confession."

"Then confess, my child," I joked.

"When I came home and saw your car gone, I was a little disappointed."

"You would have gotten over it."

"I doubt it. I would have missed you, girl," he said with fake sniffles.

"Well, I have a confession, too. I was going to leave this morning, but after speaking to one of my boys, I decided to go on vacation."

"Vacation?"

"Yeah. I can pretend your joint is a five-star hotel. Hell, it's clean enough."

Kareem laughed and touched my hair. "You looked so cute that night."

"That was a thousand years ago."

"I wouldn't mind seeing you looking classy. You know, minus the braids and adding a dress."

"Somebody watched *Pretty Woman* too much."

"Yeah, I guess you're right. You're too 50 Cent to be Halle."

I laughed it off, but secretly, my feelings were hurt. On any other day, if someone other than him compared me to 50 Cent, I would have taken it as a compliment.

"Why do you do it?" he asked.

I knew I couldn't ignore his question. "After juvie, there was nothing for me to do. I tried working at a supermarket, but the manager didn't want a convict working for him. Then I ran into Rome."

"Rome from the old days?"

Shug'ah

"When you left, you really left, huh? You forgot Rome Rawlings? He remembered you."

"Yeah, that was my boy. He played some serious ball."

"Well, he gave up running after a ball, dropped out of high school, and began running drugs and guns. When I came on the scene, he already had a crew. I think he had plans for me being his girl or some shit, but I wasn't down with that. Eventually, he asked me to join his crew. No one was more pissed than your cousin. When Rome got gunned down, I thought about walking away, but the power and dollars pulled me back. At times, it gets to me."

"Like yesterday?"

"Yeah, like yesterday."

"So why do you do it?"

"I do what I do because I can and I'm fuckin' good at it."

"How many people have you killed?"

I couldn't answer that question if I wanted to. I stopped counting after five. I just shook my head and shrugged my shoulders.

"You know what?" Kareem said, standing to his feet. "I is hungry. Is you hungry?"

"Yes, I is."

"Stay here. I'll prepare everything for you tonight."

Kareem made our plates, humming the whole time. He always had a way of making me feel at ease, even when he was the one who made me uncomfortable.

"This is some damn good chicken," he said with a hint of surprise in his voice when he took a bite. "Do you cook often?"

"No. Tiny cooks most of the time."

"I saw Tiny, and he is not tiny."

I laughed. "I know. We're thinking it's time to rename him."

The conversation for the rest of the meal was light. Then the phone rang.

"...Right now...but...And it can't wait until morning...Of course I want this client...Fine, I'll pick up Sasha and be there in about an hour...Then take her out to dinner...Okay, I'm leaving now...One."

"Everything okay?"

"That was one of my investors. A big client from Paris just flew in and wants to see my new designs tonight. I tried so hard to get her to see my designs while I was there, and now that I moved back here, she wants in. Better late than never, I guess."

"You're right about that. Why are you still here talking it up with me? Go."

"Thanks for understanding. I better call Sasha. She's the number whiz," he said excitedly as he dialed. He scratched his right temple after he hung up. "Can I use your ride?"

"No way. My ride is marked. You could get killed driving it." I laughed at the look on his face. "I'm kidding. Here." I handed him my keys. "You're just going to B.H., right?"

"Yeah."

"Then you'll be cool. Oh, one thing, though."

"I know. Don't fuck up your ride." He flashed his smile and closed the door.

Chapter 27

After cleaning the kitchen, I took my place in front of the TV, but nothing could hold my attention for more than ten minutes. I hadn't been that alone in years, and I rather enjoyed it. I lay down, grabbed one of the couch pillows, and held it close to my chest. It smelled like Kareem. I started having erotic thoughts. Thinking and talking about sex was always something I avoided. Jackson was the first and only man to penetrate me, and as a result, he made the most natural thing between a man and a woman nasty.

When around Kareem, I thought about sex. The subtle way he licked his lips made me want to kiss him. When he came near me, I wanted to ask him to touch me. Those thoughts eventually made me a little sick to my stomach, but it quickly disappeared because I wanted to know what it felt like to make love to someone…and I wanted that someone to be Kareem.

I unbuttoned my jeans and was about to ease the unusual aching I felt between my legs, when someone knocked at the door. I was a little surprised I had allowed myself to become so aroused to the point that I wanted to please myself. Someone knocked again, so I buttoned my jeans, walked to the door, and looked through the peephole. I put a smile on my face and opened the door quickly.

"Hi!" I greeted in a cheerful voice.

I was then studied from head to toe. "Who are you?"

I stared back at the five-foot-eight, mahogany-toned woman. "I'm someone who opened the door you were knocking on. Who are you?"

"I'm looking for Kareem," she said, backing up to look at the number of the condo.

"You got the right door. He's just not here."

"I saw his car. Kareem!" she yelled past me into the condo.

"He's not here. Damn! There's a 'Low Noise' law around these parts. Do you care to leave a message?"

She hesitated while tapping one of her manicured nails on her top lip.

"Going once, going twice." I started closing the door.

"Wait! Tell him Sunshine came by."

"Okie dokie, Sunshine."

"One more thing…"

"Come on. I'm not a secretary. Make it quick."

"Who are you?"

"Wouldn't you like to know? You have a good evening. Drive safe." I snickered when I closed the door and left her standing there with her mouth open. I couldn't resist singing a few bars of "You Are My Sunshine".

I caught the last thirty minutes of a cop show and was about to call it a night, when the phone rang.

"You're still up?"

"Yes. I'm about to get ready for bed."

"And I'm thinking you're waiting up for me."

"Oh, please! How's everything going with the Paris broad?"

"Everything's going great. She likes my work. I might have to fly out to Paris in a few days to look at the factory and hire some folks. We're going out for drinks to talk dollars and cents, so I won't be home anytime soon."

I was touched by the fact that he was checking in. "Oh, some woman named Sunshine came by. She didn't leave a message; she just wanted you to know she was here."

"Well, now I know. Hold on one second." I could hear him ask Sasha for Sunshine's phone number. "Sorry, I'm back."

"Well, I'm about to go to sleep."

"Okay. Sweet dreams."

"Thanks."

When I hung up, I felt something I never felt before. The feeling stayed with me as I got ready for bed; it kept me awake and had me tossing and turning. I was jealous. All I could think of was Kareem and Sunshine all wrapped up in each other. I lay back down and punched the hell out of the pillows. Sleep finally came; Melanie stayed away.

Around seven o'clock the next morning, I got up and quietly fixed myself a bowl of cereal. Kareem, who I heard come in around two, was fast asleep on the couch. Deep in thought, I chewed the Corn Flakes slowly, as if the crunch would wake him. I stopped chewing when I heard Kareem stretch and yawn. Before I knew it, he was in the kitchen fixing himself some cereal. I swallowed hard and tried not to stare at him, but it was difficult since he was standing there wearing nothing but a pair of boxers and showing off his great body.

He sat down across from me and dived into his cereal. I stared at him. I stirred my cereal and wondered how he spent his evening after the big meeting. *Did he call Sunshine? Did they meet at her place? Did he give her what she came looking for?*

He looked at me with wide eyes. "Are you okay?"

"Yeah, I'm fine," I said and took another bite. "What time did you get in?"

"I came in around two. I figured you would've heard me."

"No, I was sound asleep," I lied.

It was killing me. I had to know if he did anything with Sunshine. The thought of her was raining on my vacation.

"So did you get in touch with... What's her name? Summer? Spring?"

Kareem laughed. "Sunshine?"

"Yes, that's it. Sunshine." I looked at him as he slurped the remaining soy milk in his bowl. Damn, he was infuriating, but I fought to remain calm. "So did you?"

He got up and put his bowl in the sink. "Did I what?"

That did it. "Did you see her? Did you call her? Did you ask her to join you? Did you meet up with her somewhere? Did you have sex with her?"

Kareem gave me a half smile. "None of the above," he said while walking out of the kitchen.

I got up and followed him to the bedroom. "Then what?" I asked as he picked out a shirt to wear.

"It's killing you, huh?"

I massaged the back of my neck and took a deep breath. "What?"

"The fact that a beautiful..." He took a step towards me. "...sexy, fine-as-hell woman came to see me."

He was so close I could feel the warmth of his breath on my face. I took a step back.

"No, it's not."

"Yes, it is."

He leaned in, and I couldn't move. He had me pinned against the wall. I felt anxious and excited at the same time.

"Do me a favor?"

At this point, if he had asked for the moon, I would've tried to get it for him.

"Name it."

"I need to get ready for work. Can I have a little privacy?"

That's not what I was hoping he would ask for, but I smiled and backed out of the room. I went in the kitchen and silently cursed myself for showing him that he made me weak. I needed to see a talk show or something to clear my mind. With it being a Saturday, there were cartoons on almost every channel. So, I settled on a cartoon about some little island girl and her blue dog that was really from outer space. Kareem came out of his room, and his cologne caressed my nose before he even walked by. He knew the game and damn sure knew how to play it. He was looking sharp.

"I'll bring something home for dinner, so you don't have to worry about that."

"That's not what I'm worried about," I mumbled softly.

"What's that?"

"Uh, nothing."

"Okay. You have a good day. I'll see you later."

"Later," I answered.

I glared at his back as he unlocked the door, then quickly diverted my stare back at the TV when I noticed him slowly turning back towards me.

"Samantha?"

"Yeah?" I kept my eyes on the screen.

"Will you look at me?"

I leaned back on the couch and looked at him standing by the door. "I'm looking."

"She's a model."

I pretended I had no idea what he was talking about. I rolled my eyes and scratched my head.

"She?" I asked innocently.

"Sunshine, smart ass," he said with affection. "She did a few shows for me and a photo shoot. She wanted to go out with me, but I refused, and her coming to my home caused me to make a serious decision about her. I called her last night, but not to talk or have sex. I called to fire her."

"She crossed that line, huh?"

"Crossed it? She erased it and had to go."

"Amen, my brotha."

He left me with a big grin on my face. I got the comb and began working on my braids. *Spiderman* kept me company for a little while. During the commercials, I thought of being the beautiful, sexy, fine-as-hell woman for Kareem to desire. That thought cooled my temper every time I wanted to throw the comb across the room. The cartoons were a faded memory by the time I finished undoing my braids.

I got my two-way from the closet and was surprised X hadn't left more messages. After wrapping my wavy, thick hair the best I could, I put on a T-shirt and Lakers fitted cap. Kareem left a spare key to his condo on the counter, and without thinking, I added it to my key ring after locking the door. Then I drove slowly to the little store I went to the day before. I had to call X. The last thing I needed was to be on the outs with him.

Chapter 28

X picked up on the second ring. "Who the fuck is dis?"
"It's Shug'ah."
"Muthafucka! Where the hell you at?"
I couldn't explain it, but the good feelings I had been feeling seemed to evaporate the second I heard his voice. I was back in full Shug'ah mode.
"You're not my fuckin' keeper."
"Yeah, but you not being here is making a nigga think all kinds of fucked-up shit, like you not showing up the other night. Then that cracker-ass cop didn't show up. I started thinking the two of y'all had something going on."
If we were had been standing face-to-face, I would have punched him. "First of all, I can't stand that bitch-ass punk. I just do what he tells me and that's it. I can't believe you thought that."
"The thought crossed my mind, but I didn't think you would do anything behind my back. I spoke to Buchanan, and he said his partner is on his ass. So where you at?"
I knew he saw the area code. Plus, I never lied to him before and wasn't going to start.
"I'm kicking it in Malibu for a minute. I need to get my head straight."

"I can respect that, but you should've called a nigga to let me know."

"I spoke to Shabazz and told him to give you the message because you were asleep."

"You know that bitch-ass nigga don't remember nothing."

I felt a little better hearing X laugh. For the next few minutes, we spoke about meaningless shit.

"Hey, Shug'ah, we have to meet with Buchanan Wednesday at midnight. I'm not asking; I'm telling you. Be there!" He hung up before I could respond.

I sat in my ride and drank my soda before heading back to Kareem's. Once there, I washed and dried my hair and put on the pair of baby blue sweatpants he got me with a T-shirt. I never really used foundation, but I wanted to look my best. So, I got dolled up. I looked at my reflection in one of the little makeup mirrors and stuck my tongue out at my refection. Hearing a laugh, I jumped.

"Look at you," Kareem said with a smile. "I see you're going for the MJ look."

He went into the kitchen to put the food on the counter.

"What are you talking about?"

"That foundation is about four shades too light for you."

"Yeah, I figured that out."

"Besides, a woman with beautiful skin like yours doesn't need foundation." He tore off a couple of paper towels from the roll. "Now, let's get this crap off your face."

After a few wipes, I sat foundation free with a mountain of makeup in my lap.

"Close your eyes," he told me.

I closed them and felt him sift through the makeup. I giggled when he touched my face. He put eye shadow on my eyelids and then applied lipstick.

"Press your lips together and open your eyes, but keep still," he instructed as he unscrewed the top on the mascara. "I don't want you to look like you have a black eye."

"If I do, you'll have the black eye."

After putting the mascara on my lashes, he looked at me like an artist staring at his masterpiece. Without a word, he handed me the mirror and went to shower. He returned dressed in a sharp suit. He took a moment to put the food he brought home in the refrigerator.

"You know red lipstick doesn't go with what you're wearing, right?" He jingled his keys. "Let's go for a ride."

I didn't ask any questions. I just jumped up and followed him out the door. We cruised in his Mercedes Benz in silence and ended up in front of a store with the letters ALU on the window.

"This is your store?"

"You seem surprised."

"I'm very surprised," I said as we walked inside. I was even more surprised to see many different styles of clothing from casual to elegant. "I thought you just made the clothes."

He greeted his employees and smiled at two ladies who were browsing.

"I have another place about fifteen minutes from here. That's where all the designing and creating takes place. This is where all the money comes in, and now that we'll be in the Paris circuit, money will be endless."

"I'm proud of you."

"Thank you. I'm glad you're here with me, baby. Now, let's see," he said, eyeing me up and down. "I have just the thing for you. Wait right here."

His store was amazing. I knew he had his shit together, but this was together-together. I wandered over to a display case full of jewelry.

"Here it is."

I turned and saw him holding a simple but elegant black dress.

"Try it on." He looked in the direction of the fitting rooms. "I'll be upstairs in my office. Come up after you put it on. I'm going to make a few calls about my Paris trip while I'm here."

"So you're going?"

"Yep. I'm leaving on Friday. Now go on and see how it fits."

I smiled, but I wasn't happy about him leaving. I went in the dressing room and got undressed. The dress' straps were thin, so I pulled my bra straps off my shoulders and tucked them in on each side. The dress fit perfectly, but it advertised my scar.

When I went upstairs, Kareem was on the phone. He smiled at me before turning his chair around away from me. I looked around his office. On the wall behind his desk, there were some stenciled words. *When you think, you dream. When you dream, you create. When you create, your dreams come true!* I longed for the day when my dreams would create more than a cold sweat.

"Are you pledging allegiance?" he asked, hanging up the phone.

That's when I realized my right hand was covering the scar. "I just…you know…the scar."

He took my hand and slowly moved it away. "There. You are beautiful."

"No, I'm not."

"Yes, you are." He paused and looked at my feet. "You need some shoes."

I stared down at the fuzzy, purple slippers on my feet and had to agree. We went back downstairs to the small shoe selection, and Kareem studied it as if it was abstract art.

"What's your shoe size?"

"Damn if I know."

He asked me to sit down. Then he took my foot in his hand just like he did the previous night.

"Hmmm, seven and a half or eight."

"No high heels, okay? I've been wearing either Timbs or

Nikes for years, and I'm not going to break my neck tonight."

Kareem disappeared and returned holding a box. Kneeling down on one knee, he slipped on a simple but elegant patent leather shoe with a one and a half-inch heel. It was a perfect fit. He took my hand and escorted me to a full-length mirror. I liked what I saw. His handsome face wore a big smile, but it quickly turned into a small one.

"…and to the republic for which it stands, and all that jazz."

"What?"

He pointed to my hand covering my shoulder again. "Hold on one sec."

He went to a rack of silk scarves and pulled out a black one with silver sequins. He slid the scarf through the thin straps and draped it over my shoulders. It fell nicely to my sides. The scarf was sheer, but hid the scar perfectly.

It was around seven-thirty when we got back in the car. The sun was still hanging playfully in the summer evening sky.

"We have reservations for eight. Let's take a stroll in the park to kill time, shall we?"

"Sounds good."

The cool air from the air conditioner caressed my face. My life, or should I say Shug'ah's life, seemed to melt away. I felt like Samantha for the first time since being sixteen.

"Here we are." He got out the car, rushed over to my side, and opened the door for me.

A few minutes into our stroll, he reached for my hand and hooked my arm around his. We walked in silence. I think both of us were thinking the same thing: We were the only two people in the world, and the night should last forever.

Kareem broke the silence. "Make a wish."

I looked into the little fountain filled with coins from wishers. I couldn't help but wonder if any of the wishes that were wished came true.

"I'll make one only if you make one, too."

"Deal," he said as he searched his pocket for two quarters.

I watched as he closed his eyes and made funny mouth movements. He kissed the coin and tossed it in. The boyish twinkle in his eyes danced wildly. It was my turn. I closed my eyes and thought of what I would wish for. A thousand wishes rushed through my head, but only one seemed practical. I wished, kissed the coin, and then threw it in the fountain.

"Would you look at that? Our coins are touching each other," Kareem pointed out.

"No way."

"Yes, they are. Look closer."

In the midst of all the pennies, nickels, and dimes, there were two shiny quarters overlapping each other. I didn't see another quarter near that area, so they had to be ours.

"I guess you're right."

"Lady, I'm always right."

He hugged me and slowly danced with me around the fountain.

"What did you wish for?" he whispered against my forehead.

"If I tell you, it won't come true."

"You know what I heard?"

"What?"

"If you tell your wish with your last breath, it will come true."

I stiffened. I didn't want to hear about death, not that night.

"I'm sorry, honey. I shouldn't have said that." He kissed my cheek and held my hand as we walked slowly back to his car.

We pulled up to a swanky bistro, and the valet helped me out after opening my door. He then greeted Kareem by his first name. The maître d' did the same.

"Business or pleasure?" the maître d' inquired.

Kareem looked at me and smiled. "Tonight is all pleasure. Is the table I requested ready?"

The maître d' nodded, and we followed him to a table in the center of the restaurant five feet in front of the jazz band. Kareem then whispered in the maître d's ear.

I was grooving to the mellow sounds the band created as the vocalist filled the room with meaningful lyrics. The waiter returned with an ice bucket holding a big, green champagne bottle and two champagne glasses. I looked at him pour the champagne until the white foam blended into a pale, golden, bubbly liquid.

"Kareem, you know I don't drink alcohol."

"Shhh, baby girl. Raise your glass."

I did as he instructed.

"May all your wishes come true. If not tonight, then in your lifetime."

I clinked my glass with his and watched as he took a sip.

"One sip won't hurt. I promise."

I sipped and then laughed. "Ginger ale? You think of it all, don't you?"

"Just thinking of you, baby."

I felt so special. We were halfway through our meal when the singer came to our table. Kareem rose, shook his hand, and invited him to join us.

"Rufus, this is my childhood friend Samantha."

Rufus took my hand and kissed it. "Very nice to meet you, Samantha."

Kareem continued with the introductions as the waiter brought over a cup of tea for Rufus. "I met this cat in Paris at a little café. I was shocked he was from LA. I was there for designing, and he was there for vocal training."

"Small world," I chimed in.

"You have no idea. I walked in here one night for a business dinner, and there he was singing away."

"I must say, young lady, it's a pleasure to see this brotha in here for something other than a business dinner."

I smiled at the middle-aged man who had the voice of an angel and wondered if he would be so nice if he knew who I really was. I glanced around the room; everyone looked relaxed and peaceful. I'm sure they would have all hit the floor if my other identity reared its ugly head.

I patted Kareem's hand. "It's my pleasure to be his distraction."

Rufus downed the rest of his tea, cleared his throat, and stood. "I better get back to my band. Kareem and beautiful Samantha, the next song is for you. Enjoy the rest of your evening." He winked and strutted back to his little piece of heaven on earth.

"How are your feet in those new shoes?" Kareem asked as the band began playing our song.

"They're fine, trust me."

"Good. Dance with me."

Slipping my hand in his, we made our way to the dance area. Rufus sang a song of newfound love, and the lyrics seemed to wrap around us as we danced. We were so close that it felt as if we barely moved. I rested my head on his chest and heard his heart beating in unison with the drums. I finally found my little piece of heaven—even if it was only mine for the night. I don't think we realized our song was over until the band began playing an up-tempo jazz song. I turned and smiled at Rufus, who winked and started singing a woman-done-me-wrong song.

Shug'ah

Kareem asked for our dessert to be wrapped up to go. "You don't mind, do you?"

"No, not at all. I am a bit tired."

We listened to a jazz station on the ride to Kareem's. I didn't realize we were holding hands until he let go of mine so he could open the front door. Once inside, we sat at the table and ate our chocolate mousse cake.

"Thank you," I said.

"For what?"

"I had a wonderful evening."

He nodded. "So did I."

"Well, I'm going to turn in now. Goodnight." Not long after I went and lay down on his bed, there was a soft knock. "Yes?"

He came in and got a T-shirt, boxers, and a pair of sweats. Then he stood there looking at me.

"Are you okay?"

"Yeah, I'm cool," he said and left.

As I reached for the zipper on the dress so I could change into my nightclothes, another knock came. This time, I opened the door. There he stood with a look I'd never seen before. He wanted me.

"Now what did you forget?" I asked sarcastically.

"This." He held me and kissed me softly.

Chapter 29

I was nervous and scared. He kissed me again, this time a little harder.

"Why are you doing this?" I managed to ask as he abandoned my lips and confiscated my neck.

He looked deep into my eyes. "Why?" Smiling, he whispered against my open mouth, "Because I can and I'm fuckin' good at it."

Those were my words. He was using my words. And he was right. He was good at it.

"Kareem, baby, please wait."

He took a small step back. "What's wrong?"

How was I to tell him the only man to ever enter me was the first man I killed? How was I to tell him I wanted to be with him, but I was scared? I guessed it was time to give in. Besides, it had been almost ten years. It was time to move on.

I took a deep breath. "I've never been with a man since that incident. And I really want to be with you, but…"

Kareem sat on the bed and opened his arms. I melted into them.

"What he did was sick. He treated you like his possession. You probably see sex as something violent and hurtful." He removed the scarf from around my shoulders. "I just want to treat you like a woman, if you'll have me."

I wanted Kareem to touch me and make love to me like I'd seen in the movies before the "Jackson era".

I stared into his eyes. "I want you," I said slowly and kissed his lips.

As he stood, he pulled me to my feet. Then he turned me around, unzipped my dress, and unhooked my bra. He turned me back to face him, released my hair, and ran his fingers through it while kissing me the whole time. My hand went to the spot that bothered me the most.

He smiled, moved my hand, and kissed my scar. "I kinda like it."

"Oh, you do, do you?"

"Yes. It gives you character."

I found myself trying to unbutton his shirt at record speed. I wanted to feel his skin against mine. He must have read my mind, because he ripped his shirt open, causing the buttons to hit the hardwood floor. He quickly followed with his pants and held me close. He felt so warm. He held my breast in his hand as his lips found mine once again. My knees got weak from the touch of his thumbs rolling slowly over my nipples, which immediately hardened.

"Lay down," he said, his voice laced with sensuality.

I did, and he joined me. His lips and tongue picked up where his thumbs left off. This feeling was new; it felt like I was erupting from the inside out. He lingered on my lips, but every now and then he would gently suck on my tongue. When I turned on my side, the hardness of him pressed into me.

He smoothed the hair away from my face. "Are you ready, baby?"

I answered him by turning onto my back and taking off my panties. He then removed his boxer briefs.

"I'll be gentle. I promise."

I knew he would be.

He lay on top of me, and I opened my legs slightly. His lips teased my breasts as he entered me slowly. He stopped a couple times to reassure me that he would be gentle. I could feel my body relax. I opened my legs wider, inviting him to give me all he had to offer. I never knew sex could feel so wonderful. His movements were slow but effective. My hips rose to reach his, and I gripped his shoulders to release my stressful tension over and over again. Reaching up, I wiped the sweat from his brow. I never wanted him to disconnect from me. He leaned up slightly and looked down at me. We kissed long and deeply. I was breathless. His movements quickened and a moan escaped from his mouth. His body tensed and seemed out of breath. He lowered his body slowly back on top of me before we turned on our sides still connected as one.

"Good night, baby," he said with a satisfied tone.

I put my leg over his and kissed his shoulder. Soon, we fell asleep.

After a dreamless night, I woke at the butt-crack of dawn to a beautiful Sunday morning. I watched Kareem as he slept. His lips moved as if he was talking in his sleep and he frowned slightly. Then his lips formed a small smile. I couldn't help but wonder what he was dreaming about. I took a shower and decided to make us breakfast. Halfway through scrambling some eggs, I heard him taking a shower.

"Good morning," he said softly when he came into the kitchen.

"Morning to you, too."

He stood behind me as I buttered the toast. I dropped the

knife when he ran his hand down my back.

"Leave it," he ordered as he continued to stimulate me.

"But there's butter on your floor."

He turned me to face him. "So?"

"Well, you are the clean freak."

He leaned over and turned off the stove.

"Why did you do that? I have to add the cheese."

"I'm not really hungry. Are you? Is a big breakfast what you want?"

I looked up into his eyes. I never noticed that the smell of Dial soap aroused the hell out of me.

"No, it isn't what I want."

"Then what is?" he asked.

"What do I want? What I really want is for you to make me feel like a woman again."

"Hmmm, that's funny, because that's exactly what I want, too."

He kissed me passionately, and we left the messy kitchen behind us. Kareem introduced me to the art of timeless foreplay. We made love well into the late morning hours and then fell asleep while clinging to each other as if we were each other's salvation. We awoke about one in the afternoon thanks to Kareem's ringing cell. I handed it to him. He stretched and rubbed his eyes.

"I thought I turned this damn thing off," he muttered, answering it. "Oh, no. Not today, my brotha…Why? Because I have a beautiful, naked woman next to me in my bed, that's why. We'll hit the pavement next weekend. Wait, I'll be out of town…Yeah, I'll holla when I get back…One."

He hung up and smiled.

"You blew off basketball for me?"

"Oh, yeah."

"I feel special."

"I have something special for you to feel."

I pulled the sheet over my head and slid down. He

followed and softly tickled me under the covers. In between laughs and kisses, I invited him to become one with me. Once again, there was another heavenly moment that he made last for a long time. Afterwards, he got up and left me basking in the afterglow of our lovemaking to run a hot shower. Then he invited me in to get wet.

"You are so beautiful," he whispered, while washing my back.

I turned and watched him from head to toe. "So are you."

I never thought I would be here in my life. I always envisioned myself old and grey with an Uzi in one hand and a .45 in the other. That was, of course, if I didn't get killed before my grey years. But there I was making love and having fun, thinking of things I never thought possible like a positive future.

"Will you stay with me?" he asked, as he turned off the shower. "I want you here with me."

His hands moved to my shoulders and then around me. I placed my head on his wet chest, and his heart seemed to repeat the words *"please stay with me"* with each beat. I looked up at him. In that moment, nothing mattered but the two of us, and that's how it should have been.

"Kareem?"

He ran his hands over my wet hair and kissed my nose. "Yes, baby?"

"There's no place I'd rather be—"

"But?" He knew me too well.

"Are you sure you want me here?"

"I wouldn't have asked if I wasn't sure," he said, stepping out of the shower.

I followed while watching him dry his body.

"I'm sorry, baby. Maybe it was too much too soon." He wrapped the towel around his waist. "I just...never mind."

"Please don't do that. Tell me what's on your mind."

He took another towel and began drying me off. "I tell

you what, come with me to Paris."

Wednesday night would come before his Friday departure to Paris. His eyes searched mine for an answer. If I didn't make the right decision, I knew I would regret it for the rest of my life. *Now or never.*

"Yes, I'll stay with you, and yes, I'll go to Paris with you!"

"Is there still a 'but'?"

"Well, umm, not really. However, there is something I have to do."

"And that is?"

"I have to make my exit right."

"I'm not following you."

I went to the bedroom to put on a T-shirt. "I have to tell the crew face to face that I'm out."

Kareem said nothing as he sat next to me on the bed and put his arm around me. He stretched out on our horizontal dance floor. I lay on top of him, and soon, we both drifted off to sleep.

The smell of food woke me up. When I looked out the window, night was looking back at me. It was close to nine.

"Are you hungry?" Kareem asked as I sat at the table.

"Starving." I looked around. "I see you cleaned up."

"I had to. This place was a mess."

"It was your fault. You were thinking with your little head earlier."

"Hey, hey, hey! Be nice," he teased, sliding me a plate of food. "It's not that little. I called and got your ticket to Paris before you changed your mind. You do have a passport, right?"

I managed to tell him yes. Then I brought up a topic I knew he didn't care for. "Baby, I need to talk to the crew tonight and get it over with."

"You're set on doing that, huh?" He sighed deeply. "After we eat. Okay?"

"Okay."

As we ate, he told me about all the places we would visit in Paris. He told me over and over again how much he wanted me to meet his father. I could tell he couldn't wait for the night to be over so we could relax.

After dinner, I began dressing and grabbed my guns. My cell rang before I could get out the door.

"Are you okay?" Kareem asked, noticing my expression when I hung up.

"Uh, yeah. Everything's cool. What are you doing?" I questioned as I put the clip in one gun and reached for the other.

"I'm coming with you."

"No, baby," I replied, the call still fresh in my mind. "You have to stay here. I'll be back soon. I promise. Trust me."

"I trust you. I just don't trust where you're going," he said, looking at the guns in my hands. "I'm going and that's that."

"That's that, huh?"

He nodded as he laced up his sneakers. The truth was I was happy he wanted to come with me. He decided to take his car; I respected his wishes and put my guns in his trunk. I couldn't wait for it to be over. I knew X would be pissed. Kareem's eyes locked with mine and he smiled reassuringly as he backed out the driveway.

Fuck X!

Chapter 30

Inglewood Police Station

"Hey, Buchanan. I'll be right with you. I just have to make a quick call."

"Yeah, sure." Buchanan couldn't have his partner sniffing around, so he closed his locker and went to eavesdrop on his call.

"…yeah, I'm telling you, he is up to no good…I don't even want to work with him anymore. Tonight while I was getting changed, he watched me like a hawk…No, I was unable to put on the wire…Don't worry. I'll come with it on tomorrow, and we'll get him then…Don't worry. I don't think Buchanan is stupid, but I'll be careful."

Yeah, you do that, rookie, Buchanan thought deeply. *Be very careful.* He went outside to the police car, lifted the hood, and tugged on the wires to the air conditioning.

"Is something wrong?"

"Not really, rookie. Is something wrong with you?"

"No, I'm fine," he responded nervously. "I was asking about the unit."

"Oh. See, I tried to get out here as fast as I could, but, uh, we're stuck with the until with no A/C."

"Well, this is going to be uncomfortable. It's hot tonight. I should go and tell Sergeant we will ride a desk tonight."

"Now, come on, rookie. How will that look?" Buchanan was interrupted by the police radio.

"Unit 56 we got a call of a domestic in progress."

"You hear that? We've been summoned. Come on, just roll down your window and we're off," Buchanan said, glaring at him as he got into the unit.

After they handled the domestic case, which proved to be nothing but a heated argument, Buchanan cruised around the city aimlessly.

"Buchanan, what are you doing?"

"I'm lookin' for a place to make water. Is that okay, Ms. Daisy?" He grinned as they drove around Watts. "Ahhh, here we go." Buchanan pulled into an empty lot. "I'll be right back."

He stepped from the car, walked a few feet away, and pretended to do what he said he pulled over for. While glancing back at the car, he removed the .45 from his ankle holster. The windows being down due to him faking that the a/c was broken made his plan much easier.

"Always on time," he said quietly upon seeing headlights approaching.

He knew he had to do it now. So, he walked to the passenger side of the police cruiser.

"It doesn't pay to fuck with me, snitch." With those words, he pulled the trigger.

🌴🌴🌴

"Can you pull over here, Kareem?"

"Why? What's up?"

"I have to handle some business," I said when I spotted

Buchanan leaning against the police car. "I'll only be a minute."

"Okay," he said, pulling over a few feet away from the police car.

I got out and approached Buchanan.

"Hey, Shug'ah."

"Buchanan, in all the years I've worked for you, this has got to be a first. So, get to the point. What was so urgent that we had to meet out here in public?"

"It's an emergency," he said, glancing over his shoulder. "I need your help with that."

I peeked in the police car and saw an officer slumped over.

"Oh, no! I'm not helping you out with this one. What the fuck are you thinking? Are you crazy? There's a time and place for this shit, and this is not it."

"You don't tell me when or where I do shit! I'm the boss of you!"

I laughed. "As of tonight, I'm the boss of me. I fuckin' quit!"

"Samantha, what's wrong?" Kareem said while getting out of the car.

"Baby, please just get back in the car. I'll be there in a minute."

"Oh, my. This night just keeps gets better and better. How are you, sir?"

Kareem, oblivious to what was going on, shook his hand. "Good evening. Is there a problem, officer?"

"Well, I called Shug'ah here to help me with a little something, but I think you can be a bigger help than she can."

"I don't follow."

"See, I'm Shug'ah's boss."

"Shut the fuck up! You're not my boss! Kareem, go back to the car, please."

"Kareem, is it? The man in that police car was my

partner. Why did you kill him?"

"What?" Kareem asked, confused.

"Buchanan, stop it right now," I pleaded. "I'll clean up this mess. Just leave him alone."

"Too late, Shug'ah Cake. You had your chance. I'm talking with my new employee now. Kareem, just tell me why you did it."

"Buchanan, you don't have to do this. I can get the guys to take care of this. Leave Kareem out of this. Trust me, you don't want this."

He laughed. "Oh, yes, I do. This is how the story will play out. Pretty boy over here got upset because I told him that I thought he stole that nice ride."

Things had gotten too far out of hand. "Kareem, get in the car now!"

"I'm not leaving you alone with this asshole."

"Please tell this man I'm not an asshole, Shug'ah."

"You're right. You're not an asshole. You're a *fuckin'* asshole."

Buchanan stepped away from Kareem and turned toward me. "You and your foul little mouth are going to get you in trouble."

I glanced at Kareem, whose confusion had been replaced by terror.

"Now, where was I?" Buchanan questioned himself. "Oh, yes. I came to the car to call in the plates. Kareem approached the car surprised to find I was working with a partner, and he shot him. So tragic. Then he turned the gun on me, so I...well, you know how the rest of the story goes, don't you, Shug'ah?"

"No!" I screamed as I stepped in between them.

Buchanan hit me with the gun, and I fell to the ground.

"Run, Kareem!" My head hurt like hell. Kareem kneeled down to check on me. "No, run!"

I reached for what should have been there. My heart sank

as I turned to look at the trunk of Kareem's car where I had put my guns. I struggled to my feet.

"End of story."

I heard the sound of gunshots about a thousand times. They sounded different—more like heartbeats that got louder with each shot. He fired five times into the man who was my salvation. I fell to my knees. Kareem's body fell as if in slow motion, and every moment we ever spent together seemed to run through my mind before he hit the ground in front of me.

I crawled over to him and lay across his chest. "Why didn't you run?" I whispered against his lips. "I can't go on without you."

"I…I…" Kareem struggled to speak.

"Shhh, baby. Save your strength." I searched for his cell phone, while Buchanan went to call in and cover his ass.

Kareem reached up to touch my face. "I wished that you have a good…" He stopped talking and began choking on his blood.

Knowing he wasn't going to make it, I stopped trying to get his cell and leaned closer to listen to the faint words barely escaping his trembling lips. He wanted his wish to be told with his last breath so it would come true.

"A good life…" He struggled to breathe and held up two bloody fingers.

"You made two wishes?" I asked as tears flowed down my cheeks.

He gave me a weak nod. "That you know I love—"

Kareem began shaking and the word "you" never made it to my ears. He was gone, and I was alone again.

"Awww, is lover man gone?" Buchanan asked, putting the .45 he used to kill his partner in Kareem's lifeless hand. "Where are they?"

"What?"

"Your guns. Are they in the car? Those guns can be tied to me, and I'm not having that shit."

217

"They're in the trunk."

As he turned towards Kareem's car, I grabbed the gun from Kareem, stood up on my shaky legs, and pointed the gun at him. He turned and his gun was aimed at me, too. I pulled the trigger, but the spawn of Satan still stood in front of me. In the midst of the empty clicking sounds, I heard him laughing. He lowered his gun, went to the car, and popped the trunk. I was powerless; the almighty Shug'ah was powerless. I threw the gun at him and collapsed on the ground. After retrieving my guns, he wrapped them in a T-shirt and put them in a gym bag in the trunk of the police car. He then wiped my prints off the .45 and placed it back in Kareem's hand. The sound of approaching police cars brought that man down to my level.

"You better not say anything or I will kill you slowly."

Part of me wanted him to do it. I stared emotionless at the body that had been the host to one of the most beautiful souls in the world. I knew I had to make him pay for what he did to the man who offered me what I needed so desperately. A life. I had to clear the shit Buchanan was going to sling at Kareem's character, so I had plenty to live for at the moment.

"Do you understand?" he asked through clenched teeth as the police car pulled up next to us.

I looked deep into his cold eyes and replied, "I understand."

Once cuffed, I was placed in the back of the second car. The ambulance arrived, and the paramedics searched the body for any faint sign of life. I knew there was none. I saw one paramedic shake his head, and then the other covered up the body with a white sheet. My mind flashed back to the night they carried out Melanie's lifeless body and to the night I had to leave Rome's body lying in the street. I got a headache. How could this be happening? I knew why. I let Kareem in. It's because I began to care for him, and he for me. It seemed my life's story was if I let someone get close to me, they got killed.

Tap, tap, tap.

I looked at the window. Buchanan peered at me through the glass. As I peered back, a plan began to form in my mind for just how I would take the asshole out.

Chapter 31

"Tell us again what happened?"

I looked at the fourth cop they sent in to question me. "Like I told the others, we got pulled over. The cop ordered Kareem out of the car and then asked him for his registration and shit. Kareem said no." I paused to drink the cup of water he gave me, hoping he didn't notice me cringe as I lied about the man I loved. "Then the officer went to his car to call in the plates. Kareem followed him. I heard a shot, and by the time I got out the car, the officer fired on Kareem and he fell to the ground."

"Did you know him well?"

"Who?"

"Mr. Valentine."

"Who is that?"

"Kareem. Kareem Valentine?"

"I forgot his last name," I lied. "We weren't that close." I didn't offer anything more.

"Listen, Miss, I ran a check on Mr. Valentine, and he's what you call squeaky clean. Something I find funny is he has two firearms that he has a license to carry, so why would he be carrying a gun that's unregistered?"

I shook my head and shrugged.

"One of my guys got killed tonight." He paused and looked at the paper in front of him. "Samantha, my name is Peter Donald. I'm with the FBI."

He got my attention, but I didn't show it.

"The young man who got killed tonight, Jason Gibbs, was with the FBI. We are investigating Lieutenant Buchanan. Over the past eight years, six of his partners have been killed. Tonight makes number seven."

Knowing I was responsible for two of those deaths, I shifted in my seat. "Why are you telling me this?"

"I was just hoping you could shed some light on this case."

"I wish I could help you, but I can't," I said with fake sympathy. "It's two in the morning, and I'm tired. I just saw a friend get killed, and I'm in no frame of mind to help you out. May I go?"

"I'll be in touch."

Upon walking out of the police station, I realized I had no ride and no cell. I dug deep in my pocket for change to use the payphone.

"Tiny, where are you?"

"Handling some shit over in Crenshaw. You sound fucked up. What's up?"

"Nothing, just handle your shit. I'll see you later," I told him, then hung up.

I saw headlights flash twice and then the high beams blinded me. Ignoring Buchanan's signal for attention, I started walking to X's place.

"Excuse me."

I turned and saw a female officer walking towards me.

"Look, I can't talk anymore. I need to sleep."

"I was supposed to give you Mr. Valentine's things. You're free to take his car."

I took the envelope and the keys.

"The car is parked over there," she said, pointing in its

direction.

I sat in the driver's seat for a few minutes before starting the car. I knew he would follow me. When I stopped at a stoplight, Buchanan pulled up next to me. He rolled down his window and let my guns fall to the pavement before he ran the red light, disappearing into the night. He knew once I told the crew, his ass would be marked. I shifted into park and got what was mine. They were still loaded.

I drove around for a while. I didn't want to see X, but he had to know. I finally stepped into X's apartment around three. I planned to stay and wait for him, but the sounds coming from the bedroom told me that he was home. I opened the bedroom door, and just like I thought, he was in the middle of having sex. I flipped the light on and off to get his attention. I couldn't wait for him to finish. After both of them called me every name in the book, X joined me in the kitchen.

"You better have a good fucking reason for interruptin' my shit," he told me while adjusting his boxers.

The kitchen was dark, and he went to turn on the light.

"Don't," I told him.

"Shug'ah, you know I don't like this cloak-and-dagger shit. Plus, I have a wet pussy in my bed. Get to talkin'."

"Some shit went down earlier tonight."

"With who?"

I sat at the table and rubbed my aching head. "With Buchanan."

"Don't tell me you *are* doing shit behind my back."

"No, I wasn't. He killed two people tonight."

"What the fuck does that have to do with me?"

I got up and opened the refrigerator to get some water. The light was enough for X to see me soaked in Kareem's blood. He turned on the kitchen light.

"Muthafucka, you hit?"

I shook my head. "Kareem."

"What happened to Kareem?" X asked as he began to pace.

"He's gone."

"Gone where?"

I screamed at X. "He's gone! He's dead!"

X punched me, and I punched him back.

"You were up in Malibu with my cuz, and now he's dead?"

X continued to hit me. I matched him punch for punch. We both had frustration to let out.

A soft voice cut through our fight. "What the fuck is going on?" she asked, standing there naked. "You know what, X? When you stop playing with this bitch, call me."

She left after she got dressed, and X and I were alone staring at each other. Touching his bloody lip, he asked me what happened. For the fifth time, I told the story of what happened. It was, however, the first time I told the truth.

Naturally, he wanted to hunt down Buchanan and kill him that night. He calmed down after I told him that we had to plan it carefully. The phone rang, and he motioned for me to answer it as he sat down on the couch.

"Hello? Hold on." I looked over at X. "It's your mom." I tossed him the phone.

I found something to write on and got a plastic sandwich bag. Then I grabbed a jacket, slipped out of his apartment, and drove to UCLA, where I pulled into the empty parking lot around five-thirty in the morning. Sitting in Kareem's car, I put on my gloves and composed a letter for Mr. Donald. I explained what really happened that night and the reason why Buchanan had to be stopped. I carefully folded the letter, put it in the sandwich bag, and placed it on the passenger seat. It was then that I remembered the legal-sized envelope the woman gave me at the police station. It contained what Kareem had on his possession at the time of his death: a watch, a chain, a wallet, and a letter. I looked through his wallet past all his credit cards and slid my fingers into a hidden compartment. Inside was a folded photo. Tears filled my eyes as I looked at the picture taken so many years ago at the pool. Kareem was holding me, and I was holding Melanie. I forgot how beautiful she was when she smiled. I couldn't believe he carried the picture with him after all those years.

Calvin, the security guard, pulled into the parking lot.

"Morning, Calvin," I called out to him after making sure my bloody shirt was covered by the jacket.

"Hey, what are you doing here so early?"

I didn't answer him. "Do you think I could wait for Doc inside?" I asked, putting the letter in my pocket.

"He won't be in until ten."

"I don't care. I'll wait."

"Okay, come on. I have an extra muffin if you're hungry."

He handed me the muffin, but I declined his offer to share his coffee. I went upstairs to Doc's office, leaned against the wall, and let my body slide to the floor. After eating the banana nut muffin, I allowed my eyes to close.

"Samantha?"

I opened my eyes and saw Doc. "Morning."

"You're about ten days early for your appointment," he said, sitting next to me on the floor. "Calvin called and told me that you were here, so I came as quickly as I could. Did you dream the dream through?"

"I couldn't think of anywhere else to go." I didn't want to think about that damn dream, so I ignored his question.

He noticed the blood on my shirt because my jacket was open. His face didn't judge.

"Oh, my God, Samantha. What happened?"

"He's dead, Doc. I let him get too close, and now he's gone. I told you I'm cursed."

"Who?"

"Kareem…the guy I told you about. I ran into him after I left your office last week, and I've been with him." A faint smile formed on my lips. "He made me feel so good. He was going to take me to Paris, but that's never going to happen now."

"What happened?"

"I can't tell you. The less you know, the better. Here, hold on to this for me." I stood and handed him the letter. "Consider this my appointment for next week. I won't be here. And if I don't make it for the one after that, make sure a Mr. Donald with the FBI gets it."

I took off the gloves and put them in my pocket.

"The FBI? And why won't you make your other appointment? It's your last one, I might add." He got up slowly.

"It's been four years already? Damn, time flies. If I'm not here for that appointment, then it means I'm gone or it means…" I paused for a few moments. "Or it means I'm gone."

Doc walked up to me and hugged me. "I can't stop you. Lord knows, after all these years, I have come to know that you are stubborn as hell. I can only ask that you be careful."

I stepped back from his embrace. "You have been a true friend. Why did you keep standing by me after I told you about my life during our last visit?"

"I tell you what. I'll tell you that on your next visit."

"Goodbye, Doc," I said and started walking down the hallway.

I never say goodbye because it is too final, but this visit felt final. I thanked Calvin for the muffin and drove to Kareem's place. I wasn't surprised that the police had tossed his condo. They were probably watching his place as I pulled up. I knew his mom would be flying in from New York and his father from Paris. They didn't need to see his place in such disarray after being searched as if he was a criminal.

I cleaned, cried, and reminisced. After I put clean sheets on the bed, I slowly took off the bloody shirt and stepped into the shower. Twenty-four hours ago, Kareem had been in the shower with me. I wanted to cry, but I was empty. I scrubbed my skin raw trying to get the dried blood off.

I wrapped a towel around myself and pulled out one of his shirts from the closet to wear. I even sprayed on his cologne. Slowly and with tear-filled eyes, I packed up everything that was mine and put it in one of his duffel bags. I was going to sleep in the bed, but I decided to crash on his couch. I knew Melanie would show up; she always did when I had a fucked-up day. It was her duty to make it worse. As soon as I stretched and yawned, my eyes closed.

After a few hours of sleep, I awoke disappointed that Melanie didn't show up. Part of me was hoping for a distraction. Suddenly, I felt him there. I fixed the pillows on the couch and decided it was time to go. I picked up the bag and heard a man's voice when I got close to the front door.

Chapter 32

"The police were here earlier. I'm so sorry for your loss. Mr. Valentine was an excellent man."

Keys jingled from the other side of the door.

"Thank you," another man's voice stated.

Thankful it wasn't his mother, I sighed. I'm sure she would have been more than happy to take her grief out on me. I startled the man with the keys when I opened the door.

"Who are you?" he questioned, adjusting his robe.

"You must be Samantha." I looked into the eyes of Kareem's dad and was amazed by how much they looked alike.

"Yes, I'm Samantha."

The grounds manager handed Kareem's dad a spare key and said a sympathetic good night.

"I'm Broderick," he said, extending his hand.

I shook it. "Nice to finally meet you."

"I do wish it was under different circumstances." He paused as if remembering a moment with his son. Then he brushed away a tear that was about to fall. "Would you like to stay? I could really use the company."

"Yeah, but I don't really want it." I looked at his expression and rephrased my response. "I'm sorry. What I meant is, I'm not ready to sit down and reminisce about a man who I still can't accept is gone."

"Just tell me something."

"Yes?" I looked up, trying to keep the tears from falling.

"Did you love my son?"

Surprisingly, that question made me smile. "I did, Mr. Valentine. I did very much."

He smiled, stepped into Kareem's apartment, and closed the door without a goodbye.

It was after one in the morning when I pulled up to X's place. Before turning off my ride, I noticed two of Buchanan's hired drug pushers, Slice and skinny-ass Kilo, the two who kept dipping into Buchanan's drug supply. Somehow I knew this night had just begun.

"What the fuck y'all doing here?" I asked, approaching them quickly.

"Keep on walking, little girl," Slice hissed. "We ain't supposed to fuck with you."

"Oh, I'll gladly fuck with her," his skinny sidekick chimed in.

I reached for my gun. "Try it, Kilo, and see how fast you get fucked up."

Slice stepped in between us. "Do you have any idea just how much I would love to off you right now? But, I can't."

"Why not?" I questioned with anger.

"Because Buchanan said you spent time with the po-po, and if you go missing, it'll point to him. But, when all this shit is over, you better believe I'm personally going to smoke your ass."

After a moment of glaring at the two of them, I walked

slowly and calmly across the street. X's crazy-ass neighbor was throwing one of his fucking loud parties again. *So much for trying to get rid of my headache.*

"What's up, playa?" Shabazz greeted when I entered. "You're just in time."

"What's going on? How come y'all not at the party?"

"We ain't got time for that shit."

"You know two of Buchanan's assholes are across the street?" I informed them.

X looked out the window. "Damn, I should smoke them like a Jamaican blunt right now."

"Not a smart thing to do, dawg," Wall Street said, joining us at the window. "They probably have more of them cockroaches around here watching us."

"Yeah, you're probably right. Let's just get this shit together."

Every weapon our crew owned was laid out on the table.

"We gettin' that muthafucka tonight," X said, grabbing onto my shoulders. "We gonna get him for killin' Kareem."

"You can't just rush in and off him, X. I told you that we have to plan this shit right."

"We're plannin', baby." He pointed at the guns.

Wall Street sharpened his knives while Shabazz, Tiny, and NIC checked their guns. Someone was missing.

"Where's Baby J?"

As soon as I asked, we heard three shots. I was the first out the door and saw Baby J stretched out on the steps. He didn't even see it coming. People were screaming and running all over the place like rats on extermination day. For a second, I was frozen as I looked down at Baby J fighting for a breath just as Kareem had done the night before. X and NIC fired after Slice and Kilo and took off after them as they fled up the street. Looking down at Baby J, I could see he was shot in his leg and chest. I couldn't lose someone else.

"Shabazz, help me get him in my ride!"

"Damn, Shug'ah! Just call 911!" Wall Street yelled as Shabazz and I carried Baby J across the street.

I sat in the backseat, keeping my hand on Baby J's chest as Shabazz drove. I held on to not only my crewmate, but also someone who was my ace for life. I could feel his heartbeat getting weaker.

"Let's go! Let's motherfuckin' go, man!" I screamed at Shabazz.

"Don't fuckin' yell at me, a'ight! He's my boy, too," he said as he slowed for a red light.

"Run the fuckin' light! Run it!"

We finally pulled up to the hospital's emergency door. Shabazz hid his piece under the front seat, and I ditched mine in the back.

"Can you help us, please?" I cried out to a man with a stretcher.

He didn't hesitate when he saw Shabazz trying to get Baby J out of the backseat. After calling for someone else to help, he told us to step back.

"Hey, Shug'ah. You got this?"

"What the fuck? Nigga, you leaving?"

"You know how much heat I got on me. And you know the police are going to be asking hella questions."

"Fine. Whatever."

"Call and let me know what's up. When do you want me to come back for you?"

I rubbed my forehead. "I'll call you."

"Cool. Hey, he could pull through."

"Yeah, I hope so. Do me a big favor and tell X not to make a move on Buchanan."

Shabazz frowned.

"I mean it, Shabazz. It's not the right time. Tell him to trust me. You got it?"

"Yeah, I got it."

"Don't forget, either. Your ass is too forgetful."

"I'll holla at him right now. Go check up on J."

The bright lights and watchful eyes of the people waiting in the emergency area made me feel uncomfortable. I went to the woman sitting at the desk behind the glass window and told her a name and who I was there to see. While snapping her gum, she told me when there was news, I would know. *I hate hospital employees.* I found a seat next to a woman holding a crying baby. An older couple across from me looked at me and then to each other, shook their heads, and started whispering between themselves.

I slid down in the hard chair and looked at my hands. The blood was drying. I balled up my fist so tight that I could feel my nails digging into my flesh. I was done. I'd had enough. I needed X to wait because I wanted to kill that motherfucker Buchanan myself. I knew what I had to do. I knew what I *needed* to do. I looked over at the little, teary-eyed, red-nosed baby next to me. I saw the gum-chewing bitch on the phone looking at me while she spoke. I had a feeling she was reporting the intake of a shooting victim to the cops. I winced in pain. My shoulder throbbed from helping to carry Baby J. Growing impatient, I got up and went to the receptionist once more.

She stopped me quick. "I have no news for you, so wait."

I wanted to reach through the little hole of the glass that separated us and smack her so hard that her gum would fly out of her mouth. But, I kept cool and reached deep inside for a sweet voice.

I sniffled. "I know you're busy. I'm just worried about him. I love him, you know."

For a second, she seemed sympathetic. "I told you that I'll tell you when I find out."

"Thank you so much. Is there a bathroom nearby?" I held up my bloody hands.

She pointed to the bathrooms, and I clenched my jaw after turning away from her. I locked the door and took a much-needed leak. I then washed Baby J's blood off my hands. Looking at myself in the mirror, I tried to cry. I tried to think about all the shit I had been through up to that point. Nothing came out, though. I couldn't cry. I couldn't think about shit. All I could think about was getting Buchanan. It was time to perform for my Ghetto Grammy. I pinched my nose until it was red. Next, I rubbed a little soap between my thumb and index finger. I then rubbed my index finger in my right eye. I closed my eyes tight to soothe the burning. When the stinging cooled off, I rubbed my left eye. After a few seconds, both eyes were red and watery. *Perfect.* Right before unlocking the door and going back to the waiting room, I rubbed a little more soap on my index finger just in case.

Chapter 33

I wasn't surprised to see two cops there already. Ms. Snappy Gum pointed me out. I pretended I didn't see them and took my seat next to the woman and her crying baby.

"Ms. Jones?"

I pinched my nose and sniffed. "Yes?"

"Can you come with us, please? We need to ask you a few questions."

I blinked quickly, teasing the traces of soap still stinging my eyes. I nodded and followed them to the elevator. When the elevator door closed, the talking began.

"I'm Detective Williams, and this is my partner Detective Rivers. Your friend is in surgery on this floor," he said as the elevator doors opened on the second floor.

We walked in silence and sat down in an empty waiting room. Williams stopped to get a Coke from the vending machine.

"Please sit," Rivers invited as he sat down.

Williams stood as he sipped from the red can. Rivers took out a small notepad and jotted down my name, phone number, and where I worked. He then began his interrogation.

"First off, I'm very sorry about…" He paused.

"Joe…his name is Joe. How is he, by the way?"

"We don't know," Williams informed me. "How do you know Joe?"

"He's my boy."

Williams and Rivers looked at each other.

"Your boy as in your friend?" Williams asked.

"No, my boy as in my baby…my boo." I sighed and sniffled loudly.

"Tell us what happened tonight."

"We were at this party over in Watts, and Joe and I decided to step outside to get some air." I stopped and looked them both in the eyes. "We were sitting on the steps, and I started kissin' on him and he started feelin' on—"

"Okay, we get the point."

"Well, we decided to go home and finish what was getting started. That's when we saw this car drive by very slowly. I didn't pay it any mind the first time, but when I saw the same car come around again, I took notice. See, my father was killed in a drive-by, so I notice these things. I knew something was up when I saw the driver was white."

"White? The man driving the car was white?"

I rubbed my eyes with my soap-soaked finger and nodded.

"Then what?" Rivers pressed.

I let the soap-induced tears flow. "Then, I made a mental note of the license plate number. The car stopped in the middle of the road, and this white guy rushed up to us. Joe asked him what his problem was. Next thing I knew, he pulled out a gun and started firing. Joe fell, and people started screaming and running. Some guy told me that he would take him to the hospital, so I helped him get Joe in his car. By then, my baby was out. I swear, I thought he was dead."

"Did you know the man?"

"The shooter? No." I sniffed.

"I mean, the man who brought you here."

"No. I figured he was someone from the party just lending

a helping hand."

"Do you remember the license plate number of the shooter's car?" Williams asked.

"Oh, my God," I whispered. "I don't know if I can remember. All I can see is my boo lying there. There was so much blood."

"Can you at least try?"

I sighed, then bit my bottom lip. "Detectives, I really want to help you, but it's so blurry."

"Give us what you can and maybe a make or model of the car."

"It was a dark color, could have been dark blue or black, and a two-door. Come to think of it, it wasn't a real license plate number."

"What do you mean?"

"It was personalized, like a code or something."

I closed my eyes and let a handful of seconds go by. *Damn, I hated acting prissy.*

"I got it! I can't believe I remember it!"

Williams and Rivers looked at me anxiously.

"It was 4U2-NV."

"For you to envy? That's kind of long for a plate."

"Give me a piece of paper and your pen." I wrote Buchanan's plate on it.

Williams took out his radio and called it in.

"So Joe isn't involved in a gang or anything like that?" Rivers questioned.

I simply shook my head.

"Rivers, you're not going to believe this. The car belongs to Richard Buchanan."

"The cop from Inglewood?"

"Yeah, the one involved in that shooting last night when that cop and young designer got killed."

"I say we pay him a visit." Rivers stood. "Ms. Jones, you have been a great help. Here's my card if you think of anything else. And we know how to contact you."

When they disappeared around the corner, I found a nurses' station and asked if there was any update on Baby J. There wasn't. I had given them a fake name because I didn't want them to know I was the witness to Buchanan's crime when they pulled the report. I spotted a bathroom and washed out my eyes. I wasn't too fond of the game of chess, but this was similar. I was the black queen out to destroy the white king. Although this game was far from over, I knew I had him cornered.

"Check, muthafucka," I said as I stared into the mirror.

Then I drew in a deep breath and went to wait on news about Baby J.

"Ms. Ruiz," a soft voice said.

"What?" My hands covering my face caused my voice to be muffled.

"Sorry to wake you. I just wanted to let you know the doctor is going to come and speak with you about your friend."

"Is he okay?"

"The doctor will answer your questions." She handed me a clipboard with forms.

"Fine," I mumbled, taking the papers and pen.

The "No Cell Phones Allowed" sign stared at me as I flipped open my phone to call X.

"What's good, Shug'ah? Gimme some good news."

"I haven't heard anything yet. You home?"

"Yeah. Why, nigga?"

"The po-po may be around asking questions. I'll explain later. When I leave here, I'm going to crash at the house."

"Why they gonna be asking questions?"

"I'll tell you later. Did Shabazz give you my message?"

"Yeah, but I don't understand."

"Oh, shit! I have to go. I'll call you back." I closed my phone and smiled at the doctor.

He smiled half-heartedly and glanced at the sign, then back to me.

"How is he?" I asked.

"He's very lucky, but it's a little too early to tell if he will pull through one hundred percent."

"What do you mean?" I asked, standing.

"He's in a coma, and right now, the machines are keeping him alive."

"Fuck," I whispered. "I'm sorry."

"No, it's okay. I understand. Are there any other family members?"

I shook my head. "I'm his family. Can I see him?"

"Yes, you may. Please fill out the paperwork the nurse gave you. He's in room 207A."

"Thanks."

I walked down the hall and stopped in front of Baby J's room. I couldn't go in. I couldn't see him connected to machines. So, I walked back to the nurses' station.

"What do you want from me?" I asked the same nurse who had given me the papers.

"Excuse me?"

"This. These papers. What do you want? I don't really have the patience for forms right now."

"Do you have insurance?"

"Yeah."

"You do?" she asked, sounding surprised.

"The one with the duck."

"Duck?"

"The insurance company with the duck."

She smiled. "Oh, you mean AFLAC. Do you have the

card?"

"Not on me. I'll bring it by tomorrow." I glanced at my watch. "Hell, it is tomorrow. I'll bring it by in a couple of hours. I need to shower and sleep."

"My shift ends at seven. My name is Karen."

"I'll be back around that time then, Karen."

"Your name?"

"Samantha Ruiz. I'll be back."

It was close to four in the morning when I walked out of the hospital. I called Shabazz and was glad I didn't have to wait too long for him to come pick me up.

"What's up? Our boy good?" he asked.

"Too early to tell. Move over."

Shabazz moved to the passenger side, and I got in.

"X wants to see you."

"He's gonna have to wait," I told him. "And you can't go to X's right now, so where should I drop you off?"

"Take me by Tiny's."

I dropped him off and drove to the house, where I showered, dressed, and then dozed off on the couch for about thirty minutes. When I woke, my stomach growled, so I fixed a bowl of Fruit Loops. Afterwards, I searched for the insurance card. I guess I made too much noise, because Tasha woke up.

"What are you doing?" she asked in a whisper. "You're going to wake up Malique."

"I need that damn insurance card," I whispered back.

She went to her room and came back with the card. "What's going on?"

"Shhh, you're going to wake Lil' Man."

"All you have to tell me is to mind my business."

"Really? That's all it takes? Fine, then mind your business."

"You know what?"

"Yes, I do. What and I went to school together."

Shug'ah

She giggled softly. "I don't know why I continue to put up with your ass."

I drove back to the hospital, took the elevator to the second floor, and retraced my steps from earlier. Karen was in the same place writing in a notebook.

"Here you go." I slid the card across to her.

"You came back?"

"You seem surprised. Any change?"

"Sorry. No change."

"I can see him, right?"

She glanced down the hall. "Yeah, go ahead. I need a few minutes to fill out the information for your friend."

I walked to Baby J's room and took a deep breath before entering. He had shit strapped to his chest, a hose in his mouth, and a small tube in his nose. At least he was alive and still had a chance. I stared at him. He was so damn young. He had no business in this life, and neither did I.

"I'm sorry, man." I pulled a chair close to the bed, sat down, and held his limp hand. "It should have been me. Don't worry; we're going to get them. I wish you could take the ride with us, playa, but you just lie here and rest. We got this."

"Ms. Ruiz?"

"Yeah?"

"You're all set."

I got up and pulled the chair back to its original place.

"Good. Take care of him." I took a look back at Baby J. He had kept me going the past few years and was someone I could look after. I didn't know if I would be back, but I hoped that I would.

The early morning sun teased me about my sleepless night when I left the hospital. I called X.

"We can't hang at your place."

"Why the fuck not?"

I told him why, and we agreed Tiny's place would be our new spot.

Chapter 34

"Damn, nigga, you couldn't clean up?" I asked, entering Tiny's place.

"Why? Y'all ain't special."

"You a nasty muthafucka." I moved the beer bottles and sat next to Shabazz.

"So what's going on?" he asked.

"Wait till the others get here."

I flipped through the channels to the morning news.

"*...the same officer was present at the shooting of two people late Sunday night when an officer along with well-known clothing designer Kareem Valentine lost their lives. According to police, it was Valentine that fired at the cop and then Officer Buchanan fired upon him. It is unsure if Officer Buchanan was involved in the shooting last night where a young man still clings to life and is listed in stable but critical condition. According to police, an eyewitness puts Officer Buchanan's vehicle at the scene. Local police and the FBI are still investigating both cases. As of this morning, Officer Buchanan is suspended from duty. Tom?*"

"*Thank you, Heather. We have gotten letters, emails, and phone calls regarding Kareem Valentine. Many in the community refuse to believe he was involved in the shooting*

Imani Writes

death of the young officer. Many say he was a kind-hearted man who was following his dreams. The shootings are still under investigation by..."

I turned it off.

"Eyewitness?" Shabazz asked me with a smile.

Before I could respond, X opened the door and entered followed by NIC and Wall Street. After greeting each other, the plan to fuck up Buchanan began.

"There are six of us now."

"Still seven," I said, interrupting X. "Don't count out Baby J. He's not here, but he's still a part of this crew."

"I apologize. Okay, Shug'ah. Break it down."

I had their attention. "Last night, I told the cops at the hospital that the person who shot Baby J was white, and I gave them Buchanan's personalized plate. We just heard on the news that he is suspended, so we're going to kick his punk ass while he's down."

"What's the plan?" NIC asked.

"We hit him where it hurts…his pockets."

X jumped in. "One by one, we're going to off his little piglets, starting with Slice and Kilo."

"We know all his peeps and where they stay, so it shouldn't be hard," Wall Street added with a grin.

"We're not going to do it right away, though," I said. "We need to keep a low profile and watch them from a distance. He's going to expect us to fly off quick, but we aren't going to do that. We'll let a week or so pass, and then we'll do a weekend hit. Paint him into a tight corner, because when he's helpless, we all know he acts foolish. He knows his fellow officers will be watching him, so he'll try to keep a low profile. But, knowing his greedy ass, he'll be into something. We're also gonna focus on Snow Man because that's his right-hand. No one will think twice if his brother comes to visit him, because Snow is not on their radar. However, we know he'll be taking up the slack for Buchanan and making his money for him. They'll be hustling on the low, but we'll be even lower."

"He got like twenty assholes in his crew," Tiny reminded us. "It's not going to be easy."

I smiled and patted Tiny's round stomach. "Nothing satisfying comes easy."

"True," X agreed. "We are seven of the assholes." He smiled as a few of us chuckled. "So, that would leave the unlucky number thirteen. Add in Snow Man and Buchanan and we got fifteen. But, like my man Wall Street said, we know all of them and where they stay. If I know that cracker as well as I do, he'll make it easy for us. Instead of his usual one guy here or two guys there, he'll double up so they can watch each other's back."

Shabazz cracked his knuckles. "I'm ready to do this. When do we get him?"

All eyes were on me. I thought about my last appointment with Doc, which was over three weeks away. I wanted to keep that last appointment.

"Not this weekend, but the next one. That should be enough time to find out what they're up to. Now remember, Buchanan gets his last and we do it together. We need to split up in pairs."

"I can roll with NIC," Shabazz offered.

"I'll roll with you, Shug'ah," X said.

Surprised, I looked at him. "Cool with me. That leaves Wall Street and Tiny. We'll meet up here every night. X, you can't go home, so I suggest you get some gear."

"Yeah, I got that."

"I guess you can crash with me at the crib."

"Cool."

Thursday night found X and I patrolling in Inglewood. Just like I thought, Snow Man was making frequent visits to his brother's place. We were surprised the police weren't parked outside his place 24/7. They only drove by every now and then. I guess it was their way of giving Buchanan room to slip up, but he was smart.

"Are you coming to the funeral?" X asked me when we stopped to get something to eat.

I looked up from my fried chicken wings and shook my head.

"I thought you were going to come by since he was your boy and all."

"I don't do funerals anymore."

"I feel you on that. Well, we lay him to rest at noon tomorrow, just in case you change your mind."

I licked my fingers. "Yeah, just in case."

The next morning, I watched X get ready for the funeral. I never saw him all dressed up before.

"Are you sure you're not coming?"

"I'm sure."

X picked up the white roses he got for his aunt. "Here."

I took the single rose he offered me. When he left, I stretched out on the couch. I felt guilty not going to Kareem's funeral. *If I don't go to the church, the least I could do is go to the cemetery.*

About an hour later, I decided to go. I got dressed in the black dress Kareem had bought for me and made sure I looked like I did the night we went out. I drove to the graveyard but kept my distance. A tree sheltered me from being seen. Still, I was close enough to hear. Rufus sang his rendition of "Amazing Grace". You could hear the sorrowful quiver in his voice as he poured his heart into every note. A lot of people showed up to pay their respects to a wonderful man. Kareem's parents held hands while standing in front of their only child's final resting place. A few words were said, and as the casket was slowly lowered into the ground, the mournful cries made their way to the heavens. I stood there as the crowd thinned. Then, I walked up to his grave holding the single white rose.

"Excuse me, Miss."

I turned to the man holding a shovel.

"Please, give me a minute." I turned back to the grave and read the marble headstone:

Beloved son,
May you rest in peace knowing…
You thought, you dreamed, and you created.
God Bless You.
Kareem Tyrell Valentine
December 12, 1979 – June 6, 2004

Chapter 35

I sat down next to the six-foot hole in the ground and peered in.

"How did we get here, my love? I wasn't going to come, but I had to talk to you for a second. I replay the time we spent together, wondering when was the right time I should've left you. I can't think of one because I would have missed you too much. I don't regret one second I spent with you. I wish more than anything that I could go back to that night and change what happened. I need you."

The tree branches above me rustled. I smiled and stood.

"I will make your wish come true. I will make a better life for myself as soon as I deal with the muthafucka that put you here. I need a favor from you. If you happen to run into Mel in the spirit world, tell her to give her big sister a break. I love you, Kareem."

I put the soft petals to my lips and kissed them.

"Thank you for loving me." I tossed the rose on top of the casket. "Goodbye, my love."

I felt a mixture of sadness and hate with a side order of anger as I drove away from the graveyard. I drove to Inglewood, and with each passing minute, my anger grew more. Buchanan had to pay. I drove around his block for a while. Each time I got in front of his house, I slowed almost to a stop. On my fifth time around, I stopped in the middle of the road with his house to my right. With me blocking the traffic, many drivers honked their horns, which is exactly what I wanted. Buchanan opened his front door, and he stood there looking like the devil had him up all night playing poker.

He stepped outside with his arms open as if daring me to do something in broad daylight. I rolled down the heavy tinted window and glared at him. He glared back.

"What are you going to do, bitch?" he shouted.

I gave a half smile, put two fingers to my lips, and made the motion that I was shooting him. Then I hit the gas and screeched out of sight. I drove straight to Tasha's salon, parked in the back, and slipped in the side door.

"Oh, my God! Look who had an extreme makeover."

"Fuck you, Jackie," was my quick response.

"My bad. She's still a bitch," Jackie shot back and laughed.

"What are you doing here? You come to work?" Tasha asked, eyeing me up and down. "Where did you go?"

"I went to a funeral. I just came by to cool out, but it looks like y'all busy up in here."

"There's some show going on tonight. I had to send Malique home with my mom because he was getting on my last nerve. Do me a favor and wash out chair number three for me before what hair she has left falls out."

While walking up to the woman in chair number three, I happened to look out the window. A black SUV pulled up in front.

"Get down!" I yelled.

Bullets and glass flew everywhere. I looked to the back of the salon at Tasha standing frozen in disbelief. I yelled at her to get down, but she couldn't move. I got up and ran to her, pulling her down to the floor. Bullets continued flying into the salon as the women screamed. Once the vehicle sped away, I got up. Although I could see women crying, sound escaped me again. Chair number three was empty, and the woman that had been sitting there was on the floor dead. Another woman clutched her dead son and screamed, but I still heard nothing. Slowly, the sound came back, and the screams cut through me like knives. I wished I couldn't hear them. Tasha dialed 911, but the approaching sirens let me know someone had already called.

"I have to go," I told Tasha.

I ran out the side door, dipped around the block, and got a taxi. On my way to Tiny's, I called the rest of the crew and told them to drop everything, leave their rides, and take a taxi to meet me. I asked to get dropped off a few blocks from Tiny's. I was the first to get there, but everyone else came shortly afterwards. I knew X was doing family stuff and would be a while.

"What's going on?" Wall Street asked.

"Tasha's salon got hit."

"My son!" He reached for his cell.

"Malique wasn't there," I told him, but he called anyway.

He spoke to Tasha for a minute and then hung up.

"What she say?" Shabazz inquired.

"She said about four people got killed and six are injured."

"That's fucked up."

Wall Street looked at me. "You were there?"

I nodded.

"Who the fuck did this?"

I looked at them. "Who the fuck you think?"

My head throbbed in pain. I went into the kitchen to take some painkillers and then I changed my clothes. We were sitting around discussing what we were going to do to Buchanan and his drug crew, when X walked in.

"Somebody please tell me what the hell is going on?"

We all started talking at once.

"Shut the fuck up!" X yelled. "Shug'ah, talk to me."

"Buchanan's drug boys shot up Tasha's salon."

X's eyes went to Wall Street.

"Lil' Man wasn't there," Wall Street informed him.

X looked back at me and motioned for me to keep talking.

"It's kinda my fault. I drove to the Wood mad as shit and went by Buchanan's house. When I stopped, he came out and pretty much dared me to do something to him. I pointed two fingers at him and let him know he was marked. I then drove straight to the salon and parked in the back. Within seconds, they shot the place up."

"I don't need this fuckin' shit today, Shug'ah," X said. "I just put my cuz in the ground. You had no business going there. You know what? We fuck them up tonight."

"No," I replied.

"Muthafucka, did you hear me? We deal with them tonight."

"I guess you didn't hear me. I said no!"

X rose to his feet, but Shabazz blocked him from getting in my face.

"Shug'ah, you make a nigga wanna kick your ass!" X said, backing down. "You acting like you run shit up in here."

"Nobody runs anything up in here, and that goes for me, too. We made a deal when Rome died that no one was in charge, but we mainly look to you because you've been here from the beginning. But, you're wrong, playa. They're expecting us to go after them tonight. If we hunt them down now, it will be suicide. Them shooting up the salon was a fuckin' invite to sign our death certificates. If you run out there shooting, we'll be burying your ass next week."

"How did you get so smart?" X asked with a smirk.

"By protecting your ass all these years, nigga."

X and I looked at each other, and an unspoken understanding flowed between us.

Shug'ah

"Okay, we do as planned, but we move it up. We don't go anywhere together, and if we need to make a move, we do so during the day."

I cleared my throat. "What do you mean move it up?"

"We can't sit and plan for next weekend. The longer we take to make our move, the more shit they'll do to our families, and I'm not having that shit. We hit Buchanan first."

NIC stretched. "So when do we move?"

"Sunday and Monday."

I was a little surprised. "Sunday as in the day after tomorrow? And what's this shit about hitting Buchanan first?"

"We hit him first, plain and simple."

"Bullshit! If word gets out that we took out Buchanan, we'll be at the mercy of his other assholes. They won't like that because we'll be fucking with their money."

"Do you have a better idea?"

"I say we do the guys first and save Buchanan for last, the same as we planned before. They crossed the line today. You know if they hit the salon, it's just a matter of time before they hit where we stay. I say we check into a motel or some shit like that, get a map, and plan this hit effectively. There's no room for mistakes."

Wall Street massaged the back of his neck. "Y'all know a lot of Buchanan's punks hang out in Crip territory, right?"

"Yeah, and the rest of the muthafucka's hide among the Bloods," NIC replied. "What's your point?"

"Nothin'. I was just pointing that shit out."

X took a deep drag of his blunt. "We never had static with the B's and C's, and I don't plan to start now. So, we make it swift and clean. We hit who we have to hit, and we're doin' this shit in a day. No crazy shootin' and shit, because if we hit a B or C, game over."

Tiny raised his hand. "I have a question."

X laughed. "You're not in school, nigga. Speak."

253

"Wouldn't Buchanan move his guys knowing we're going to hit them?"

"Good question." X thought for a second. "We don't know what to expect. He may move them, but that would be a coward move. I've known that muthafucka for years, and one thing is for sure, his ass is not a coward. He'll leave them out there on the streets to dare us, seeing if we have the balls to fuck with them. No offense, Shug'ah. I insist we do Snow Man first. Consider it like making a sandwich. We have the Wonder Bread brothers as the bread and the other fuck-ups are the meat. You feel me?"

Tiny smiled. "I feel you, dawg."

"What's the plan for tonight?" X asked me.

I got up and locked the door. "Tonight we stay here. In the morning, I'll find a place for us to stay, and then during the day, you guys get y'all asses there."

"Sounds good." X put out his joint in the ashtray. "I need some sleep."

Sleep. Yes, I needed some, too. Within the next few hours, one by one, we fell asleep. We were used to roaming the streets till the early morning hours, but those days were gone for the moment. Tiny crashed in his bedroom, and X took the other room. Shabazz fell asleep on the floor in front of the TV, Wall Street on the couch, and NIC on the loveseat. That left me Tiny's broken-down recliner that his fat ass always sat in. As I tried to get comfortable, my cell rang.

"Hello?"

"Ms. Ruiz, this is Karen from the hospital."

"Yes, any change?"

"No. I didn't see you come by tonight, so I wanted to tell you that he's still holding on."

"I appreciate it. I'll be out of town for a few days. I'll come visit him as soon as I get back."

"I'll call you if there's any change."

"Thank you."

Shug'ah

I made a quick call to Tasha to see how she was doing and to make sure she took my ride to Manny's. Aside from still being shaky, she was okay. She told me my ride was where it was supposed to be. After hanging up with her, I turned off the TV and closed my eyes. I didn't realize how tired my body was. I had a full night's sleep with no dreams. I slept peacefully.

Chapter 36

The next morning, I got us a room at a motel on Long Beach Boulevard. Wall Street showed up with his collection of ties and knives. I didn't know which he had more of. He got on his cell and called one girl after another like he was a damn pimp. NIC arrived equipped with his frown, guns, and a map. Shabazz walked in with his clothes stuffed in a plastic bag, his radio, and his CD collection. Tiny arrived with his arms full of groceries. I knew he would make sure we had plenty of chow. X rolled in with a duffel bag filled with guns.

We put the map on the wall and went to work. X put the call in to Manny for three new rides. Tiny made sandwiches, while we made a list of all the assholes that worked for Buchanan. Wall Street placed his little razor knives in the map to show the spots where they always hung out. There were thirteen marks, and six of us in teams of two. Tiny and Wall Street had four hits, so did Shabazz and NIC. X and I had five. All had to be done in one night. On Monday night, we were to pay a visit to Buchanan. We finished going over the plan after midnight right when Manny dropped off the rides. X suggested we get some sleep. While the crew slept, I lay there going over the plan again and again.

X was on the move around four in the morning.

"Where the fuck are you going?" I whispered into the darkness.

"Damn, Shug'ah. You gonna give me a fuckin' heart attack. Change into something a girl would wear and meet me outside."

I didn't really have anything but the baby blue sweat suit. So, I put it on and brushed my hair into a ponytail. After grabbing my gloves, I joined X outside.

"That is ladylike?"

"Hell, do I look like a fuckin' lady?"

"Hell no, but I guess it'll work."

I looked at him and our temporary rides. "A fuckin' mini-van?" I laughed.

"Well, no one in their right mind would expect us in this."

"You have a good point." I got in the passenger seat. "Where are we going?"

"It's a hot morning." X looked at me. "But, it looks like snow."

"Amen to that."

We arrived at Snow Man's at almost five-thirty. We drove around the block and parked across the street. Didn't seem like the police were watching his house.

"Alright, Shug'ah, we're waiting until his ass pops out of his crib to get his Sunday paper. Then we take the party inside."

"I could be taking a jog and just happen to twist my ankle in front of his house."

"He might recognize you."

"I doubt it. We met a few years ago when I came here with Rome. I think it'll be cool."

"I hope so."

"You hope so? You got my back, right?"

"Yeah."

We sat there waiting for time to move. Finally at six-forty, the newspaper was thrown on Snow Man's lawn. I

Shug'ah

secured my guns under the big jacket and began my morning run. I worked up a sweat running around the block, and on my second time around, I figured he wasn't coming out for his Sunday paper anytime soon. I needed to get in his house before the neighbors woke up. I ran to the mini-van.

"X…" I paused to catch my breath. "Don't flip, okay? But, I'm going to do the twisted ankle shit."

"Naw, just wait a little longer."

"Just let me do this. Once I'm inside, you knock on the door."

"Shug'ah…"

"Have a little faith, my brotha. It is Sunday after all."

I ran to the front door and rang the doorbell. I knew X was having a fit while waiting. I turned my back to the door and bent over to massage my so-called twisted ankle. The door opened. It took him a while to speak. I figured he was checking out my ass. I moaned in fake pain.

"Can I help you?"

"Yeah, I think I twisted my ankle. Can I use your phone to call my sister?"

"I don't think so."

"Pretty please? Ow! It really hurts. Besides, I'm harmless." I added a bubbly smile.

Snow Man eyed me up and down. "I guess so, but make it quick."

I followed him into his house. He turned to look at me as I limped, so I made sure the smile was still a little bubbly.

"Wait here," he instructed and went into the kitchen.

I put on my gloves and took out one of my guns and held it behind my back. He walked up to me and handed me the phone. I took it from him.

"You know…" My expression changed to a cocky smile. "…I was wondering if your big bro forgot to have the don't-talk-to-strangers talk with your dumb ass." I hit him with my gun so hard that he fell to the floor unconscious. "That is for what your asshole brother did to me."

X began knocking.

"Oh, please don't get up. It's for me anyway." I opened the door. "Hurry up."

"What did you do?" a gloved X asked.

"I hit him with my gun. Check out the rest of the house."

X quickly went through the house.

"Anything?"

"No, just a porno on in his room."

I kicked him. "You horny fuck."

"So?" X asked.

"This is your party, X. Do your thang."

"Let's get him to his bed."

I tuned out the sounds of empty, fake desire that flowed out of his TV as we got him in the bed. X then went to look in the bathroom.

"This man has more shit in his cabinets than a pharmacy. Look what I found in his first-aid kit." X held up a bag of cocaine. "I guess someone is going to OD today."

X got the needle and was about to inject it into his arm.

"Wait! There's no track marks in his arm, so he doesn't shoot up there. Check between his toes."

"You know a lot about this shit," X commented while checking.

"My mom worked at a rehab place."

"I don't see anything."

I lifted Snow Man's shirt. "He shoots up here!" I pointed to the marks on his stomach.

After X injected him with a concentrated hit of cocaine, he left the needle in Snow Man' stomach. Before leaving, I moved his head to the corner of the nightstand.

"What are you doing?"

"Well, when the police show up and find him dead, they'll see the cut on his head and scream murder. I have to make it look like he hit his head on the table after overdosing."

"Oh, come on. A hit from a gun is much different than a little bump from a nightstand."

"I know, but it'll buy us time."

"Let me guess, you learned that from your momma, too."

"Nope. I got this shit from TV."

X laughed. "Get your ass up out this house."

"Wait a sec. Look at this." I held up a bunch of sealed, stamped envelopes.

He took one and held it open to read it. "Oh, shit! Bring those with us. Grab that laptop, too."

"So you think we bought ourselves some time?" I asked as we drove away.

X glanced at me. "I think we did. One down, fourteen to go."

"Will you please sit the fuck down?" Wall Street mumbled at Tiny as he did his routine pacing before a hit.

I chuckled a little. "Leave the brotha alone. This is the most exercise his fat ass has had in a long time. NIC, hand me my extra clips."

Besides the faint hip-hop beats coming from Shabazz's headphones, the room was dead quiet. I looked around at my boys. Tiny retired to the couch with his double-barrel shotgun across his lap. Wall Street busied himself with picking out a tie for the occasion. NIC glared at me when he realized I was looking at him, followed by a nod. X entered the room zipping up his pants from handling his business in the bathroom.

Damn, I really miss Baby J, I thought while placing a .45 in my ankle holster and putting the extra clips in my back pockets. We planned to leave at midnight.

I went out to the mini-van and reclined in the front seat. I thought of Kareem. It had been a week since he got killed, since I heard him laugh, since I felt him inside of me, and since I kissed his lips.

"What you doin'?" X interrupted my thoughts.

"Just waiting for it to be time."

"Anxious?"

"No, not really."

"Good, because if you were anxious, you could fuck around and do something stupid."

"I need to pee. I'll be right back." I closed the car door.

"Shug'ah…after you flush, tell them it's time to roll."

"Alright."

Chapter 37

We were on our separate missions ahead of schedule. Kilo and Slice were two of the guys on our list. I must admit that I was a little anxious to get rid of them since they were the ones who shot Baby J. I told X that Kilo would be easy to find because he was probably doing his weekly Sunday night visit to his crack ho. That asshole was a creature of habit. X said he would wait in the car.

When I slipped into the apartment, I heard the shower running. I walked quietly through Kilo's crib. His woman was laid across the bed passed out. I opened the bathroom door and could see his silhouette through the shower curtain. He had his piece on the toilet tank; I took it. Then I leaned against the sink waiting for him to finish.

He slid open the shower curtain. "Oh, you gotta be fuckin' kiddin' me."

I eyed him up and down. "Damn, playa, shower must've been cold, huh?"

He reached for his gun.

"What? Looking for this?" I aimed his gun. "Is this the same gun you fired at my boy with?"

"Fuck you."

"Get out."

He repeated himself. "Fuck you. I'm stayin' right here."
"Fine, suit yourself." I fired.
"B-baby?" a muffled voice called out from the bedroom.
I dropped his gun, ran out of the apartment and down the stairs. X was waiting for me in front of the building.
"All good?" he asked as we pulled away.
"Yeah."
Around one in the morning, we were driving around Watts. I wasn't surprised to find two of the assholes dealing out of their car. We waited until they pulled away and then tailed them for a while. Just enough to make them suspicious, but not enough for them to make a phone call. They hit a turn and sped up.
"Think we got spotted?"
I chuckled. "I do believe you are correct."
"If these guys are doin' what I think they're gonna do, they will come to us. Roll down your window."
I wasn't sure what he meant, but I trusted him.
"Ahhhhhh, right on cue. Get ready," X said, looking in the rearview mirror.
I cocked my gun.
"Be cool," X whispered to me.
I looked in my side mirror and saw one was coming up on my side with his gun in his hand. I figured the driver was approaching on X's side.
Before they got to our windows, one spoke. "Seems like you niggas are lost, or maybe you just wanna die toni–. Oh shit!" He yelled when he saw us in the car.
X and I fired at the same time before they had a chance to raise their guns.
After driving for a few minutes, X told me it was my turn to drive.
"Just curious. How did you know what they were going to do?"
"We call that spot 'The Turnaround'. When Professor was

trainin' some of the dealers, he told them about that spot. The road is a circle. He said if they felt they were being followed, lead them there and floor it. Then come around and rear-end the very car that was following them."

"Nice."

"As you see, it worked."

"Worked for us."

"Amen! Hey, let's head over to Long Beach. I have an idea where we can find another mark."

"Got it."

As I drove, he called the others.

"How they doing?" I asked when he closed his cell.

"Seems like everythang is everythang. Turn here."

We were in a neighborhood known as Crip territory.

"Don't slow down, but look over there. Do you see what I see?"

"I see him."

We were looking at Chedda Cheese, the top seller for Buchanan.

"Okay, pull around the corner and stop. I need to think."

Chedda Cheese was known to have strong gang ties in Long Beach; his cousin was a Crip. He stood on the porch with his cousin and a few other guys smoking weed.

"Pull up right here."

I stopped in front of a yellow house directly behind the one Chedda Cheese was at.

"Have to do this quietly. Last thing we need is Crips up our ass."

I reached into the backseat and grabbed my duffle bag.

"Here." I handed him a pistol with an AK attachment and a silencer.

He laughed. "Damn, girl. Scared of you."

"There's a pathway leading from this house to the back."

X got out and walked down the path. I waited.

When I saw X run towards the car, I slipped the car into

drive, but X ran around the other side of the house. A few seconds later, X jumped in the car.

"Drive!"

Once we had Long Beach behind us, X began to laugh.

"You okay?"

"Whew! Yeah, I'm cool," he said between chuckles.

"Okay, what the hell is so funny?"

"Let's just say he got caught with his pants down. He went around the side of the house to take a piss, and it couldn't have been more perfect."

We stopped at a twenty-four-hour gas station for a fill up.

X tossed me a bottle of water. "I'll drive."

I finished pumping the gas and jumped into the passenger side right as my cell rang.

"Talk to me."

It was Wall Street. "Shug'ah, you and X on your way here?"

"Not yet. We still have to find Slice."

"Y'all haven't found that nigga yet?"

"Found who?" I heard NIC ask in the background.

"Slice," Wall Street told him.

"Let me talk to her. Hey, Shug'ah."

"Hey, NIC."

"Where you two at?"

"We're over here in Stanton."

"On our way back here, Shabazz drove through Huntington Park, and we saw Slice's whip by a strip joint in Bell."

"How long ago?"

"Not even an hour ago."

"Thanks."

"No problem."

"So what's the plan?" X asked when I hung up.

"NIC said Slice was up in Bell by a strip club."

X glanced at his watch. "It's almost three."

Shug'ah

"Take us about twenty minutes to get there."

X sped out of the station. He and I both knew we had to get to Slice soon before he found out his boys had been rubbed out. We drove straight to the strip club, but we were too late.

"Damn it!" X said, hitting the steering wheel.

"Don't sweat it. He probably hooked up with a female and is taking her back to his place to seal the deal."

"We could go to his crib over in West Compton."

"Or maybe we'll get lucky and spot him on the way."

The traffic was light, so we were able to run a few lights and press our luck with the speeding limit.

"Where is this stank muthafucka?" X said.

As soon as he said it, I spotted Slice coming out of a nightclub in Rosewood with a female.

"There he go right there!"

X followed him for a while, keeping his distance. When Slice stopped at a red light, we pulled up next to him. He was so busy sliding his hand up the passenger's skirt that he didn't realize just how close we were. I leaned over and tapped on his window with my gun. The look on his face was priceless. By the time the light turned green, all that could be heard was the sound of his passenger screaming. The job was done…for tonight.

We pulled into Manny's after four. Tiny and Manny were playing cards; the rest were just relaxing. Wall Street loudly cursed about the blood on his shirt.

X shook his head. "Well, if you pick up a gun, you won't get your clothes fucked up, you half-breed knife lover. We need to go get some sleep, but we need eyes on Buchanan."

"I'll do it," I volunteered.

"Naw, you need some sleep."

"No, I don't! I'm fine."

"Shug'ah, don't argue with me, please."

I didn't say anything else. Actually, I was tired. So, I sat on Manny's funky old couch and closed my eyes.

"I'll do it," Shabazz said. "I'll need a ride."

"There's a house across the street from Buchanan's that's being remodeled," I informed them. "So, Manny can hook him up with a plumbing van or something like that."

X grunted. "You don't miss anything, do you?"

"I can't afford to."

X's voice faded a little as I fell asleep. Suddenly, her voice began taunting and begging me to play with her. Someone shook me. I threw a punch and then opened my eyes.

NIC stood there rubbing his stomach and shaking his head. "Time to go," he said, pissed that I hit him.

All of us were tired on our ride to the motel. As soon as we got in the room, I collapsed on the bed. Hours later, the smell of BBQ hit my nose.

"Well, lookie lookie. Sleeping Beauty woke up," Tiny advertised.

I grabbed the rib from his fat fingers. "Yes, and I'm fuckin' hungry."

NIC came out of the bathroom with a towel wrapped around his waist. I sat next to X as he rolled a joint.

"Sleep good?" he asked before running his tongue across the paper.

I thought for a second. "Yeah, I did."

"Good." He took a drag and let it out slowly. "It's on the news. Look."

Pictures flashed on the screen of some of the faces we had on our hit list followed by the news reporter saying, *"These faces are not strangers to local police..."* If we were watching this, then so was Buchanan.

X seemed to read my mind. "Shabazz called in and said Buchanan left his place to go to his brother's crib, but the cops were there. So, he kept driving. He stopped and picked up a ho and some booze."

"He knows he's fucked."

"You right about that," X agreed. "I had Wall Street relieve Shabazz about three hours ago."

My cell rang. It was Wall Street.

"What's up, playa?"

"We got problems. Two cops are parked in front of his house. I think his bitch ass called for the protection."

"Yeah, I bet he did. This *is* a problem."

"Wait, wait, hold on. He's coming out to talk to them." Wall Street began laughing.

"What's so fucking funny?"

"No worries, Shug'ah. They're not staying. Buchanan's ass is mad as fuck, too."

"He can't ask for protection without giving them a reason. Good for his ass. Just keep a look out."

I hung up and told X what happened, and we had a good laugh. The beauty about the whole thing was that word traveled fast. Buchanan couldn't buy protection on the streets no matter how much he offered.

Much to Tiny's dismay, I swiped another rib. He chased me around the little room and I jumped on the bed, which happened to be the bed NIC was relaxing on. NIC grabbed my leg and pulled me down to the bed.

"Y'all fuckin' play too much!" he yelled, taking the rib from my hand and putting it to his lips.

Tiny laughed.

"Oh, you think that shit is funny, huh?" I got up and grabbed the plate of food.

"Gimme back my food, Shug'ah!"

I shoved a fork full of potato salad in my mouth.

"Shug'ah!" His voice was filled with warning.

"What? Here." I handed him back his plate.

Not long afterwards, Shabazz came in with Mickey D's for all of us. He had also stopped off to get some rope and duct tape. Halfway through eating my food, I got a sharp pain in my stomach. I figured it was Tiny's potato salad since the pain left as quickly as it came.

We lounged around for the rest of the afternoon. Later on, X drove to Inglewood to be with Wall Street. We all were going to meet there shortly, so I took a shower and got dressed.

"You ready?" Shabazz asked.

"Just about." I put on my hat, shoved my gloves in my front pocket, and grabbed my jacket. "Let's go."

We piled into the SUV and hit the 405 a little after ten. I shared the backseat with Tiny. Shabazz slipped in his CD, and the three of them grooved to the beats. I was in my own little world, my mind a thousand miles away from this life.

One more job and I'm out. I've lost too much and can't afford to lose anything or anyone else. Besides, I have Kareem's wish to make come true, and a promise I had to keep to him and to myself.

"Drive around the block," NIC told Shabazz.

We slowed next to the carpet van we got on loan from Manny. My cell rang.

"What's good, X?"

"Everything. One of LAPD's finest rolls by every hour or so. One just went by about ten minutes ago. Park up the street and meet us around back."

"Is he alone?"

"Yeah, pretty much. He still has that bitch in there with him."

"Okay."

I told them the plan. A few minutes later, we were standing at the back door of Buchanan's house putting on our gloves and making one last supply check.

Chapter 38

NIC was about to break the glass, but X stopped him.

"See…" X turned the knob. "It's open. I think someone was expecting us."

The sound of a television guided us through the house. Buchanan was in his underwear passed out drunk in a recliner, and his strung-out lady was in the kitchen searching for something to eat. Spotting us, she headed straight for me.

"I'll suck your dick for a twenty," she offered me.

"I don't have a dick, bitch."

"Sure, you do," NIC said quietly.

"Fuck you, NIC," I told him, rolling my eyes.

"Please, I'll s-s-suck it real, real good."

"Suck on this!" I said and hit her with a left, then a right. She collapsed to the floor.

X gave an approving nod. "Come on. Let's do this shit."

After Tiny tied up Buchanan nice and tight to his chair, Shabazz slapped his face, yelling at him to wake up.

"Hold up. I have a better idea," I said, stopping him from giving Buchanan another slap. "Wall Street, work your magic."

He loosened his tie, rolled up his sleeves, and adjusted his gloves. Wall Street worked like an artist. He opened his case of knives and pulled out a small razor knife. He then pulled the coffee table closer to Buchanan's chair and sat on it. Next, he very skillfully cut into Buchanan's skin.

Shabazz paced. "What the hell is that gonna do? Let's kill this bitch now."

"Patience," Wall Street told him without looking up.

The razor knife was so sharp that very little blood exited the tiny cuts. He made cuts all over his body. Finally, he retrieved alcohol from his case and wiped the blade off with a white cotton cloth. The razor knife was then returned to its spot and the case was closed.

"Tape his mouth," Wall Street instructed.

Shabazz did as told. "Now what?"

Wall Street simply handed him a half bottle of beer.

Shabazz smiled. He knew what to do. He shook the warm bottle of beer and sprayed it all over Buchanan's body.

"Mmph…mmmnn!" The tape muffled Buchanan's screams and grunts. His body jerked and shook as he tried to speak. His eyes went from face to face.

X took center stage. "Keep still. Stop acting like a fuckin' baby. Stop!" He sat on the edge of the coffee table inches away from Buchanan's face. "Now do I have your attention?"

Buchanan nodded.

"You crossed the line. You know that, right?"

Another nod.

"When we signed up to be your hired triggers, all of us, including you, signed a contract that we don't fuck with family."

Buchanan's eyes widened.

"Oh, you don't know, do you? The man you killed last week in front of Shug'ah was my cousin." X pulled his gun out.

Buchanan whimpered and squirmed like bait on a hook.

"You taught us well. Bet you wish you didn't. In case you don't know, but I'm sure you are aware, your other boys are dead. Thanks to all of your info over the years, none of them could hide from us." X stood and put the gun to Buchanan's sweaty head. "Killin' your faggot-ass brother was a bonus."

He tensed and tried to talk.

"X, wait!"

"NIC, I'm about to pull this fuckin' trigger. Why you stoppin' me?"

"Shouldn't we get a confession out of him or something?"

X thought about it for a second. "No." He put the gun back to Buchanan's head. "Shug'ah, come here."

I stepped to X's right side.

"You deserve this one after what he did to Kareem that night," he said, then stepped away.

He was right. I promised Kareem that I would kill the man who killed him. It was my turn to sit in front of Buchanan.

"You never liked me, did you? Thought a woman had no place, no business in your world. But, you couldn't risk getting rid of me because Rome wouldn't stand for it. By the time Rome got killed, I knew too much. You knew I was in too deep. You tried to end the crew after he died, but we made sure you kept us on your payroll because if we weren't on your payroll, then we were on your hit list. I knew you wanted me dead no matter what. I could see it in your eyes; see it even now. You killed what little part of me I had left when you shot Kareem, you fuckin' son-of-a-bitch. I wanted you to pull the trigger when you had your gun to my head, but then I wouldn't be able to enjoy this moment with my gun in your face, witnessing firsthand your end. We won't get caught, if that's what you're thinking. Your dear ole brother didn't get to mail off the letters you had him write up." I turned and motioned for Tiny to hand me one of the letters. I held it up for Buchanan to see. "To whom it may concern. If this letter has been sent to you, it means I am dead...blah, blah, blah. You know you're fucked."

He began crying.

"I'm going to kill you, and for the second time in my life, my actions will be justified. The good book clearly states, 'An eye for an eye'."

I stood. "A tooth for a tooth."

I aimed. "A life for a life, muthafucka."

I fired five times, the same number of times he fired into the man I loved. I turned and faced my fellow crewmembers. Then I turned back to Buchanan and fired one shot right between his eyes.

"That's for Baby J."

We put our guns away and walked through the kitchen.

NIC was the first to speak. "Hey, Shug'ah. What about your dick-sucking girlfriend?"

A few chuckles turned into laughter, and just like that, we were back to normal.

I smiled and looked down at the woman sprawled out on the floor. "Leave her. By the time she wakes up, she won't remember a damn thing."

"Except maybe wanting to suck your dick," X said, laughing.

"All y'all are full of shit."

We stood by our ride and took in the night air. I removed my gloves, flexed my fingers, and cracked my knuckles. X decided to call Manny about picking up the van. After he finished his call, we all got in the SUV and drove back to Long Beach.

Chapter 39

I wipe my brow; it's too damn hot. I look down at my bloody shirt, and then take it off so I can take a long, cool shower. Afterwards, I grab a slice of cold pizza, but my stomach starts to turn from the first bite. I take my seat back at the window. Life goes on, but for us, time was standing still. I'm not even sure how long we will have to be here.

Doc calls again; I ignore it.

It's week three since we took Buchanan down, and we are all crazy from being locked away from the rest of the world in this crappy motel. So, we decide to move the party over to X's crib. As usual, NIC and Tiny are fighting over the remote for the TV. X is at the table smoking a joint. Wall Street is on his cell trying to explain to one of his women that he wasn't cheating. Shabazz is writing rhymes in his notebook. And me? I'm missing Baby J.

"You good?" X asks when I sit next to him, away from the fistfight over the damn remote.

I yawn. "Yeah. Just tired."

"How the fuck can you be tired? All we do is eat, sleep, and shit."

Imani Writes

"I know, right?" I can't tell X that ever since we killed Buchanan, every time I close my eyes, she shows up. "Give me a hit."

X peers at me through the thick smoke. "For real?"

"Yeah."

He hands the blunt to me. "Take it. I'll roll another one."

We sit side by side getting fucked up. Damn, it feels good to detach from reality. I don't even care about the Texas-size headache I know I'm going to get from smoking. I need sleep. I need to feel good.

X stands up. "Come on. You can sleep in my room."

I follow him to his room where I kneel on the bed and let my body fall. After taking off my shoes for me, he joins me in the bed. When I roll over, he moves the hair from my face.

"You know, you're not a half-bad looking woman."

I laugh and hit his hand away from my thigh. X leans in to kiss me, and I kiss him back. I need this. I need him. I need.

"Kareem," I whisper into the darkness.

The touching and kissing abruptly stops. I open my eyes, and I am alone. I cry myself to sleep.

"Samantha. Samantha. Sam. Wake up, silly?"

"Melanie?"

"Samantha, come play with us."

"Us? Who's us?"

"Hey, beautiful."

"Kareem?"

He smiles, picks up Melanie, and walks away. I follow them through the thick trees.

"Can you slow down?" I ask him, out of breath.

Kareem disappears. I trip and fall. When I look up, all the trees turn into hundreds of Jacksons laughing.

"Melanie!" I scream.

"Sam, help me. Please." Her voice is so weak.

"She's my new thing." Jackson's voice burns my ear.

Shug'ah

I see Melanie in his arms and feel the knife in my hand. "Let her go!"

"I can't. She belongs to me now."

Melanie seems to be gasping for air.

"She will never be yours!" *I yell, holding up the knife.*

I close my eyes as I feel the knife meet flesh. Jackson's laughter is all around me.

"What have you done?" *Melanie asks, taking short breaths.*

I open my eyes. Melanie lay there with the knife in her chest. I can't move. I can't speak. She holds up her arm and points at me, her eyes wide with fear.

"It's your fault. It's all your fault."

I close my eyes once again and tell myself to wake up.

"Samantha, dream it through," *Doc's voice echoes in my ear.*

I ignore it. "Wake up!" *I scream to myself.*

Jackson's laughter gets louder.

Melanie repeats, "It's all your fault."

I feel lips on my lips and my eyes open. Kareem is giving me the sweetest kiss.

"What are you doing?" *I ask when he takes a step back.*

"I'm kissing my girl," *he replies with a smile.*

Jackson is quiet. Melanie sits with the knife embedded in her chest and her arm still extended, her finger pointing at me.

Kareem takes my hand. "Come with me."

"I want to, but I can't. I have to save Mel."

"Just come with me for a second. I want to show you something. Just take my hand."

I look at Melanie, who is still blaming me. I have to get out of there. So, I place my hand in his, and we walk a few feet away. The trees still represent the towering figure of Jackson.

"Are you ready to see what I have to show you?"

"Yes."

When Kareem turns me to face Melanie, I close my eyes.

"Oh, no, my love. Look," he softly instructs.

I reluctantly open my eyes and wasn't prepared for what I saw.

"You see, beautiful? It's not your fault," he whispers in my ear.

Melanie wasn't blaming me. She wasn't pointing at me after all. I didn't know Jackson was standing behind me. I stand there while looking at my sister point at the man who killed us both. I fall to my knees. How selfish of me. I've been blaming Melanie for almost ten years of sleepless nights and was keeping her spirit restless with that son-of-a-bitch Jackson. I walk over to Melanie and kneel beside her.

"Mel, I'm so sorry." I lay my head in her small lap.

"Get away from my new thing!" Jackson yells.

I grab the knife from Melanie's chest and turn to Jackson.

He laughs maniacally. "And you plan to do what with that knife?"

I look over my shoulder and watch Kareem as he picks up Melanie to hold her close to him.

"You may have killed Mel..." I yell, raising the knife, "...but you can't have her spirit anymore." I keep my eyes open as I stab into the blight of our lives. "Let her rest in peace!"

Jackson falls face down on the ground. I roll his body over with my foot and see his eyes fill with fear.

"When I get to hell, we'll finish this." I plunge the knife deep into his chest.

Jackson's body bursts into flames, and the trees disappear. I look toward the heavenly sky, and then suddenly, I feel a little hand in mine.

"Samantha, thank you."

I pick her up and kiss her soft cheek. "No, my love, thank you. I should have known you would never blame me." I put her down and look out into the field of blooming wildflowers. "I'm so sorry I wasn't there to protect you that night."

"And who was there to protect you all those nights?"

Her voice is different. She looks different. Just like the flowers around us, she blossoms into a beautiful, grown woman right before me.

"I've watched over you all these years. I was very sad about the choices you made in your life."

I am so overcome by emotion that I can't speak.

"The night you got shot scared me. The times you would go to the cliff and think about jumping, I would persuade you not to."

My hand touches my left shoulder. Whenever I went to the cliff, I never knew why I would be in my car driving back to Compton with no memory of leaving.

Melanie put her arms around me. "I tried to come to you so you could stop blaming yourself. I soon realized you would never allow me to come through to you." She held my face in her hands. "When Kareem died, I knew he could help me get through to you. I'm so happy you found love. Even though he's gone, you'll carry that love with you always. Do the right thing, Sam. Live for yourself."

Right before my eyes, Melanie reverts back in time to her ten-year-old state.

"I'll live for you, too."

Her hair dances in the wind and her eyes sparkle. She can finally rest in peace.

Kareem, who is standing a short distance away, joins us. "You can cancel that hell appointment with Jackson. Mel and I are going to keep a place just for you in heaven. Carry me with you always. Remember, I love you."

"I love you, too."

I hug Melanie long and hard. I then hug Kareem and kiss his lips one last time.

"I should have been able to save you."

"No more blame. I wouldn't change the time we got to share for anything." His hand touches my heart, trails down to my stomach, and then to my waist. He smiles. "You'll carry me with you always."

Melanie and Kareem smile at each other.

"What are you two smiling about?"

Kareem didn't bother answering my question. "I think someone is here for you."

I turn. "Doc," I say with a sigh.

"Come on, Samantha," Doc urges, extending his hand to me. "It's time to let them go."

"But, I don't want to."

"I know, but it is time."

Doc and I stand there as we watch Kareem and Melanie walk away. I laugh through my tears as Kareem tries to catch a butterfly for Melanie. They both turn and wave at us. I wave back.

"Doc?"

"Yes."

"Let's go."

"All you have to do is wake up...wake up...wake up!"

"Wake up, Shug'ah," X says, shaking me. "It's over."

"What's over?" I question, my head throbbing in pain.

"It's on the news. Get your ass up so you can see it."

I get out of bed and jog into the living room. Tiny, NIC, Shabazz, and Wall Street are huddling in front of the TV. I stare at the screen and listen to the FBI agent I met that night at the police station.

"It is tragic when we lose a good, young agent, but when it is at the hands of a dirty cop, it makes the tragedy that much worse. To the family of Agent Jason Gibbs, we send our deepest condolences. To the family of Kareem Valentine, we send our thoughts and condolences, as well. Due to new evidence, it is evident that Mr. Valentine was as much a victim in this tragedy as our agent. We apologize for slander that was brought to this young man's character. As far as the death of Lieutenant Buchanan, we, the FBI, and the LAPD have exhausted all leads in this case. We have come to the conclusion that his murder was a random act of violence due to the double life he led. This case will be considered closed. I'm not taking any questions from the press at th..."*

X turns off the TV.

"Just like that? So soon?" I question. "It's only been three weeks."

"Trust me, Shug'ah," Tiny says. "The last thing the government wants to do is waste money looking for the person that killed a dirty cop."

X holds me for a second. "Smile, muthafucka. It's your birthday."

Chapter 40

It's my birthday! I'm twenty-five. I actually made it to twenty-five.

"I need to see my son," Wall Street announces.

NIC and Shabazz grab a basketball and head to the pavement. Tiny mumbles that he needs to cook something. With those four gone, that left X and I alone in his small apartment.

I take my holster off the kitchen counter. "It's been one hell of a ride, huh?" I ask, taking a seat on the couch.

"Amen to that," X agrees, handing me a cold glass of water and a painkiller.

I take a drink and then swallow the pill. "It's time for me to get out, X." I place my guns on the messy coffee table.

"What the fuck you talking about?"

"I need to do something with my life."

"You are."

"No, I mean something positive."

"Like what?" he asks.

"I thought I'd head out east."

"East coast, look out. You know you'll always have a place here when you come back."

"That's just it, X. I'm never coming back."

X leans against the wall and looks out the window silently.

"I'm going to pretend these past years didn't happen. I'm going to forget about everything and everyone," I tell him as I button my jeans.

"Even Kareem?"

It's my turn to be silent. I pick up my duffel bag and turn toward the door.

"You know, I saw you that day at the funeral." He pauses and rubs his chin. "Kareem's mom didn't want me to say anything at the service, so I was going to have a word alone with my cuz after everyone left the cemetery. But, you were there sittin' and talkin' to him. It was kind of nice you two found somethin' together."

"Now I need to find myself. You understand that, right?"

X exhales and paces a little before sitting next to me on the couch. "I guess so."

"Don't look for me after today, because for the first time, I won't be there."

X nods. I head to the front door.

"Shug'ah?"

I stop and face him once more.

"I didn't really like your ass when you first joined up."

"That's not news. Truth be told, I couldn't stand your ass, either."

X smiles and walks over to me. "Over the years, we have grown to respect and trust each other. I'm going to miss looking over to my right and seeing you there. Most of the time, you made a nigga forget you were a fuckin' female."

"Except for last night?"

He smiles. "Yeah, except for last night. You're a hard-ass nigga, girl. I stand here proud to call you…" He pauses as his voice cracks. "Proud to call you family. And no matter how fucked up your family is, you can't forget them. You can never forget family. Never."

Shug'ah

In all the years I'd been with the crew, I never saw X get emotional.

"You never forget fam," I repeat to him and open the door. "Take care of yourself."

"You're leavin' now? What about the other guys?"

My cell rings. "Hello?"

"Good afternoon, Ms. Ruiz."

"Who is this?" I ask the female caller.

"This is Nurse Karen at the hospital."

"Oh, is everything cool?"

"Are you back in town?"

"What? Oh…yeah. I got in last night."

"Then I think you need to get down here as soon as you can."

My heart starts to pound. I can't lose someone else.

"I'm on my way."

"What's up?" X inquires when I hang up.

"Nothing to worry about. I got this."

I breathe in the hot air as the morning sun hits my face. "Tell the guys…" I try to find the words. "Just tell them to be safe."

"You go find yourself, Shug'ah," are X's last words to me as I step outside.

When I hear the door close, a part of me felt like I was betraying the crew, but a bigger part felt liberated. I jump into my Escalade and roll down all the windows. While driving slowly by the basketball court, I see Shabazz getting his short ass beat like always. I turn down the music to listen to their laughter. I know I will never forget them. Just like X said, you never forget family. I drive away without looking back in the rearview mirror.

I slip in the back door to make my final withdrawal from the wall safe. I am on my cell finishing up making plane reservations to Chicago, when Tasha makes herself known by clearing her throat.

"So, that's it? You leavin'?" she asks as I put my cash in the bag.

"Yeah."

She responds with a lengthy sucking of her teeth.

I smile. "You're not going to miss me, so stop acting like you are."

"Miss you? You damn right I'm not gonna miss you." She laughs loudly. "Bitch, I never really liked you."

I pause from packing my cash. "Here." I hand her a few stacks of bills.

Her smile disappears and she shakes her head, making the unbeweaveable curls dance to the Ludacris song playing on the radio. "I can't take your money."

"You know you can."

She stares at me.

"Okay, fine. I'll leave it here, but you know your girls would steal from the Pope if given a chance."

"Amen to that," Tasha says quickly, scooping up the money.

"Now that's the bitch I know." I pick up my bag. "I need a favor."

"Name it," she offers without hesitating.

"Here's about twenty-five grand for Baby J's hospital stay. The insurance will pay most of it, but I told them to send the bill here for the rest. Just pay them a little a month. It shouldn't be too much. Use some to fix up your shop and save some for Lil' Man."

As if on cue, Malique runs in begging me for a dollar for ice cream. I hand him a few bills I had crumpled in my pocket.

"How's Joe?" she asks.

"I'm about to find out. You take care."

I walk through the front of her house. Her living room serves as a temporary salon, and the smell of relaxer is making me feel sick. I can't open the door fast enough, but the smell outside isn't much better. I throw the bag onto the backseat.

"Hey, bitch!"

"Takes one to know one," I shoot back as I turn to face her.

Tasha stands there with Malique attached to her leg. "I'm gonna miss you." She flutters her glued-on lashes to prevent herself from crying.

I hug her. "I'm going to miss you, too. Now none of that crying shit. You know it took you an hour to put all that crap on your face."

She laughs.

I drive off slowly. This time, I do look back.

Chapter 41

"Karen, how are you?" I greet when I get to Baby J's floor.

"Fine, Ms. Ruiz. I'm glad you could make it down here."

"Just tell me. Just tell me if he didn't make it."

"It's quite the opposite. He's going to be fine. It was touch and go as you know, but he's going to pull through."

I don't know if I want to laugh or cry. "Can I see him?"

"Of course. That's why I called you. He's been asking for you."

I thank her and rush to his room.

"What's up, Baby J?"

"Me, playa-playa," he responds weakly.

I share with him all the shit that went down, including the end of Buchanan. Now for the hard news.

"Damn! You're leaving?" is all he can say.

We sit in silence for a while. I think we are both thinking about the past years and the fun we've had together.

"We had good times, playa."

He agrees wholeheartedly.

"Joe…" I pause.

"Oh, shit. This is going to be serious. You never call me Joe. Let me sit up for this."

I help him. "Joe, I'm going to miss you, man. You're my heart. You're the lil' bro I never had. I'm not going to sit here and preach to you about what you should do with your life. Reminding you that you just turned twenty-one, but you lying up in here alive after a bullet hit your chest should be a wake-up call. I'm not going to be checking in or any shit like that. When I leave, there's no looking back. I left some money with Tasha to help pay for your medical bills and shit."

"I got money."

"I know you do, but if you keep hitting the poker tables, you won't. Listen, take that money and do what you always talked about. Go to film school and do what you are passionate about."

"I feel you, Shug'ah. I'm really going to miss my homie."

I lean over and kiss his cheek. "See you, Baby J." I turn to leave.

"Hold up."

I face him with my tears fighting to fall.

"You just said, 'See you, Baby J'. You told me once that when you say goodbye, it's final, but you didn't say goodbye to me."

I smile at him. He's right; I can't say goodbye. Not to him.

He smiles back, showing off his Fabulous look-a-like chipped front tooth.

Tears hit the corner of my eyes. "Keep your cell on," I manage to choke out.

He nods his head. "Fo'sho."

I have one more stop before the airport. Well, one more appointment.

He's sitting in his office reading. He doesn't even look up at me when he turns the page.

"You're late."

"Better late than never. Right, Doc?"

He places a bookmark in the book, adjusts his glasses, and looks at me with a smile.

"Better late than never. Have a seat."

"I'm surprised you're here. Thanks for waiting."

"Something told me you would come by. So what happened?" Doc questions. "You know what? Don't tell me."

"After four years, you're now going to stop asking me questions?" I laugh.

"It's so nice to hear that, Samantha. I haven't heard you laugh much."

"It's over, Doc. It's finally over!"

"The dream?"

"The dream, the crew, the ridiculous so-called curse. It's all over."

I proceed to tell Doc everything, and he practically smiles the whole time.

"What are your plans now?"

"I'm going to—" I stop and rub my stomach.

"Are you okay?"

"Oh yeah. I've just been eating crap these past few weeks. I think it's catching up to me. You have any water?"

Doc grabs a bottle of water from his little refrigerator.

"So?" He urges me to continue.

"So I'm thinking of going to Chicago. I might go to school."

"Chicago?"

"Yep, from Cali to Chi-town. I don't know why. I just pulled a location out of my hat."

"It's going to be quite a change. What are you going to study?"

"I want to do what you do. I mean, who better to know

how to tame a young mind gone over to the dark side than someone who has danced with the devil?"

He looks at me as I take a drink. "What school?"

"I'm not sure. I'm going to check them out when I get there."

"I'm sure you will do great wherever you decide to go. What about money?"

"I have a bit and I'm going to do something good with it."

"I can't find fault in that."

I sit up straight in the chair and look deeply into the face of the man who never judged and never turned his back on me.

"Doc, I—"

He put up his hand as if to silence me.

"No, please, let me say this."

"Go ahead."

"I often think of the first time I met you. I know I was a pain in the ass." The look on his face lets me know that he agrees. "No matter what I said, you always stood by me. I know you covered for me when I missed meetings. You've been just like..." I clear my throat and place a box on his desk. "Just like a father. I've never really had a full-time father, but these past four years have given me a glimpse of what it would be like to have one. Consider that a late Father's Day gift to replace the one I broke."

He grins and opens the box. "An hourglass. I love it. Thank you."

"There's real diamond dust in there, too. Now every time you have a client come in and you turn it over, you'll think of me."

Doc moves to sit in the chair next to me. "I won't need to turn it over to think of you, Samantha. I've never married and never had a child, but if I was fortunate enough to have had a daughter, I would've hoped she would be as strong, smart, and passionate as you. You are an amazing young woman, and I can't tell you what a pleasure it has been to get to know you. I always tell my students when they get out there in the real world with their patients, care, but don't get in too deep. I didn't heed my own advice." Doc chuckles. "Look at the two of us sitting here pouring out our hearts as if we aren't going to see each other again."

"But, Doc, we aren't. I'm not looking back to this time in my life. This is it."

"Nope." He rises. "You are not writing me out of your life."

He opens his arms and I stand to embrace him.

"I love you, my child," he says softly.

I brush away a tear from my cheek and walk to the door. "Doc?"

He dabs his moist eyes with his handkerchief. "Yes?"

"I love you, too."

He closes his eyes to soak up the sediment. "By the way, Happy Birthday."

"Thank you."

I leave his office feeling reborn. Goodbye to Shug'ah, and hello to Samantha. Well, more like welcome back!

Epilogue

Chi-town proved to be one hell of a place to find myself. I didn't go to school right away as I planned. Instead, I purchased a little house and volunteered at a youth center. The first winter was brutal, but spring filled my life with hope and meaning. I went to school that fall at the age of twenty-six. I continued to counsel at the youth center while taking many classes to fulfill my credits.

Keeping my promise to Baby J, I call him every weekend. He quit the crew and is now studying at USC, working on getting a degree in filmmaking. I'm sure his name will be up in lights soon enough. He and I never speak about X or the crew, but I know he thinks of them, just as I do from time to time. Tasha got my address from Baby J, and she respects my wishes not to know about the guys. She sends me pictures of her and Malique, though. He's going to be a heartbreaker just like his uncle Rome.

Doc is now retired as a professor and lives in North Carolina. He still works, but he does it out of his home office. He told me most of his clients are family members. We email each other all the time and talk at least twice a week. He comes to visit about three or four times a year.

Along the way, I found a love that I thought I would never find again after Kareem's murder. During my second year of school, I looked up one day in Psychology 105 and there he was. Isaiah Miles asking to borrow a pen. He was the smartest guy in the class, and I'm pleased to say I was a close second. I dug in my bag for a pen while looking into his hazel eyes, and I immediately knew he was the one.

One night, we stayed up late, and after many chocolate chip cookies, he knew all about my past and me. He eventually moved in, and we became a family. Two years later, right before my thirtieth birthday, he proposed on the morning of my graduation. I was in shock. I said yes over and over again.

That was a few short hours ago, and here I sit on the stage looking out into a sea of smiling faces. I'm a little nervous because I've been through so much to get to this point. As I look down at my engagement ring, I'm instantly filled with courage. *Baby J and I will have a lot to talk about tonight.*

The Dean introduces our guest speaker David Hollis, who gets the crowd excited as he speaks. Then he introduces me to address my graduating peers.

I clear my throat. "Another hand for David Hollis." I wait for the crowd to get quiet. "As I look out among my fellow graduates today, I am filled with pride and honor, as you all should be. I am proud of the steps I have taken to improve my life, and I am honored to have taken this journey with all of you. We are not going to look to our future with doubts or what ifs. We know what is in store for us. We have been prepared for life outside these university walls by some of the toughest, but nicest professors. For that, we all thank you."

The crowd shows their appreciation with applause.

"Congratulations to everyone! And by the way, you're all invited to my wedding!"

My classmates get out of their seats and cheer louder than anyone else.

Everything was perfect. The diploma certificate ceremony went smoothly; no one tripped or fell. Afterwards, we sat through the closing statement from the mayor of Chicago.

"Well, well, well."

I turn quickly and there he was. "Hey, Doc."

"You really thought you were going to graduate without me attending? You've accomplished so much. I am so proud of you."

"I'm so happy you're here," I exclaim happily and embrace him.

"Mommy, Mommy!"

"Hey, sweetheart." I pick up the best accomplishment of all, my daughter Kareema.

"How's my little girl?" Doc asks her.

"Hi, Papa Luke."

Doc beams as he looks at us. "She just gets prettier and prettier, Samantha. She's growing so fast." Doc kisses her cheek as he takes her from my arms. "You are a big girl. You must be ten already."

Kareema giggles from the tickle of Doc's moustache. "I'm only four," she corrects him, but holds up five fingers.

A breathless Isaiah joins us. "Baby, she spotted you and took off."

"It's okay, love."

"Hey, Doc. How have you been?"

Doc shakes Isaiah's extended hand. "So you're ready to marry my Samantha?"

Isaiah holds me and kisses my lips. "Yes, sir."

"Well, it's about damn time."

We all share a laugh.

"When will I get an invite to the wedding?"

I look lovingly at him and say, "I was going to ask you if you would give me away."

Doc puts my daughter down to hold me close and whispers in my ear, "It would be my pleasure. My honor."

"Thank you."

"No need to thank me."

"Hey, let's all go to that fancy restaurant we went to in April for Kareema's birthday?" Isaiah suggests.

"Sounds good. We can meet you there at eight, Doc?"

Doc agrees before rushing off to talk to an old buddy—my first year psychology professor. How very ironic.

Isaiah, Kareema, and I walk to our car. Two butterflies dance in front of me, and I stop. Over the past few years, I've been seeing signs, like two flowers growing side by side, one smaller than the other, and I would think of Kareem and Melanie.

It's kind of silly, I guess. Signs are there when you want them to be there. Today was no exception, because one butterfly was smaller than the other. I think of the final dream I had and can't help but to smile.

"Mommy, come on!" Kareema calls to me.

"I'm coming, sweetheart."

Kareem wished for me to have a better life and for me to know he loved me, and that night, I had wished Kareem would live in my heart forever. Both our wishes came true on April 2nd, four years ago. The upset stomach I thought I had kept getting worse. I had mixed emotions when I found out I was pregnant two weeks after arriving in Chicago. The day she was born and looked at me, I knew it would only get better. I also knew that, no matter what, I would always stand up for her and be a mother that she would be proud of. Honestly, I thought of my mom that day and wondered what she was doing and how she was. The thought quickly passed.

As Kareema gets older, there are things she does that remind me so much of Melanie. The sparkle in her eyes, the way her hair dances around her face on a windy day, her utter distaste for peas, and her giggles are classic Mel. The way she puts her arms around my neck and tells me that she loves me, just like Melanie did, makes my world peaceful. The quiet moments when I watch her sleep remind me of Kareem. The way her lips move, and the little frown that appears on her face and is quickly replaced by a faint smile is her daddy's trait. Not to mention she has to be the neatest four-year-old alive. She has a bit of them both.

"Mom," Kareema whines.

I smile at Isaiah holding her. He opens the back door and buckles Kareema in. I get in and start the car. Kareema tugs at the collar on her dress, while Isaiah adjusts the A/C vent for her. He then glances at me and kisses me tenderly. I slip the car in drive. The setting sun reflects off my car keys. *The golden key.* I still have the key to Kareem's apartment on my key ring. To me, it's not only the key to unlock Kareem's door, it's the key that unlocked a door to a new start. I'm just thankful I had the strength and courage to walk on through.

THE END

Artistic Words Publishing, LLC
"A Gallery of Literary Masterpieces"
www.artisticwordspublishing.com